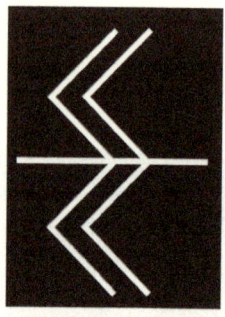

A Broken River Books original

Broken River Books
10660 SW Murdock St
#PF02
Tigard, OR 97224

Cover art copyright © 2017 by Matthew Revert
www.matthewrevert.com

Interior design by J David Osborne

Special thanks to Andrew Wilmot

ISBN: 978-1-940885-36-0

Printed in the USA.

THE HEARTBEAT HARVEST

by
Mark Jaskowski

BROKEN RIVER BOOKS
PORTLAND, OR

Here's to front porches and old friends.

*And they cried aloud, and cut themselves after their manner
with knives and lancets, till the blood gushed out upon them.*
—1 Kings 18:28

*Dust off the idols, give them something to eat
I think they're hungry.*
—"Elijah," The Mountain Goats

ACT ONE

CHAPTER ONE

Jessica has a key for a post-office box and an appointment with the men who own what's inside. She won't be keeping the appointment, and the men will load their guns. When they come knocking, hammers cocked, Jessica will be long gone. It won't deter them, but not even Colorado Jack's reach is infinite.

Given a choice between a long-shot run for the highway and a short discussion with unregistered pistols, Jessica's always known which she'd take. Even if it means following Floyd to the hideout he says he's got set up, where nobody's ever going to look for them. The idea is to hole up and wait until Colorado Jack and his crew decide that they must have left town, which was expected, and too quick to be noticed, which was not. What they'll do then, she doesn't know, but she figures it'll involve a leisurely cruise down some interstate highway, windows rolled down. An easier life ahead, by far.

She hasn't allowed herself to think like this in weeks. It's all been moment-to-moment, keeping herself above ground between sunset and sunrise then hoping to do it again.

Then Floyd shows up, and he's actually bought two bus tickets to Wichita. While Jessica gets ready, Floyd peels the receipt from his wallet and sets it real casual on the counter, tears the paper sleeves the tickets came in and drops them in the trash. Puts the tickets in his wallet. He's wearing his father's leather bomber jacket. Means business. Jessica, for the first time, starts to feel that this might work.

With the bogus travel plans displayed like a new neon sign pointing west, Floyd leads the way out of the apartment. He pauses at the stairs, waits for Jessica. She doesn't close the door. Everything she's not carrying with her has been pawned, or was already there when she moved in. No loss.

She shrugs, does a little lady-in-the-city pose on the railing, real Mary Tyler Moore. Thumbs the key up from her jeans, waggles it between her fingers.

Floyd shakes his head. Maybe he smiles, but he turns to the ground and she loses his face in shadow. She'll get to the bottom of that come the freeway, and the subtly different air of any place that's not fucking Boston. Figure out what in his murky past makes him look down when he smiles, to the side when his nostrils flare.

But then he'll start asking questions about her. Not about why they're running; he knows that well enough. Wouldn't have been fair to rope him into her getaway without his knowing, at least partly. But everything else: where she grew up, why she does what she does. The sort of questions he probably figures she has concrete answers for.

Why she doesn't join in when he starts talking about fuck the cops.

There are questions he could ask that'd lead to answers to make him think twice about this.

The prospect's rough for sure, spending time together in the car, but it's better than the paranoid wait. It's out and away and who knows what all's ahead of them, and for that she'd spend a week in a '97 Taurus, even with someone she wasn't getting used to having around.

With Floyd, maybe it won't be so bad.

So she lets it ride for now, lets him look up in his own time, follows him when he trots downstairs and turns down the street. They walk fifteen minutes before Jessica doesn't recognize the part of town they're in anymore. She looks over her shoulder and the skyline's so similar they can't have gone more than a mile. Back in front, the street gets more foreign by the step.

She gets nervous for a second, but that's the idea: to find a crevice in the endless folds of the city where a posse of men who've lived here their whole lives won't think to look.

She jogs a couple steps to catch up.

Floyd stops across from a boarded-up storefront, a couple stories of empty-looking apartments above. He game-show-hosts his hands. "Welcome to our very own hideout."

"Who owns it?" Jessica asks.

"What?" He follows her eyes up, to the apartment windows. "No, here."

She looks down. "Door number two."

It's a sewer grate. The large kind, square, not leading anywhere but sewer. She looks at Floyd. He gives a smile that's real pleased with itself. She glances to the grate again, kneels down to get a better look. Dark down there, but dry. This seems odd, but then she doesn't know her way around the sewers very well.

She stands up. "You're kidding."

"Nobody ever comes here."

"No shit." She looks up and down the street for a better option. "Why would they?"

Floyd shakes his head and threads his fingers through the grate. "Ye of little faith," he says, mixing movie-announcer bravado with boyish swagger. Jessica smiles behind his back, decides she'll follow this lark for a bit. Humor him. He's been eager enough to help.

Floyd gets the grate off and vanishes down into the sewer all at once. Jessica squints, like she's missing the trick here.

His head pops up, grins. "Come on in. The water's fine."

Jessica crinkles her nose. "Water?"

"It's an expression. A fucking—oh, man, what's the—an idiom. Come on."

He drops down again. This has gone on about long enough. They've time enough to walk around a little, may-be, but staying on the street would be inviting the kind of disaster that comes fast and hard and unannounced.

She checks the curb for oil or gum, finds a clean patch, and lowers herself down. The ground is farther than expect-ed, so she lands hard, pitches forward. She puts her palms to a wall of concrete and looks around.

"Hey."

Jessica turns. Floyd's crouched, arms out to the sides, the dramatic hero. Presumably he's been holding that pose, waiting. Wouldn't want her to miss it.

Behind him, an honest-to-god tunnel. Floyd can barely stand; for her, it's fairly roomy.

"Come on. It goes on. Plenty of room. You're not going to believe this."

She looks around, already doesn't. The light from the grate's only a couple feet above her head but looks much farther away.

Floyd's right. Nobody's going to look for them down here.

"All right. Let's check it out."

Floyd hops up, presses his palms against the concrete ceiling, springs off the floor. He jogs a few yards and turns to Jessica, grinning. She shakes her head at the kid Floyd still is, will probably always be.

It's endearing, sure, but it doesn't boost her confidence in their plan. He did find this place, though; he's come through enough for now.

She strolls forward, tries for a bit of a spring in her step. They walk farther down the tunnel than she would have thought possible.

Floyd touches her shoulder, stops her. "Look." Pointing to the right.

There's something there that Jessica wants to shrug off as just a rock formation—some leftover vestige of archaic construction techniques. But she can't. Smooth rock, almost to the ceiling of the tunnel, polished and shaped by hand. She tells herself it's in the shape of a tombstone, but keeps thinking *jukebox* instead. It makes her smile.

Floyd picks up her smile and returns it tilted.

"What is it?" she asks.

"Dunno. Saw it down here when I found the place. Looks like a clock or something, but it doesn't move at all."

Floyd's right. Four needle-shaped strips of stone, all the same length, suspended, wedged by their loops on a notch against the smooth rock face. They point in four different directions and are just far enough from the rock that their shadows give them the look of being always about to move.

They wait. No motion.

"Crazy, right?" Floyd backtracks a few yards, to where the floor is a little more level, and sits down. Pulls his backpack onto his lap, and slides a little black case and some rubber tubing out of some hidden pocket.

"What are you doing?"

Floyd pops the case open, extracts an ampule and needle. "Celebrating."

"Don't you think we ought to look around more? Check for exits, make sure we're safe here?"

"I'll put the grate back where it was. There's no other exits. It goes down a ways, then just drops off in this little shaft. To the rest of the sewer, I guess." He pulls the morphine into the needle, holds the tubing tight on his arm with his teeth. "We're all good, man. Just need to lie low a bit."

Jessica nods, halfway accepting this. She sits down across from him. Gets a cigarette going, wondering if the smoke will still be visible when it finds its way back up to the entrance. She glances at the light creeping down, decides it's definitely too far for that to tip anybody off.

Floyd finds a vein and slips the needle in slowly. Reverently. Jessica's never gone for needles herself. She prefers other delivery methods. Frankly, she's terrified by them. There's something savagely elegant to needles that makes her fear turning them on herself.

Still, she watches Floyd closely. She's always found the process fascinating.

He gets the needle where he wants it, bobbing his head like he's still hearing the ska tape from his car. Keeps the tube steady. He looks up at Jessica and grins.

A little bloom of bright red blood backs up into the tube.

Floyd's grin stretches a little too wide. The tube snaps out from between his teeth. He reaches after it, tearing the needle from his skin. It clinks and clatters down the hall, shatters against the sculpture.

"Fuck." Floyd presses his hand against the blood oozing from the crotch of his elbow.

Jessica sighs. "For chrissakes. Maybe keep it together until we know no one's going to find us here, okay?"

"No one will." Floyd gets up, dusts off his pants. "Anyway, doesn't matter much now."

He walks to the sculpture and leans down to inspect the syringe. Uses his bleeding arm to brace himself against the stone, comes up holding a needle trailing shards of glass. He turns it around in front of his eyes and flings it down the hallway, winces and puts his fingers in his mouth.

He's cut himself on the glass.

Where his arm braced against the stone, a smear of blood.

A rumbling grows from down the hallway, like an angry train coming.

Jessica blinks in the dark. The stone floor is slick, slides away under her fingers like a thing alive when she tries to push up to her feet. She tries again, fails again. Can't move her left arm, either, or see it next to her in the dark. She can just make out, in the last stubborn bit of light dripping through from the street above, Floyd sprawled unmoving in the middle of the floor.

Or, she can see his father's jacket, draped over what can't possibly be his body, not with the shape the jacket's making on top of it. It does look to be his head, though, poking out from under the leather.

"Floyd."

Nothing.

Louder, hissing. "*Floyd.*"

Something down the tunnel shifts, slithers. Close to her and huge, or far away and echoing, she has no way to tell.

Her ears prick up. Her heart slams against her ribs.

She rolls to one side, pushes her good arm under her. The floor holds for her a second, two. She gets halfway up before the traction fails and her hand slides free. She thumps back down against the floor.

Her breath comes shallow. A smell oozes from deeper down the tunnel—neither organic nor inorganic but heavier than air. Something burnt. She stops trying to push herself up and instead pulls herself along the floor with her good arm. She makes it only a few feet before she snags.

Her dead arm, pinned to the floor by something.

She scuttles her feet around, walking while lying down. It would be funny, but whatever her sneakers are smudging against feels less and less like the algae she assumed; it's not slippery until she puts a certain amount of pressure on it. She gets her feet out in front of her and twists onto her back. Floyd's backpack is closer than he is. She jabs out her leg as far as she can.

It takes a few minutes. She's ready to scream with frustration before she gets her toe through the loop at the top of the backpack. She drags it a little and her toe slips out. She pounds her fist on the floor. Soft slick of blood between her fingers. She throws both legs out. The bag is close enough now that she can pin it between her feet and pull it all the way to her.

The smallest pocket is empty, as is the next largest. Jessica's nerves jump and tighten her chest. If Floyd doesn't have a lighter, she'll be sitting here in the dark. Sudden claustrophobia. It wasn't as bad when she didn't think she had a light, but with the possibility there and gone her blood presses her temples like deep water and her movements get frantic.

The main pocket has plenty in it—clothes, a water bottle, assorted paraphernalia. No lighter. She grips the strap to hurl the bag at Floyd, figuring he must have it on him, and feels the bulge there against the foam padding. She stops. Her fingers find the bronze zippo lighter. She fumbles with it one-handed until finally a blue and orange flame scalds her eyes.

She takes a deep breath and looks at the arm she can't feel. Gasps ragged air and drops the zippo. It goes out. She finds it again. Steels herself, deep breath. Flicks the wheel.

Her fingertips have gone purple. Long threads of black hair, damp with grease, wrapped and knotted around themselves in thick braids, crusted inside their folds with white mold, jab out of red puckered wounds in her arm. No fewer than six holes.

She clenches her jaw and holds the flame to the hair.

From down the tunnel, the noise kicks up again, a rapid shuffling and a deep bass throb like the howl of a terrestrial leviathan. Her dead arm screams back to life and the pain blurs her vision. The hairs twist and seethe, pushing farther through her arm, snaking up atop her skin to her shoulder.

A tendril creeps along her jawline, prodding at her mouth. She clamps her jaw shut. The burning static in her arm intensifies. She will not, must not open her mouth. The tendril moves faster, sliming her lips with grease. A deep crack from her arm and Jessica goes dark.

CHAPTER TWO

Papa Louie's is haunted. Elijah sits in the corner booth, picking at the cracked vinyl, watching the people whose dishes he used to scrape laugh over globs of tomato sauce. There's a table, twelve people around it, and he recognizes a handful of them from the tip-less delivery jags Lou would send the dishwashers out on. What he's really seeing, though, is the way he and Donny would talk about them in the back, tossing insults while scraping their food into the dish pit, waiting for the next knock on the back door, which they'd answer furtively, passing through a baggie and taking in cash. The past is thick in this kitschy, primary-colored kitchen.

The people at the table look mildly happy and a little drowsy. Oxford shirts and smart pleated skirts. They finish their food and get ready to leave. Elijah's sure they've left nothing for the server.

Office parks were always a time- and money-sink.

Elijah watches the twelve-top crumple their napkins, drop them into the red plastic baskets, and file out the door. He taps his fingers on the table, marking out seconds until the new guy strolls out from the back of the house to gather their trays. He has trouble balancing them, drops one on the way to the kitchen.

Elijah smiles. He remembers how Lou likes to slip out of his office at times like this, to startle the employees into toeing the company line.

Sure enough, by the time the new guy gets the trays all stacked and through the swinging doors, Lou's voice doesn't quite boom from the side of the kitchen opposite his office, but it's getting louder.

Elijah lets him get a couple sentences in, really working up a rage-lather, before he stands from the booth and strolls to the back.

Lou cuts off mid-tirade. Stares at Elijah with disbelief. The new guy looks back and forth between them, sensing the heat shifting off him and onto this new person he doesn't know, doesn't care about.

"You gotta lotta fucking—" Lou falters, waves at the new guy. "The fuck you waiting for? Get to work. Time to lean, time to fucking clean."

New guy scampers off.

Lou pushes his office door wider. "You. Get in—"

"Don't think so."

"The hell you say to me?"

"I'm not going into your office. I'm not having a little chat, and I'm all good without another life-coaching session from you."

"Get out of my kitchen. Now."

Elijah thought he was ready for this moment. Like he didn't have to throw his weight around—like he was so untouchable. Instead: "Look, mighty pizza lord. Pay me. You owe me a week and a half."

Lou waves his hand, starts walking away. "You didn't come in, you didn't call. No call, no show, no fucking pay."

"I already worked the hours. You know it." The door's swinging closed, so Elijah shouts, just loud enough that the people in the dining room could hear.

Lou glances at the swinging door, at the people eating behind it. "Get out before I call the cops."

Elijah raises both hands, takes a step back. "Give me my paycheck."

"I don't owe you a paycheck."

"Labor board might see it different."

"Fuck your labor board. You quit."

The tone of his voice flashes Elijah back to any number of other kitchens. He cycled through a few before landing at Papa Louie's. It was a rough prospect landing even this job, and then only under-the-table. For all that, though, the tone of the imperious restaurateur is universal, a blend of perfect confidence and permanent outrage.

"Or, okay. I'll just make a phone call. IRS. The boys in suits. With briefcases. Maybe they count how many employees *they* think you have, see if it matches what you say."

Lou scoffs, but it's a different kind of scoff. "Lou" isn't even his real name. He started going by it when he took over the place after the original Lou died.

Elijah clears his throat. "Or you could go get me the money I'm owed—"

Lou grabs him by the arm, finally remembering the presence of the new guy scrubbing dishes, scoping him for signs of disloyalty. Elijah doesn't have to see the kid's face to know exactly the kind of smirk he's choking back.

Lou drags Elijah into his office and slams the door behind him. "The fuck did I ever do to you, huh? Offer you a job? Give you a paycheck?"

"I'm not going to argue."

Lou pounds the table, to scare the backroom staff with how he's giving Elijah hell, putting him in his place. "Then get out. Leave. Come back and I'll call the cops."

Elijah flips open his cell phone. No way Lou falls for this bluff—probably—but there's only one way to find out.

He thumbs Lorelei's number, lets it ring a couple times.

She comes on the line. "Internal fucking Revenue Service."

"Yes, I'd like to report a—"

Lou lunges across the tiny office and swats the phone from his hand. It smacks against the wall.

"Fucking kids," Lou grumbles, digging in his desk for the checkbook. "Always out for a fucking handout, trying to get something for nothing. Don't even show up for their fucking *shift* . . ." He scratches out a check, thinks better of it, crumples it unsigned. Digs an envelope of cash out from the drawer and peels off a few bills from the top.

"Here." Slides them across the desk.

Elijah picks them up. His stomach clenches. He's holding three twenties and a ten. It's, generously, half of what Lou owes him, and Lou knows it. The choice he's giving him is to surrender and walk out with something, or fight him and risk not getting anything.

It's half calling Elijah's bluff, half falling for it. Elijah never said he wasn't slick.

Elijah crumples the bills and stuffs them in his pocket, watching Lou's horrified expression. He raises his eyebrows, stares at Lou over the money. Walks calmly to the wall and retrieves his phone.

What he wants to do is toss a one-liner over his shoulder on the way out the door. But he's seen Lou throw knives at cooks for less, and Elijah has a gun in his pocket now. Lou came at him, it would end pretty much one way. And Elijah's not looking to kill anybody; he's just looking to finally get paid.

The man across the counter steams. Lorelei can feel it coming, the tirade over how his employer fucked up the reservation, how he's going to have to put the room on his personal card. She smiles her way through something about hotel policy. Yes, they got the reservation; no, they don't have a card on file, and if you want the room for the weekend you'll have to put down your own. Yes, she's sure the receipt can be annotated to reflect this. No, she can't call your employer and double-check.

Yes, she's sure. Company policy.

The smile makes her throat itch. She holds it down. Keeps smiling.

The man puts on his best type-A scowl and leans real casual against the counter.

"Look, honey, I don't know how you do things here, but that's not my job. That's *your* job, and if you wouldn't mind doing it, maybe I'll get some sleep tonight, hmm?"

"If you'll just give me your card, I'll get you all set up." It's not policy, not in the script, but Lorelei pulls the key cards from the drawer and slides them into the sleeve, holds them up so the man can see them.

His face flushes. "Do you propose to hold my . . . my *damn* room hostage, so that you can—"

The manager rushes over. He's some new guy, fresh out of Courtesy College. Lorelei doesn't know his name. She knows his expression, though.

"What seems to be the problem, sir?"

"Thank god, someone who can help me. Well, I'll tell you, sir, the problem is that this *person* you've hired is telling me that she—"

Lorelei isn't listening as the man rants. The baby-faced manager listens and nods and follows the book. He gives the guest the same spiel Lorelei had, and the man listens, nods, says that he knows what that's like, when corporate's got some policy that gets in the way of honest folks like the two of them doing business. He slides a fresh new credit card across the counter to the manager.

The manager holds his hand out for the key cards while the credit card runs, gets approved. Lorelei makes him reach down and pick them up himself.

The man rolls his luggage toward the escalator.

The new manager turns on Lorelei. "Do you see what I did there?"

"You did the same thing I was trying to do."

"No. See, I practiced *customer service.*"

Lorelei drifts through the next couple minutes of earnest coaching, following just closely enough to nod at the right points. He gets it out of his system, repeating a couple of things. After the third iteration of *we have to give the customer what he wants*, he raises his eyebrows to signify that he's done.

"So, what do you think went wrong there?"

"I guess I see your point."

The manager nods far too enthusiastically. "Good, good. We're all always learning, right? So, what are you going to do in the future?"

"I suppose," she says, recalling some dim meeting months ago, "that really the question is going to be listening to the customer, right? Letting him tell me what he needs."

"Good, good! Okay, great. Get back to it, then."

She keeps herself from spitting as he saunters away, but just barely, and returns to the desk. She's been going over the plan in her head, wondering what they're going to do with Slim. He beat the shit of Donny at the pizza shop, it's true, but that doesn't mean he's onto them. Doesn't mean he's counted up all the missing pills and pinned them on Elijah. But it does mean he's suspicious of *some*thing, and if he was willing to turn on Donny, he might be willing to turn on them. She's been reluctant to give up a steady job to take care of the problem. It seems like a drastic solution to a situation that might not need one.

But, leaning against the varnished wood, flipping through the logbook so it looks like she's doing something—*proactively* applying potentially wasted time, the handbook says—it doesn't seem like there are all that many places for her to go.

The overnight girl comes in, which means Lorelei's off in thirty. She looks around conspicuously enough and comes over to the desk.

"You, uh, you're that Lorelei, right?"

"Yeah. I know you?"

The girl flushes and looks over her shoulder again. If Lorelei wasn't expecting her, she'd be thinking the girl was a cop.

"No," the girl says, "we just met the once. I heard, you know—"

"Yeah, I know. I'm off in a half-hour. Catch me in the break room then, before I leave."

The girl frowns. "But I'm supposed to be on the desk in thirty."

That kind of detail is important to going unnoticed, flying under the radar. Never calling attention to yourself.

But Lorelei's not thinking long-term anymore.

"So? You want it or not?"

The girl shakes her head and apologizes. Lorelei waves her off.

Forty minutes later, she slides the paper bag with the yellow bottle in it to the girl, under the break room table. It's a clean transition, purse to pocket. There's no reason to assume that the hotel actually checks the security cameras in the break room, and Lorelei can't say for sure that they even work, but there's no need to leave her ass hanging out. Not over a fifty-dollar transaction.

Lorelei walks to her car, pretending not to see the manager's farewell nod.

There will be a much larger payday soon. They just have to get through the next twenty-four hours.

Elijah comes strolling out of Papa Louie's like he's dethroned the champ. He taps his hand on his pocket, doesn't seem to notice he's doing it. Ernie sees it and knows he got the pay he was owed.

Or, more likely, he got some fraction of it.

It was a stupid move, but he said he needed a ride, and Ernie needs his ears.

Elijah gets in, stretches himself along the back of the seat like he just worked a full day. "Sometimes, man, sometimes life's all right."

"Yeah? What, you come into some real money? You got yourself a job?"

"Nah, I got what's mine."

"You get all of it?"

Elijah stares off into the distance, not letting Ernie ruin the moment.

Still, Ernie's intent on it. "You figure out what the fuck you're gonna do about Slim?"

"About Slim how? What do you mean?"

Elijah's never told him, but there's no question that he's running some kind of scam. Ernie doesn't mind much, since it isn't cutting into his own business with Slim—at least not directly—but the situation is escalating. Elijah's probably not the entirety of it, or even a major part, but he isn't unrelated, either.

"You know how I mean. He beat up Donny, what, two months ago? You seen him since?"

Elijah nods. "Yeah."

"And?"

"You know better than I do. It's the same."

"It's not the same. It's worse."

They drive in silence. Ernie's taking him to the pawnshop, the way Slim asked, to talk things over. *Reorient*, was the word Slim used, since Elijah quit working at Papa Louie's two weeks ago and surely needs the income.

Thing is, Elijah doesn't seem too worried about it.

There was something in Slim's voice, though, that worried Ernie.

He parks in front of the strip mall and goes to unlock the door of the shop. The sign just reads *pawn*. Everything's nondescript, from the red light-up lettering and the bars over the windows to the cheap guitars and stereo equipment on the shelves. Ernie gets the door open and waves Elijah in. Elijah hovers a second, then goes through fast, to try to cover his hesitation.

Ernie closes the door behind them and locks it. In the middle of the room, checking for whatever double-cross he was expecting to be there, Elijah looks suddenly very old indeed. The dim red security light casts the shadows on his face deeper and darker. Relief and exhaustion poke through the carefree bluster he was laying on in the car.

More than anything, that convinces Ernie that he knows something's up.

It's not a great sign.

Ernie leads him to the back office, watches as he clocks the sleeping bag on the floor. Elijah looks to Ernie, eyebrows raised.

"Yeah. That's another thing. Slim's been staying here, you know."

"No shit? Sleeping on the floor? Like, what, he couldn't make rent?"

Ernie ignores the joke. "No. Like he left his apartment, got himself gone. He's pulling up roots, man."

Elijah stares. "You know why? Or where to?"

"Nope. To hear him tell it, nothing's gonna change here. We'll keep doing what we've always done. He wouldn't say more than that."

"And that makes you nervous."

"It doesn't you?"

Elijah rolls his eyes. "You think there's some problem? Heat from the cops or something?"

Or something, definitely, but Ernie can't say that. Instead: "Could be cops, sure. But he's been coming a little loose, lately."

"Yeah."

"He thinks somebody's been ripping him off, selling it somewhere else."

Elijah snorts. "Like anybody's gonna get away with that, the way he keeps an eye on his stash."

"Didn't say they would get away with it. But yeah, it would have to be one of the crew."

Elijah looks everywhere but Ernie.

"And, whoever's doing it, you know Slim's gonna come down."

"Yeah. Well, that's what happens." Elijah's bravado is slipping.

"Anyway, what he wanted me to talk to you about: How do you feel about working again? Now that the set-up at Louie's is blown."

"Yeah. Yeah, okay."

"He'd want you picking up prescriptions."

"Okay."

"You haven't done scrips in forever. You're sure you're up for it?"

"Look, I said I'd do it, okay. Money's been . . . money's tight."

Ernie nods and shows him out. Slim shows up ten minutes later.

Elijah collapses on the couch, stays that way, waiting for Lorelei to get home. Wants to sleep but can't. He gets up to get a beer from the kitchen and finds himself moving precisely, opening the fridge and taking the can and popping the tab a little slower than usual. Careful, like he's performing surgery.

He looks at his hands, decides that a little caution right now might not be the worst thing.

Best to get in the habit.

The conversation with Ernie has forced their hand. They'd talked about tonight, planned on it, but if Slim's sniffing around, it has to be tonight. Before he can do whatever he's planning to do in retaliation, or pick up and leave the state, and their supply, dry.

That last option dries Elijah's mouth, moistens his palms. Every possible outcome that has them getting out of central Florida depends on Slim's presence.

Slim likes to present himself as a meal ticket, a quick way out. Maybe he'll even appreciate the irony that they've found a way to make him just that.

Lorelei slams the door before Elijah registers the sounds of her entering. She drops her purse on the floor by the door and collapses into the recliner.

"Honey, I'm home."

"Roast's in the oven."

"How'd it go?"

"We gotta move, now."

"What? You get the money from that pizza fuck?"

"Yeah, and I saw Ernie."

Lorelei sits up straight.

"Like I said, we gotta move."

He fills her in on the conversation with Ernie, how Slim's almost certainly onto them.

"You think Ernie knows?"

"Yeah. Pretty sure he does."

"Then the whole thing might be fucked."

"No, I don't think so. I think he's sandbagging Slim on this one."

Elijah doesn't have to say why. Ernie's history with Lorelei is fraught, but it's still history. He sees that history happen on Lorelei's face, a kind of frowning wistfulness, and wants to ask how she feels about it—about Ernie sticking his neck out blindly, even after all this time.

He wants to, but he doesn't.

Lorelei clears her throat. "Assuming that's right. Slim suspects, and Ernie knows what he's not telling. We keep to tonight then?"

"I don't know what other choice we have."

She nods. They get up and change clothes—black jeans, black sweatshirts, running shoes. Lorelei gets a backpack and a duffel bag from the closet. Elijah takes the gun from his pocket, checks that it's loaded.

They stand in the bedroom like that, Lorelei with the bags and Elijah the gun.

"There's no way to know what we're walking into," she says.

"I told you, Slim's staying there. He'll be there tonight, unless he's out doing whatever."

"Yeah."

"Even if he's not there, we can wait, get the drop on him."

Lorelei rolls her eyes. "I'm not worried about who *gets the drop on* whom, Eli. More like, what if he has friends with him?"

The gun in his hand. He holds it out to her; she's the better shot. She drops the bags and takes the gun. He picks up the bags and slings them over his shoulders.

They look over each other, their supplies.

Elijah drives.

CHAPTER THREE

Father Abatangelo keeps a bottle of Malbec in the lower left-hand drawer of his desk, a revolver in the right. He opens the left and ferrets out the bottle and two glasses. From the other side of the rectory desk, Hector gets the sense that the second glass threw off balance by a hair what was normally a fluid, secondhand motion. Father Abatangelo sets down the glasses and pulls out the cork, pours two frankly un-clergy-like drinks.

Not that Hector can blame him. It has been some time.

Father Abatangelo sits and drinks. Hector nibbles at his wine. It's probably best not to make the joke about the body and the blood, all things considered. Father Abatangelo finishes his wine and pours some more.

"Father."

The priest winces. "Did you come to confess, Hector?"

"Nah, Tony. It'd take all night."

"Good. Besides, we do have a place for that."

"The little booth."

"Confessional."

"Right."

Hector drums his fingers on the arms of his chair. Catches himself, stops. He takes down the rest of the wine and tilts the empty glass toward Father Abatangelo. The priest obliges.

"Remember Gutter Street?"

"Mmm." Father Abatangelo doesn't quite nod. "Flashbacks?"

The flashbacks, the dreams, Hector could handle. "Being followed."

Father Abatangelo gives him a long look, pours himself more wine. "By whom?"

Hector stares hard.

"It's been fifteen years," Father Abatangelo says.

"Uh huh. Long time."

"You think you saw them?"

"I did. One of them."

Silence.

"No," Father Abatangelo says, very slowly. "You didn't."

"I know what I saw."

Hector glances around the room. The rectory is small but not bad for a basement church flanked by tenement buildings and rot. He looks to Father Abatangelo.

The priest shakes his head. "You can't stay here, Hector."

"I know."

"We don't have those kinds of facilities."

"Yeah, I know. That's fine."

"Then . . .?"

"I was wondering . . . could you go check on the clock?"

Father Abatangelo sighs, rubs the bridge of his nose. "That clock, it doesn't do what you think it does."

"Come on, Tony. Just go look at it."

Father Abatangelo looks up. Hector puts on a desperate look. He doesn't have to work very hard at it.

"Okay."

Hector nods. There should be something for him to say, here. There doesn't seem to be. Father Abatangelo gives him a look he can't quite put a name to, but he knows what he's thinking. He's seeing a red sky and a black stone archway, and three much younger men sweating and bleeding. Remembering the smell that doesn't occur in nature, and the thick knots of greasy mold and hair that clung to their boots for days after. He's seeing the third man's body, remembering how they never spoke of it after but saw it when they closed their eyes. Hector knows he's tried to keep them closed for fifteen years.

Father Abatangelo looks away first.

Hector stands and goes for the door, turns back. "Tony, does Alan still live in the same place?"

Breath hisses through Father Abatangelo's teeth. "The flat by the docks? I think so."

"Was thinking of going to see him."

"Don't do anything stupid."

Hector nods. "Just, you know. He should know."

Father Abatangelo shakes his head.

"Unless . . . You don't happen to have anything?"

The priest's eyes dart up. Hector regrets saying anything.

"I'm clergy now, Hector."

"Well."

"It doesn't work if you half-ass it. You know that as well as I do."

Hector nods. There's nothing much else for him to say. He leaves the rectory and climbs the musty steps up to the street.

* * *

Alan's five radios, arranged in a perimeter around the studio apartment, spit talk shows and commercial jingles and sportscasts, all at the same volume. Not music—never music—but a smooth gray cream of noise that's as much a part of 7-C as the cheap linoleum and jaundice-yellow wallpaper.

It's to keep out unwanted voices, he says. Fine for him, but Hector's having a hard time fighting the urge to try and track one particular station. He paces a tight path in the middle of the room.

Alan sprawls on a recliner, wearing the same distant grin he had the time Hector asked why the radio was never tuned to music stations.

Then, his answer was that it just doesn't work the same.

Now, he's surely wondering when Hector will come to the point. Probably already knows what it is, or has guessed.

The speedball Hector copped off Alan scrapes its way through his brain, his heart, doing its thing.

"Alan, those loud enough?"

Alan sighs. "Don't complain. They're necessary."

Hector stops pacing a second, meets his eyes. "Nothing flashy. I don't want to be followed."

"Oh, man." Alan leans forward, slouches his elbows onto his knees. "Old Hector's looking for the heavy shit." He stands and lopes into the kitchen, pulls the tools out from under the sink. When he moves, his too-big rag of a shirt flutters behind him. Hector closes his eyes and tries to unfocus his ears the way you'd do your eyes with a magic-eye painting. It starts to work, like the radio signals have blurred together and become physical. His heartbeat is suddenly in his ears.

Hector opens his eyes.

Alan turns and sets the equipment on the floor. The chair sits in the corner, broad and heavy and throne-like, covered by a beige tarp. He flourishes off the tarp, exposing sticky varnished wood, and motions for Hector to sit.

Hector realizes that Alan's rushing him. Lest he should change his mind. Hector sits. Alan loops a twisted pendant on a leather cord around his neck.

"You know," Hector says, easing himself in, "more like the heavy shit came looking for me."

This should give Alan pause. It doesn't.

Father Abatangelo opens the lower right-hand drawer of his desk. A rosary sits atop the leather-bound lives of the saints. He sets both on the desk and pulls the wood box with the steel corners from the drawer. The wood's dull, the corners gleaming. He takes a deep breath and opens the box and removes the revolver, reaching back into the drawer for bullets.

He closes the box and sets the revolver on top of it, pours six bullets into his hand. He sets the first upright on the table. Once upon a time, he thought that carving little crosses into the tips helped for mystical reasons, but soon convinced himself that it more likely encouraged the rounds to fragment on impact.

He's less sure of that now.

Once, soon after Father Abatangelo had taken his vows, Hector asked him what it was like, preaching the gospels, when he knew. He'd seen.

"The Lord works in mysterious ways," Father Abatangelo said.

They laughed a bit over that, the tired, strained sort of mirth that led them to not see each other for years.

Hector cleared his throat. "Does it help, though? The people you, ah, save?"

"Well enough. Not really how it's supposed to. It's not about transcendence. Not in this area code, not from me. We can't afford grace here. All we can do is maintain ritual, keep out the devil."

Father Abatangelo learned quickly not to say such things, not to think them too loudly. Whether God knew what was in his heart, he didn't know. His lack of faith didn't cause problems so long as he kept it diligently to himself.

The cracks in the barrier only show when he starts thinking about it. One has to do something to keep out what needs keeping out. He remembers Alan's absurd radio set-up, Hector's narcotics, or whatever he replaced them with when he got sober.

He'd preferred the cloth to all that. Street theology was an unstable beast.

Father Abatangelo strips off his priest blacks and puts on a rare set of civilian clothes. He hefts the revolver, wondering if he can conceal it. It's a huge gun that radiates a certain youthful masculine foolishness. The word *Python* engraved on the barrel doesn't help.

He gets it levered into his pocket and un-tucks his shirt to cover it, puts on a jacket for good measure.

He pauses on his way out the door. The cabinet there—dark old wood with heavy tarnished hinges—hasn't been opened in years. The locks on it are the only ones in the church, besides those on the front door.

Father Abatangelo slowly, reluctantly puts his hands to the crucifix around his neck. He knows full well what's on the other side of this moment.

He removes the crucifix and unlocks the cabinet. There's nothing inside but a pendant on a cheap chain. He takes the pendant and puts the crucifix in its place.

The pendant rests on his chest in a familiar heavy way. Twisted steel, looping patterns folding into themselves inside a thick outer circle—a far older symbol than the crucifix he now prefers. A decade ago, he took he pendant off for the last time but couldn't bring himself to dispose of it, even if it meant risking the presence of such an artifact in the house of the Lord. He sighs, tucks the pendant under his shirt. If Hector's right about the clock, there's no place for his adoptive Lord where he's going.

Hector comes to in fits and starts. The room looks different somehow. Empty. His chest burns. He looks down, sees his shirt in tatters and the pendant gone, its shape burned into his skin. He winces forward. The knuckles on both fists are raw. Shreds of a gray leather under his fingernails. The back-alley ritual is over and it's time to leave.

He stumbles forward from the chair. Muscles ache. He gets halfway across the apartment and trips over the body of Alan, eyes burned and smoldering, mouth open in a sneer.

Alan's corpse is clutching the pendant to the side of his face. Hector can smell the scorched skin.

He scuttles back, back, until he hits the refrigerator against the near wall. His skull thumps against the door. He doesn't even really feel it. The world goes indistinct at the edges. He hauls himself to his feet using the handle.

The door swings open as he stands. Inside the fridge are no shelves or food, only dripping stinking vines of the hair he'd hoped not to see.

He glances desperately around the apartment, looking for the thing's body. It's nowhere to be seen, and he realizes that the whole thing, tendrils and body and all, must be coiled in the fridge.

He grabs the door and tries to shove it closed, but the hair has pushed out, uncoiling and expanding, like it's leaking through a hole in the wall. He turns and sprints out the front door and down the hall.

It takes Father Abatangelo two hours to get to the Gutter Street alley. Fifteen years ago, he resolved to set up as far from there as possible. If he found himself somehow unable to leave the city, then at least he situated himself on the far side. Now, looking down at the sewer grate pried up and laid to the side, it's like he's stepped back through the years, his vestments gone, the old pendant around his neck.

And someone's down there.

He puts his hand on the gun in his pocket and crawls through. The tunnel beyond is exactly how he remembers. Carved damp stone and a roof a few inches too low for him to stand upright.

He takes a few steps down the tunnel and stops. Feels a sound in his bones before it registers aurally—a low rumble and a slithering, far away but discernible. He tells himself it must be a train passing. Hector could not have been right about the clock.

A hundred yards down he finds the bodies. Two of them, a man and a woman. The woman's emaciated, with a junkie's frame, and run through with the hair. There's a tendril jammed into her mouth and out the back of her head, where it loops around and plunges into the back of her skull, protruding from a ragged hole in her face, right above the eyes.

He only guesses the other is a man from the clothing. Limbs stand out at no relation to one another, the body broken and lumped in a pile underneath a tattered leather jacket.

Father Abatangelo steps carefully. It shouldn't be much farther to the clock.

It comes up on the right. His breath catches in his throat.

When they found it fifteen years ago, the clock stood abandoned and still. It filled the side of the tunnel from floor to ceiling, heavy stone shaped like a tombstone. Four hands sticking out from a flat, unmarked face, and a stone gear the size of a truck tire just above the floor. They'd poked and prodded at it, trying to find a mechanism or purpose, until their priorities got rearranged.

Now, the three hands swing up to twelve o'clock and pendulum down. No particular rhythm, not in time with each other. The scrape of stone on stone. The gear at the bottom spins slowly in a pool of blood, like a riverboat pinwheel in shallow water.

Hector was right.

Father Abatangelo watches for as long as he can stand, waiting for some sign of the device's purpose. The rumbling down the tunnel gets louder. He turns around.

The woman's eyes snap open, bulging yellow and bleeding.

Father Abatangelo pulls the gun from his pocket and cocks it, but keeps from firing. She doesn't seem to have registered his presence. They stare at each other. Her face is unnaturally still. He keeps the gun on her. The barrel wavers. His skin crawls.

He creeps past her. Her face turns, watching him leave. He keeps his footsteps as quiet as he can. If he turns his back on her, he's certain she'll make a move.

He gets almost out of sight. The woman's mouth creaks open, wider than natural, and the sound from down the tunnel comes out of her mouth.

Father Abatangelo forgets himself. He turns and runs.

When the tape finishes, the sergeant lets the player run for a second before reaching over and switching it off. The static gives way to sterile silence, but gradually the hum of the air conditioner creeps in, smooth and less obtrusive than Hector's home unit. It's quiet enough that he almost suspects what he's hearing is the fluorescent lights and tries to tune his ears to it, to make sure. The sound fades before his attention. Ears start to ring.

The sergeant plops his boot heels on the table. Hector starts so hard the cuffs dig into his left wrist, where he's fastened to the table. The sergeant smirks.

Hector had been staring at the tape player, trying to listen to silence. Something's wrong, though, something he can't remember. He'll have to ask Alan when he sees him.

"So," Hector says, lips cracking, bleeding, "that was my voice."

The sergeant nods.

"No, I mean, that was my voice? A question."

The sergeant tilts his head like he's assessing just how much shit Hector's going to give him.

But he's not giving him shit. Not on purpose, anyway, though God knows he'd like to. But while Hector's heartbeat was in his ears a minute ago, now it's in his face, pulsing through what feels like bruises. It's the same in his chest. He truly does not know where he is. A police station, yeah, but beyond that. Last thing he remembers is Alan's radios. The chair. The leather cord looped around his neck and the pendant heavy on his chest.

Then, the sergeant. And that tape. Christ.

The door to the interrogation room whispers open and a woman appears sporting uniform blues and red knuckles. The sight of her knuckles triggers something not quite a memory. She rubs at them with a cold smile. Hector's jaw twitches. The cuts he's feeling on his face start to make sense. She shows him some teeth.

"You remember Officer Filbert."

Hector tilts his head, thinking he's going to be here for a spell. "I think we've met, yeah."

Filbert's show of teeth bends into something a bit more like a smile that some dumb, reflexive part of Hector's brain wants to return. He refrains. Her mouth keeps bending, even as the sergeant starts talking again. Hector's not listening. The corners of her mouth split, blood dribbling dark and clumped down her chin. The jaw stretches and severs, and Hector stares down the void at the gray leather skin pushing its way out.

The sergeant doesn't seem to have noticed. He's going through the rigmarole of threats and cajoling to get Hector to cop to something, anything.

Back to Filbert. A growing pouch of the gray skin hangs down to her knees. Hector gets up to run but it's far too late. A rope of black hair catches his ankle from underneath all that skin and he sees in the leather a single yellow eye peel open.

* * *

Father Abatangelo sits in his rectory, pistol in one hand, rosary in the other. The crucifix back around his neck, forbidden pendant wrapped around his gun hand.

He's fingering the beads, trying to meditate on the Luminous Mysteries, but the rumble coming from below the church grows louder and louder. He grips the revolver.

The sound chased him all the way back from the tunnel. He'd pull ahead for a while, but it would always catch up, rattling from a building he passed or rumbling up from the sidewalk. He kept his eyes straight ahead, not wanting to see anything reflected in windows.

The church entrance is barricaded, the filing cabinet shoved in front of the rectory door.

These are surely useless measures.

Father Abatangelo grinds his teeth, forces himself to concentrate.

Holy Mary, mother of God, pray for us sinners, now and at the hour of our death.

Grant us the wisdom to save the last bullet for ourselves. Amen.

CHAPTER FOUR

Slim turns out the light, pulls the little silver case from the desk drawer where he left it. The headlights cut off just before they turn into the lot. Amateur hour. The driver's not expecting Slim to be watching.

First mistake.

The car's tired. Slim can hear it from inside—jangling springs and whining brakes, the kind of heap that'd go for five hundred if the guy selling didn't much like you. It makes the move with the lights a little funny. That, and the driver doesn't seem to know there's a rear access road they could've taken.

Slim dusts off the case, places it carefully in the middle of the desk. Starts checking off his mental list for the ninth time: the sandwich shop and the liquor store closed hours ago; only Ernie's Pawn is left, and Ernie's in the back room, taken care of. The office is in his name, of course.

Slim's got the whole strip mall to himself. The visitors have more considerate timing than expected.

He smiles. Their voices carry even before they close the car doors. Footsteps are light but audible. The murmuring dies off. They're getting serious.

The Sirkos have come calling.

Slim adjusts the silver case on the desk. Blood wicks up into the white thread of his shirt, joining the brown criss-crossing already coagulated, fabric plastered to his bleeding arms. He made the cuts long minutes ago.

The knife drips from the edge of the desk. He won't be needing it again tonight.

The door eases open. A quick jerk and then a pause, slow creaking, like they can't quite believe it's unlocked. Two people silhouetted in sodium yellow. They enter and spread out, each to a side of the room.

Slim thuds his feet up on the desk next to the case.

The two intruders freeze.

"Elijah Sirko," Slim says, because everyone only ever calls him Eli.

Lorelei pulls something unsurprising from her belt.

"And, of course, Lady Lorelei."

Lorelei's stiffening is damn near audible.

Having appropriately stoked pet peeves, Slim waits. Lorelei raises her hand. Click of a hammer cocking—always disappointing, if you've seen enough movies.

She tilts her head. Waits for last words.

Slim bites down on the inside of a smile. "Well, fuck."

It's enough for Lorelei.

The gunshot is stupidly loud. Hurts more than the dull blast in his shoulder. Slim doesn't hear the next two over his ears' ringing. He feels them, though, in the chest. The wall behind him is surely a mural of his viscera.

He tips back in his chair, hits the floor. Scuttles toward the office to make it look right.

The trick now is keeping that lead from his skull.

Lorelei drills another into his lower back and Slim doesn't have to pretend to go limp.

He hears Elijah tramp forward, start rummaging through the desk. Nothing much of interest except the shiny case set carefully on top. Importantly.

Elijah grabs the case, fiddles with the lock. It's comically baroque and nearly impossible to open. From the sound of it, he doesn't make much progress, just stuffs it in his pocket and ransacks the desk for what cash there is.

Lorelei walks to the back room. Slim waits, frowns into the stiff green office carpet. She hasn't reacted yet.

Then: a muffled gasp, Elijah's name hissed across the darkness. Elijah stomps toward the back room, meets the door, pushes against it. A wet impact; the door's obstructed from within.

"Fuck me," Elijah says. "Ernie."

"You said you didn't think we could trust him."

"I said I wasn't sure."

"Well." Lorelei pauses, looks at Slim. "I guess Slim felt about the same way."

Elijah curses again, under his breath.

"Hey," Lorelei says, "this means he knew, right? He'd've been coming for us next. We'd be leaking out in some closet somewhere. Looks like you were right."

They heave against the door until Ernie's body slides far enough for them to slowly step over. Slim feels like laughing. They won't be sure they avoided stepping in his blood until they get somewhere with better light. They make quick time in the back room, though, come back out nearly immediately. Know where everything is, or anyway what they're looking for.

They hurry to the front door, all business now, stifling jitters under a pretension to professionalism. Ernie's body shook them. The weight of the duffel bags dangling from their hands and thrown over their shoulders must be comforting about now.

Slim plans to do more than shake them. Very soon.

Elijah holds the door open for Lorelei. She hesitates in the doorway, looking at Slim on the ground. Hand drifts to her pistol again. Maybe thinks it's not done. A feeling in the back of her mind, he hopes, that her eyes aren't quite dispelling.

Slim suspects she'll make it a good deal longer than her husband.

Elijah hooks his head toward him. "He's gone, Lori. Look at all that blood. Come on."

She nods, but keeps her eyes on Slim a second longer. The door closes behind them.

Truth is, it's dark enough in the office that Slim could probably have opened his eyes all the way, instead of the peeking-through-the-slits routine, as if pretending to be asleep.

But the temptation to jack-in-the-box up, startle them briefly and pointlessly, was already pretty strong.

And Elijah is right, for once. Just look at all that blood.

Slim rolls over on his back. The holes tunneling through his body howl. More than a couple things inside him bend in new and wrong directions. He grips the bottom of the desk and pulls himself under it.

Taped to the unvarnished wood, a thin black sheath the width of an eyeglass case, where Elijah had no reason to look for it. Slim reaches up and fingernail-picks the tape loose from one corner. It's slow and his nail bends back, but even the runes cut into his arms won't keep him alive forever.

The main thing to remember is you can still bleed out, even if it takes far longer.

He gets the tape peeled halfway off and yanks the case the rest of the way free. It plops open onto his chest. The syringe inside stares back at him, plunger already drawn, barrel wrapped in even more duct tape.

Slim doesn't want to see what seethes inside the glass. He looked into it when it was first filled, to make sure. One look at the shapes shimmering within the ash-gray liquid was plenty.

He takes a deep breath. Finds the vein inside his elbow and plunges the needle in.

His arm blazes, the spark pure and black and spreading fast, down to his fingers before doubling back and striking at his chest. Quicker than morphine, than blood. He seizes upward and lands back on the floor, gasping, nerves afire, blood churning and foaming in him, but alive.

Very much alive.

Leaving the house will be the hardest part. Elijah sits on the floor, sagging floorboards creaking comfortably. Lorelei sits next to him and he rests his head on her shoulder. It would be sacrilegious to sit on the furniture now, just to leave it in the morning. What little they've packed to take with them sits in a pile by the door. It's not much. They haven't discussed that they aren't sleeping tonight, but Elijah feels they owe each other that much, and is hugely relieved when Lorelei sits next to him to keep this vigil.

They've made the house into a physical map of their last two years. It has scars aplenty. The hole in the cabinet from when Elijah pulled a double shift and had to put his foot through *something*, the gnarled laminate on the counter Lorelei would pick at while drinking her morning coffee. Chipped linoleum in the kitchen where someone smashed a plate. The house has bent around them, like hard leather molding to the shape of a foot, and the prospect of a new home has Elijah's nerves going.

So when the sun breaks they're up not early but late. They carry the luggage to Lorelei's dying Pontiac in one trip. Elijah goes back to the house and locks the bolt, the doorknob, and peels the key from the ring, holds it in his palm with Lorelei's. The orders were to leave them in the landlord's mailbox, but Lorelei pulls up next to it and Elijah rolls down his window and sets them on top instead. Not actively fuck-you-ing the guy, but leaving the world the opportunity to do so, appealing to the gods of cosmic irony.

Elijah watches the towns pass in a blur of memory that threatens to harden into nostalgia, his eyes on all the wrong places. What can he do, though? He's dug himself into central Florida deep enough that those wrong places are endless.

The Pontiac cuts down through Winter Springs and onto the state roads, south and then east. Soon the land flattens out, relaxing for the long stretch from the suburbs to the beach. They could get there faster by paying a toll, but Lorelei likes the way 50 weaves forever through short walls of trees, and she is the one driving. Elijah's in no mood to complain, anyway. Barely in a mood to stay awake, except he's sure this is an important moment. It's the starting-over that will finally stick.

He falls asleep in spite of himself, head suspended on the seat belt, warm wind whipping his face. He dozes until Lorelei brakes, gets off whichever road they're on. Highway gas stations and motels drift by. They come by way of a two-lane road through what looks like fallow farmland to a sudden burst of houses, a cluster of roofs with nothing around them for a half-mile. It's the kind of development that anticipated the next town stretching out toward it, but got stranded when the market suffocated under its own weight and the construction crews stopped.

Lorelei pulls the Pontiac into the subdivision. Elijah watches the scenery change abruptly and perfectly. They pull up to a house. Holes still in the front lawn from the for-rent sign. From the moment the tires cross the plant-less brick planters on the side of the road, they may as well be in the middle of the suburbs.

Elijah takes the duffel bags out of the trunk. The money and the Dilaudid aren't leaving his sight.

Lorelei opens the door and they go in to take a look around.

The house is too clean. There's a ravaging that takes hold of Floridian structures, with living-in and the right sort of neglect, that's nowhere to be seen. The floor is neat tile and smooth hardwood instead of planks that give underfoot, or even age-yellowed linoleum. It makes Elijah feel like he has to tread lightly, like his neglecting to take his shoes off at the door is an act not of comfort but of rebellion.

The kitchen is all gleaming granite countertops and steel appliances. He can't imagine a couple eating, fighting, fucking in that kitchen. He can't imagine a dishwasher and his hotel-receptionist wife even remotely affording to live there.

Not if they were keen on saving their blood money for a later date.

Lorelei leads him around. The place isn't as large as he'd supposed, but still a far cry from where he'd envisioned lying low.

"Two bedrooms," Lorelei says, "one and a half baths."

"A half bathroom?"

She shrugs. "Fucked if I know. Maybe it means the one that doesn't have a shower?" She's grinning like she's waiting for him to catch on.

He shrugs. "Never knew you were so domestic."

"Oh, motherfucker." She turns on him, the edge back in her eyes. "Who's gonna look here, right? Here of all places. You hear about us, you think a shack off the interstate, somebody's aunt's place in the woods. The middle of some new development? Fuck off, no way."

"Well."

"Especially since we haven't sold the shit yet."

Which raises the question. "Okay, sure. I'm unclear on that point myself. How *did* we wind up here?"

Lorelei flashes a grin and points out back, does her best realtor voice. "And, as you can see, there's plenty of backyard, if you decide to get a dog for the kids."

"Lori."

"Do you and the wife *have* kids?"

Elijah flashes that maybe there's a real question under her shtick, but Lorelei twists a nasty little smile and he knows where he stands again.

It doesn't mean he's going to talk first, though.

She sighs. "I've got that friend in real estate, remember? I had her set it up."

"Hell."

"Relax. Under a different name, from an agent for a client and so forth. There's enough dead ends that no one's going to be able to follow it. And if they do, it ends up at her sister's father-in-law."

"Huh." Elijah looks around again, slower. "Wait. Doesn't that make him *her* father-in-law, too?"

"No. Um. Actually, I don't know."

They spend the evening in different rooms. Getting the house used to their smell like it's a dog. Trying to bend the rooms around them.

It's not the same. It's not ever going to be the same, but Elijah figures it could be a lot worse.

Three days later, Elijah crouches by the front window, staring through the blinds, head and body shielded by the wall. The peeling brown sedan is there again. Mazda, looks like, or Honda, from the eighties, when all those makes looked like malnourished Buicks. The driver's in no hurry, looking everywhere but to Elijah. Lorelei comes down the hall. Elijah hears her turning in place, looking for him, and hisses her name.

She doesn't hear.

"Lorelei."

She comes into the living room and shakes her head at him. "What are you doing?"

"There's somebody outside. Somebody who—"

Lorelei takes two long strides to the window and grabs the little stick to open them. Elijah grabs a fistful of her blouse and tugs her down next to him. The blinds rattle. Lorelei curses, drives her elbow into his ribs.

Elijah wheezes, sways back on his heels, but keeps his hold on her blouse.

"Somebody's who's fucking *been* here before." He takes a pained breath. "Look. Look at his hat."

Lorelei's scowl smolders. "Couple days and you're already getting stir-crazy?" She turns from him and presses her cheek to the wall, looking out from the side of the blinds. "Yeah. Big doofy fishing hat. Gray. So what?"

"Guy was here yesterday. Didn't see him the day before, but I passed him day before that."

"You *passed* him?"

"On the sidewalk. I went to the gas station. That's not the point. Same gray hat, same falling-the-fuck-apart car. Look at him. See his face?"

She looks again, face hardening. "No. Did you?"

"No. He keeps that hat pulled down. I haven't caught his face. He doesn't *want* me to catch his face."

"Uh huh. Or he's waiting for his friend to give him a ride to work, or he's trying to catch somebody who's been stealing his morning paper. Or maybe the radio in his house is busted and that's the only place he can listen to his Duke Ellington tapes."

The way she says it, though, means she doesn't believe it herself, is already starting to think ahead to the next five steps.

He's relieved. It's what he wants to hear. He doesn't know what the hell they're going to do.

"You're sure it's the same guy?"

"Same guy, same car. No question. Just sits there. He's circled around a couple times today, but he keeps coming back, parking in a different place. Wonder the neighbors don't say anything."

"Neighbors?"

"Sure."

"Eli, have you *seen* any neighbors? Not for a couple blocks, and barely then. It's one of the perks. You haven't wondered about where they're keeping their cars?"

He hadn't wondered, hadn't even thought about it. "I figured they have garages, right?"

Lorelei stands, paces back from the window, still watching. Feels for a chair, sits. Elijah takes another look. The man dips his head below the wheel, fumbles for something, then rights himself and fiddles with the radio. Miming a tape player. Not looking in Elijah's direction.

"Well," he says, "who do you think it could be?"

Lorelei lets the silence stretch, like she's making sure he really wants to have this conversation. "Well, can't be Slim, at least."

She says it like a joke. Elijah's not laughing. Not smiling, even.

No, it's not Slim. As of a week ago, Slim's taking some time off from his usual illicit haberdashery due to a rather serious lead problem.

Lorelei clears her throat. "Maybe he's, what, that guy of Slim's? Always in those muscle shirts?"

"Asher."

"Yeah, Asher. But he's kind of an idiot."

Elijah shakes his head at this. He isn't about to start underestimating Asher, but it's not really the time to argue about it. "Yeah, I don't see him tracking us down."

"Well, Jo? Donny? Maria?"

"Jo's solid," Elijah says. "And anyway, I didn't tell her anything. Donny's off in his own little world, last I heard."

"Last you heard was a while ago."

"Maria, maybe. I don't know. You hear from her lately? I mean, before?"

"It's not Maria."

Elijah lets that old fight ride for the moment. "Okay. So, I don't know, could be anybody. Slim had all sorts of new friends toward the end, right? Kept meeting with guys I didn't know. Could be one of them."

Lorelei nods. They watch the car a while longer before Lorelei stands and says it's not getting them anywhere. She's right, but Elijah doesn't know what else to do. He'd planned exactly as far as reaching this hideout, and imperfectly at that. These are new, uncharted waters.

Lorelei leans her elbows on the table and looks around, taking in the house they've barely started getting used to. The way she moves her head, just a touch of a smile on her lips, Elijah's got a pretty clear idea of what's coming.

"We need to do this faster," she says, not looking at him. "If anybody knows we're here, we need to get going."

"But we can't move anything in town. You *know* that. We show up someplace with an armload of the shit, some bells are gonna go off, one way or the other."

"In town, yes. In the state, probably."

Elijah opens his mouth, stops. Put it together. No time to wait around for the heat to die. They're going to have to improvise.

So they watch until morning. The car leaves in the middle of the night. It hasn't come back, and the sun's already broken clear of the horizon. Elijah piles in the car after Lorelei and she drives around the block. He gets out a street over, behind their house, in case someone's watching the house from a more hidden vantage, and they kiss over the gearshift. Lorelei's lips are dry, chapped. Elijah gets out and watches the car for as long as he can, trying to cement it in his memory, before cutting through the vacant yard and in through the back door.

If anyone's watching, hopefully they'll think the house is empty and follow Lorelei, thinking she has their whole take wither her, not knowing she's onto them. Maybe tip their hand in pursuit.

He's going to keep all the lights off and not poke his head out that front door. He's got food and beer enough to last, and he's not expecting Lorelei to be gone more than a week.

That is, if her old friend Hector up in Boston is solid. If he's still alive, still even a little bit interested. If he doesn't turn tail and run from the something's-wrong smell coming off Lorelei when she shows up with a friendly smile and more hillbilly heroin than they've even had time to count.

She's got the gun. If anything goes wrong, no police department in the world would bother making the ballistics match between drug dealers in distant states.

He's got a bowie knife and time to kill. He sits on the couch with the silver case from Slim's office on his lap. It's oblong, shaped like a flattened miniature football. The polished metal stuck out in that office, but he couldn't figure out how to open the clasp. The better light in the living room doesn't help at all.

The case opens after an eternity of absently focused fiddling. Elijah puts pressure on various sides with two fingers and a thumb, the other thumb against the opening. The box eases open only to snap down.

Elijah frowns, tries again. It doesn't give. The mechanism holding the lid shut gives a little when he puts both his thumbs around the back of the case, but it still won't let him open it. He runs his fingertips along the case, looking for more pressure points. He finds four more, two on top and two on bottom, spaced irregularly. Eases it open, glances inside.

Nothing. Gears and braces and struts, all the same gleaming metal. He can see where thin strips are positioned near the sides. They can be bent, opening the box, but only if the pressure's in the exact right spot.

He eases off his fingers. The lid clamps shut again.

It's a box built solely to keep itself shut. Slim's style has developed a sense of humor. It makes Elijah nervous. He stashes it in a high kitchen cabinet and sits on the couch some more.

Four days later, there's a knock at the door. Asher sidles into the living room like they're drinking buddies, like they spent last Friday shooting the shit. He actually says *an offer you can't refuse*.

It hurts, but Elijah has to admit that he's right.

Elijah takes up Asher's offer a week later, makes the party at the right point. Still on the upslope of people arriving but not so early that they stand out. Asher parks down the block out of necessity; the street's clogged with cars. He gets out first. Elijah takes a deep breath and follows, wondering if Asher has a fishing hat to go with his upscale gym-rat getup

"Now," Asher says, looking over Elijah's shoulder like there's something terribly interesting there, "we'll go in separately. Play it cool. Give me five minutes or so, then follow."

"Five minutes."

"Smoke a cigarette."

"Don't smoke."

Asher stares at Elijah like he's just noticed he's there. "Yeah, never could figure that." He threads one from his pocket without removing the pack and sets it and a lighter on the roof of the car. "Here. Fake it." He does a getting-prepared shoulder thing, halfway between a shrug and a pantomime lapel-straightening, and starts toward the house.

Elijah's impressed, despite himself. It's a good thought. Nobody's going to corroborate stories of their arrival—anyone who sees Elijah come in will assume that he arrived later, and anyone watching now will assume he hung back to have a smoke.

Could be he ought to cease his thinking of Asher as a second-rate hanger-on, cruising by on animal charisma. The thought makes his skin crawl.

He does what Asher says, though, and lights the cigarette. After one coughing try at a real drag, he puffs shallow, pretends to enjoy it.

The smoke takes longer than it probably should, but he relishes getting to do the grind-it-out-with-the-toe move. The idea is that there's a guy at the party who walked off with a dozen or so scrips, unwisely made his way back to town. Asher will keep his mouth shut about where Elijah's been holed up if he helps solve the problem. Elijah's supposed to be perfect because these are new people, won't recognize him.

Elijah shoves his hands in his pockets and walks toward the lit-up house.

The trick is to focus on just one face, blur out all those moving and looking and emoting behind it. Bodies in the living room, throbbing and dancing. Elijah feels old. The crowd brings on the familiar pressure in his temples, on top of his heart, that his recent weeks of solitude have at least spared him from. Or de-familiarized him to. He didn't have to deal with rooms full of people hiding out alone. He's lost the knack.

It takes him a few minutes after entering to even remember to breathe, the press of people is so strong. He winds his way around the living room, looking at shoes instead of faces, and finds a wall where people are just leaning. Still too many of them, but it's a step.

The table with the cheap liquor and plastic cups is right next to him. He pours a dollop of gin, exaggerating the motion so anyone watching will think he's pouring more, and fills the cup the rest of the way with tonic water. He now has at least something to do with one hand as he sticks the other in his pocket, leans against the wall.

Still two years shy of his thirties, he's thinking that everybody here needs to get off his lawn.

The guy leaning next to him says something about a band, but Elijah's far enough out of the loop he doesn't recognize the name. He plays the out-of-towner, manages to pass a couple minutes in conversation. Focus on the eyes—it helps some. He tells the guy he's from Indiana, in town visiting some fictitious friend.

He sips to fill the silences between sentences, between conversations. Turns out he didn't know until now how straight tonic water tasted.

He's waiting for the signal from Asher. For when the target's arrived. The .22 revolver Asher gave him is smaller than he's used to but heavy in his pocket. It's too hot for a jacket but he's wishing he had one anyway; his pants verge perpetually on sliding right down.

In another conversation, lying about being from Michigan this time, he says he's fascinated with the Spanish moss here in Florida. The other person nods, semi-amused, and he gets a glimpse at how he looks when tourists say it.

Asher appears a couple of times, flitting from upstairs to the backyard, dipping into rooms and then out of sight. It's like he's occupying some other plane of the party, knows about places Elijah can't.

The party starts to thin, a steady drip of drunks heading out the front door and onto the back roads, and still no signal from Asher. Maybe Elijah will get off easy after all. Though he hasn't much moved, he's exhausted. An Asher-led interrogation might well be beyond him.

It's down to the hostess and a couple of friends. Asher drifts into view from somewhere. The hostess flicks on the lights. The living room's wreckage stands out in incandescent relief. Elijah takes the hint, moves toward the door. Asher slides in front of the exit, grinning through clenched teeth. Elijah stares at him. He never gave the signal.

Asher reaches back and pulls a gun from his waistband. He holds it behind his back where only Elijah can see it. It wasn't on him when they got here; Elijah was going to be the muscle.

Unexpected, was the idea.

Asher briefly meets his eyes then looks to the hostess's boyfriend, who's doing an exaggerated time-for-bed yawn.

Elijah takes a deep breath.

Asher steps forward, whips the gun out. Calls everybody motherfuckers, and can he see some hands, please.

Elijah realizes a little late that, hooray, they now have a hostage situation.

The hostess's boyfriend crashes onto the couch. Hand over his nose, blood trickling out between his fingers. Asher checks the butt of his gun for residue. Elijah holds his revolver on the hostess and a profoundly stoned man in a Phish tee-shirt. He glances to Asher.

Asher stares back, sees something in his expression and shrugs. *What did you expect?* all over his face.

From the couch, Phish's eyes balloon but his face doesn't move. Hostess moves her hands a little too much.

Asher takes one step forward. "Right. Hands where I can fucking see them, and no more of that." He tilts the gun Host-ward. "And I wanna see cell phones on the table, in a nice little stack. And slow."

Three sets of hands poke into three pockets and extract three phones, build a merry little tech pile on the coffee table. Boyfriend breathes through his mouth. Asher looks at Elijah, at his gun. It's not shaking so much. He nods.

"Anybody hanging around outside?"

Elijah checks the peephole. Two guys on the sidewalk, lounging against streetlights and smoking cigarettes, doing a good-night sway. Elijah starts to speak, stops. Thinks about how fast things could go even further south if a hostage starts making noise, attracts the boozy cavalry.

He shakes his head. "Nope." Places one hand deliberately on the door, two fingers extended. His body blocks the couch-goers' view.

Asher glances to the hostages, to Elijah.

Elijah taps the fingers once.

Asher nods. "Okay then. My associate here is going to keep y'all company while I take care of things." He gets halfway to the stairs and turns. "And don't go making trouble, hear? We'll be out of here soon enough."

He disappears up the damp-floorboard stairs. The three on the couch stare at Elijah.

Phish opens his mouth. Elijah shakes his head, lifts the gun like he's testing out its weight, and Phish closes his mouth again.

Boyfriend groans.

"Hey," Hostess says. "The fuck do you think you're doing?"

Elijah takes a step forward, slowly lifts the gun. "You heard the man. Quiet's the name of the game."

Hostess fixes him with a look to melt chrome, purses her lips.

Boyfriend leans forward. "Hey, man. Shit, look." He sniffs, spits blood. "You and fucking Asher—"

Elijah turns, tensed to break Boyfriend's nose again, to make concrete the threat of imminent bodily harm.

Which takes his eyes away from Hostess.

The beer bottle arcs through the air. Its base smacks against Elijah's temple. He stumbles back but manages to keep a grip on the gun. Hostess slams into him, knocks him against the wall. The gun hits the carpet. Hostess rears up, aims her fist.

A roaring pop like the ground breaking and a hole bursts in Hostess's shoulder. Blood flecks Elijah's face. White noise rings in his skull.

Hostess falls. Asher at the foot of the stairs, gun in hand, a backpack slung over one shoulder. He shouts something Elijah doesn't catch and he plants his back against the wall. Phish leans and twitches like he's trying to break a physical bond with the couch. Asher clamps a hand on his shoulder and pushes him back.

Elijah gets to his feet, slowly. Hostess moans in front of him.

"You get what we came for?" he says.

Asher smiles. "Almost."

Boyfriend gets to his feet and lurches toward the door. Asher points the gun at him. Boyfriend's expecting it, but it doesn't matter. The first shot hits the shoulder, the second the head.

Elijah picks up his fallen weapon.

Hostess's scream tears hot holes in the air, gives way to coughing.

Asher stands behind Phish, pops his brain all over the coffee table.

Hostess shields her head with her arms. Elijah turns his gun on Asher.

This isn't an ambush, isn't about recovering anyone's stolen property.

Asher smiles at the barrel of Elijah's revolver.

This is an execution.

Elijah squeezes the trigger.

The report does nothing to ease the ringing in his ears. Nor to drop Asher.

He squeezes again. Fires all six rounds at Asher's chest.

Asher smiles. The revolver was loaded with blanks.

Hostess gets her knees underneath her, props herself up. A huge pool of blood on the carpet behind her.

Asher sights down his gun. Takes his time. Fires.

Hostess's throat bursts backward. Spatters the wall.

Elijah flings the revolver at Asher.

Asher doesn't have to move much to make it miss. He licks his lips, taunting. Elijah freezes. There aren't any outs he can see. He can't pretend he had Asher's back, can't possibly make it to the door before he gets off a shot.

Assuming Asher has any bullets left. Which Elijah isn't sure. He stares at Asher, gathering himself, and darts toward the front door.

Elijah's a step and a half away when the door opens. His chest slams into the outstretched palm of a man in a gray fishing hat.

Elijah bounces backward, falls. The man in the gray hat tilts his head. He is no doubt the man he saw through the window outside the house, in the sedan. Who forced Lorelei out of town and Elijah here.

The hat's dipped too low to make out most of the face, but Elijah can see the goatee, as full as the rest of the body is scrawny, like the man's facial hair has been sapping sustenance from the rest of him.

The mouth in the midst of the goatee twitches. "Mr. Sirko."

"Slim," Elijah says.

Another blast from Asher's gun. Elijah's hip buckles like there's a new joint. He hits the floor.

He watches through a haze of adrenaline and fuzzy panic as Asher places the gun in the hand of Hostess, angles her so it looks like she was shot by Elijah. Asher nods, fires off another.

It divots the floor near Elijah's stomach—a near miss. Elijah twists in anticipation, jerks his injured hip. White light flickers over his eyes. He pitches to his side and vomits into the carpet.

Words spoken above him. A vague sense of surprise that he's even conscious. Footsteps in the carpet and something strong takes hold of Elijah's skull, wrenches so it faces upward.

Elijah opens his eyes and sees Slim.

"Oh, Eli." Slim does an avuncular little sigh. "We had such a good thing going. This really is a shame."

Elijah remembers it differently. The witty response escapes him.

Slim clamps his fingers down hard on Elijah's head, pulls a long, curved knife from his belt. He drags the business end of the blade along the top of his own forearm, into fresh skin, between a complicated history of such cuts. He pries one of Elijah's eyelids open with his thumb.

The blood comes fast and hot, sluices over Elijah's eyeball.

Elijah screams. The world slides out of joint; the image skips, like the projectionist in charge of beaming our lives from the stars down onto the surface of the planet showed up for work hungover, his work jittery, out of focus. The feeling slides through the ocular cavity to the skull.

Slim releases the eyelid.

Elijah blinks hard. Succeeds only in getting blood all over his face, beading off his eyelashes.

The room commences to spin. Elijah holds to it as long as he can, digging his fingers into the carpet, but the dark starts at the edges and worms its way to the center.

CHAPTER FIVE

No sign of Jessica for two weeks. The kids she runs with have heard, same as Lorelei, that a guy named Floyd's been gone about as long, so they're reluctant to tell her much. But it's not that kind of situation, Lorelei thinks. It wouldn't be, even if it were. Not for Lorelei. But she needs to find her all the same, and maybe that need bleeds through in her voice and spoils whatever leads she might pick up.

Still, Jessica maybe knows how to get in touch with Hector. Lorelei wouldn't so much as mention his name to a stranger in this town. But he's the only person she can trust with the kind of weight she's looking to move.

Five days up north, here in the city, and she's already itching to get back to Florida, to streets she knows, people she can read.

There's exactly one possibility left. And so Lorelei fights down her instincts again in order to get on the subway and holds the triangular loop hanging from the roof for thirty-five minutes, to the stop nearest the last address.

It's a long enough walk from the subway stop that Lorelei sees the change in the buildings, the slope that's not so much a gradient as a series of sudden shifts. She doesn't put her hand in her jacket pocket, doesn't hold Elijah's revolver out of sight. She doesn't, but she almost does.

The address comes up first. It's a narrow apartment building, a staircase with two doors on either side, uninspired lighting and threadbare carpet. A single digit on each door. Lorelei hits the second floor, double-checks what's written on the scrap of paper. Knocks on number seven.

A shuffling comes from the apartment behind her. Lorelei straightens up, doesn't look behind, lets whoever's back there keep on not seeing her face through the peephole. She listens close as she can and doesn't hear anything more.

Which, likely as not, means the watcher hasn't moved from their door.

Lorelei raises her hand to knock again. The door yanks open, catching on the chain.

"What do you want?" An indistinct face from a dark apartment.

"I'm a friend of Slim's."

The woman snorts. "He doesn't have any friends left in this town."

"I'm not from this town." Beat. "You knew I was coming."

The woman sighs and closes the door, pulls the chain and opens it again. She's a head and a half shorter than Lorelei. Lorelei tries not to loom, but also not to look like she's cowering. Gives up and just stands there.

"Well, come in if you're coming."

Lorelei slips through the opening. The woman closes the door behind her. Clicking and sliding of various locks. Lorelei's eyes adjust to the dim living room. There's nothing much to see but a bare wood table with a couple chairs. The first thing to Lorelei's lips is something about how she loves what she's done with the place.

She catches herself just in time. "I'm Lorelei."

"Bet you are. Lorelei, friend of Slim. Haven't heard his name in a while."

"I never did catch yours."

"Hm." The woman tosses some clothes off a recliner and sits. She doesn't offer a seat to her guest. "See, I'm disappointed. Last I heard from down south was somebody'd ripped Slim off. Made off with a bunch of money. Drugs, too, depending on who you talk to. Names that get mentioned, one of them is Lorelei. And here you are. Same name, and a friend of Slim."

"It's a funny coincidence."

"I'd sure love to talk to that other Lorelei."

"I'm sure plenty of people would."

The woman laughs, showing teeth for the first time. "Yeah, but I haven't got a bullet for her. I'd like to shake her hand. I'm Stacy."

"Stacy." Lorelei wanders to the window, looks out at nothing. "I've got to talk to Jessica. You know the Jessica."

"Yep. She's a friend of Slim's too, once. Maybe you could ask him."

"I don't imagine that conversation would be much fun."

Lorelei doesn't have to turn. She can hear the smile.

"Maybe not. But I haven't seen her in a month or so."

"Neither has anybody else."

"But I can tell you where she'd been hanging around, with that Floyd guy. You know. He told me once he was gonna take her there."

* * *

Lorelei stalks up and down Gutter Street, checking the sewer grates. Stacy said she'd know it when she saw it. She described how the grate over the entrance wasn't even bolted but wedged in. People would pry it up to get into the tunnel and replace it when they left. She'd never been down there, though, pleaded crippling claustrophobia in the face of the contrary evidence of her dim apartment.

She told her it was right in front of an abandoned storehouse. Lorelei's taking that to have been a joke. She walks six blocks down, six blocks up, both sides of the street, past any number of former businesses, and some still clinging to life. Shopkeepers eye her the second she's in front of their doors and forget about her the next.

She settles on one last go-round, pretending to be looking at addresses. The second grate she sees stops her cold. It's in a dead space in the street, between two rows of boarded windows. Someone would have to crane their neck or happen to be passing by to notice anyone slipping down into it.

Lorelei looks around, crouches in front of the steel. It's fresh, un-grimed, with four shining new city-maintenance bolts in the corners. The concrete behind bears scars from previous gouging.

If anyone had been hiding out down there, they're certainly trapped now. And while Lorelei has never met her, Jessica doesn't strike her as the sort of person with tools, a contingency plan.

A smell like burnt hair comes from the grate. Lorelei tries not to consider what that means and puts her face right up to the steel. She hisses Jessica's name as loud as she can without her voice carrying too far.

No reply, but a thump and rattle from deep below.

She gets out a scrap of paper and writes down the closest address.

When the white-haired man limps into the convenience store, Stacy puts down the cigarettes she's been stocking and leans against the counter. Head down like she's reading a magazine, eyes tilted upward to cruise the guy. It's not usually the older ones she has to worry about. More often it's kids, giddy to be where they're not supposed to be, nicking food and knocking over shelves.

Still, though. The way this guy's moving, it'll pay to keep watch.

The man hobbles his way down one aisle and along the back wall. Drunk, maybe, or something else, something synaptic. Stacy edges to the side and peers down the aisle. The man stands in front of the cooler where the water's kept, looking up and down, up and down, like all the labels confuse him.

Stacy can relate. She has to stock those shelves, somehow get each identical bottle into its specific slot.

The man tugs at the cooler door. It doesn't give. He tries again, then tries to slide it. Still nothing. He peers at the handle, at the hinges, finally slides it the right way. He reaches in for a bottle, taking both hands off the door. The door slides back, almost knocking him off his feet. He braces one hand against the glass, pushes the door to the side with his knee, and reaches in with the other hand. Finally, triumphantly, he pulls out a bottle.

Stacy knows better than to be looking at him when he turns around. That's exactly the bait he might be looking to take, to start himself a little scene. She looks to her side, at the security camera feed. It's as much static as not, the camera leering at the wrong wall anyway. She counts to ten in her head. Still the man's not at the counter.

She jerks her head back around, thinking she let the guy slip by without paying for the water, but he's swaying now in front of the juice endcap. He scans and scans. Finally he reaches for a bottle and sends half the shelf clattering to the floor. He looks from the lemon juice in his hand to the bottles on the floor and sighs, steeling himself to lean down and pick it all up.

Stacy doesn't figure she can endure the time that would take. She was supposed to be on break twenty minutes ago, but the next shift's late, or quit. The very least she can ask is to not be part of this scene.

"Don't worry about it," she says. "I'll get it."

The man looks at her dubiously. Like she's the one who might not be up to the task.

He finally makes his way to the counter. Stacy slowly rings up the water and the lemon juice. The man surprises her with a couple of crisp dollar bills.

Counting his change, she meets his gaze. Dull recognition, the sense that she knew this man. Like seeing a distant relative on the street.

The man cocks his head. His eyes burn bright. The rest of him slips into their shade; the unkempt hair, the size-too-big clothes he wears like he's recently shrunk.

"Do I—" Stacy starts.

The man looks down, back up at her, squinting. The feeling fades. Stacy hands him his change. He jingles the bell on the door on his way out.

Stacy's skin goes numb. Chill on her face.

She shakes it off, brings herself back around. Outside, a group of people turn the corner up the block. She flips the be-back-soon sign around on the door and retreats to the stockroom.

The old lady isn't paying her enough. What else is new.

Lorelei returns to the Gutter Street grate, the supposed last known location of one Jessica Roberts. There has been no missing-persons report, no police investigation. Her friends believe—or claim to—that Jessica has run off with a known drug dealer named Floyd. Lorelei has been running in circles for nearly a week, talking to friends of Jessica's, and friends of friends, circling back and tracing cold crash pads, abandoned squats.

The only potentially useful information spouts from Stacy, about whom little is known. Or, about whom little has been forthcoming.

And that little information has Lorelei crouching in the gutter of a dark street in an unfamiliar city, one hand holding a socket wrench, the other gripping a revolver inside her jacket pocket.

She grunts, has to take her hand off the gun to even pretend to get the bolt started. The only bolted-down sewer grate she's ever seen, perhaps the only one in town, and the city crew seems to have done their job properly.

This is the last stop on her tour of the city. Money isn't the concern; there's enough left to sustain her for a while yet. But she and Elijah stole more than money from Slim, and can't move it back in Florida. Not with Slim's people still around.

The bolt budges the smallest bit. Lorelei grinds her teeth, wrenches harder. Jessica is at best a long shot. But getting back on the interstate empty-handed, that would be too much.

Fifteen minutes later she's loosening the last bolt, sweating in the cooling air. Footsteps down the street. She stands quickly, makes to look like she's just out for a casual stroll. Not a convincing act, on this half-dead commercial block, but what she's doing is for sure illegal, and definitely hard to explain.

She walks a handful of paces and turns. No cop there, no flashlight or patrol car. Just a man slowly approaching from down the alley. She can't see his face, but he is almost certainly watching her. He stops, sways a little. Lorelei watches him. The man finally dips back to the intersection and heads around the corner.

Lorelei exhales. The last bolt is so close to coming out. She kneels and gets it the rest of the way without even taking the wrench back out of her pocket. The bolt slips from her fingers, rings against the concrete. She sticks her fingers through the slats in the grate.

Footsteps pound from around the corner. She looks up and sees the man careening toward her, all white hair and wide eyes, mouth flopping open. Lorelei stands. The man gets within a dozen paces.

"You," he says, from the back of his throat. "You."

Lorelei can't tell if he's starting a sentence or calling to her. He's close enough to smell, arms outstretched. His eyes strain, bloodshot, and draw her attention from the rest of his face.

She takes a quick step forward, brings her elbow up, going for the nose, but hits his chin instead. The man staggers back. He gathers himself and comes back toward her.

Lorelei curses and draws the revolver.

"You."

"Yeah, fucking me. Time to find someone else to bother, old man."

"You. You don't want to—"

Lorelei makes a show of pulling back the hammer. Wonders whether she's still a decent shot. Can't be too hard to not miss, though, at this distance.

The man's hair hasn't merely grayed but is a shocking white, standing nearly on end, a sea of dead reeds sweeping back from his head. Lorelei braces the gun with her other hand.

"You—"

"I said fuck off."

The man takes a step back. Lorelei takes two forward. The man turns and runs.

Lorelei returns to the grate, trying to keep her hand from shaking. It was only a matter of time, she supposes, before she ran into some character, poking around ill-traveled parts of an unfamiliar city, but still. Those eyes, that hair.

She shakes her head and pulls free the grate, lets it clang to the sidewalk. Arranges herself in the gutter, guessing at the best angle of approach.

She puts her hands on the concrete and lowers herself carefully down.

Stacy finishes the last hour of her accidental double shift. The afternoon guy didn't show, and the old lady screamed at her over the phone until Stacy agreed to cover for him, just to end the conversation. It'll take a week of solid badgering just to get the pay she's owed for the extra hours. This time she's going to do it. No more of this under-the-table shit, these unpaid extra hours keeping the place afloat.

Not like the old lady or her husband ever work anything but weekend mornings, after all. They've got some mysterious way of knowing, though, about too-long lunches or unauthorized store closings. Stacy suspects one of the other Chamber members on the block spies for them, but hasn't been able to narrow it down.

No keeping the old lady from railing at her, anyway. She made a big production of what a service she was doing by employing Stacy, but that doesn't forestall her digging into the past for dirt to use in whipping Stacy back in line. Stacy could just as easily be on the street. She's not unaware of this. It stays her tongue when the old lady calls her a kid.

"May the Lord keep you for your good fucking works," Stacy says, and pockets two packs of cigarettes before locking up.

She lights one on the half-mile walk back down the economic ladder. It's at least a small blessing that she's not required to wear a uniform, can pretend for those first few blocks that she belongs on this street and not as a servant.

Before this she'd worn a bright blue vest for her brief stint at a big liquor store, where she had to take classes in order to give customers wine recommendations, and which ended when the results of her background check came back and exploded her very fraudulent resume.

The trick then had been figuring out how to stash the vest the moment she got out the door, so she could walk home without broadcasting how she'd spent her last endless hours.

She reaches her block and stares up at the lit second-floor window of her complex. The curtains are open a touch, and lamplight flares out the opening. She walks around to one corner of the building, then to the other, rigging a map of the floor plan in her head. Surely it must be a different room.

But it's not. No matter from which angle she checks, the lit window is hers. She makes sure she's out of view from anyone looking through the crack in the drapes and stands, watching, finishing her smoke. Sees no movement behind the drapes. No shadows. Nothing at all amiss except the lamp she didn't turn on this morning, let alone leave burning when she left for work.

She looks around again. No one on the street that she can see. She wishes she had a gun, a knife. Hell, a corkscrew would be serviceable, if there's not too many of them.

As-is, though, she's not going up that staircase tonight. Or ever again.

The thought of her very little money makes her worry. She turns and exits the block at the quickest walk she can manage. Maybe she could call in some old favors, some ancient debt made to bear fruit. Except, she cut those ties a while ago. Which only further raises the question of why whoever's in her apartment is there.

Maybe Lorelei really was who she said she was. Maybe she was followed. Maybe somebody figured out Stacy had helped her and wasn't happy about it.

Except that doesn't make any sense. If they'd been following Lorelei, surely they'd have taken one of any number of opportunities to jump her, make her disappear before she got to Stacy. Extract from her whatever information they wanted.

But the fact of it is, the light is on. And there's no reason Stacy can summon for it, except that conversation with Lorelei yesterday.

She slips away, down the street, taking a roundabout route in case.

* * *

Father Abatangelo does not know exactly where he is. He's aware that he's been wandering for some time, perhaps days, but the specifics are murky. Much of his attention is focused on walking; it's hard to put his feet into the right positions. If he lets his concentration slip for even a second his balance wavers. Twice today the ground has come rushing up.

It's getting better, he tells himself. It can only get better.

Except, that's not right.

The last clear thing he remembers is the rectory, the basement church that had been his for six years. Sitting in the chair, waiting to go down fighting. Sighting down that huge pistol at the door, certain it was a matter of very little time.

He was right about that, but not the way he thought.

But that waiting, that's the clearest thing. After, as the walls started shaking as though filled with massive snakes, bricks tearing loose, ceiling planks splintering and raining paint and sawdust and insulation on his shoulders, his mind was a broken movie camera, only imprinting images on a fraction of the frames.

This must have been the lost time Hector told him about.

One frame that burns bright, if blurry, is the door finally splintering, a pillar of hair and mold and the smell of the end of the world pouring through, then pulling themselves out just as quickly. The shifting wall of gray leather, roiling over the pulpit and the pews.

The yellow eye that filled the hole in the wall and stared. Unblinking.

Father Abatangelo didn't even pull the trigger.

The eye continued to stare. He doesn't know how long he sat there, watching it watch him as the church crumbled around them. He remembers his vision blurring and dimming and coming back again, and the eye was still there. New holes in the church.

He waited for the three floors above to come crashing down and kill him. Woke in an arm's-length bubble underneath a mountain of wreckage.

A shoulder bumps rough against his. He pinballs into the brick wall of the building next to him. He's not on the same street he was a moment ago. The light's different, the buildings taller. He catches a snatch of profanity from the departing pedestrian. It worries him little.

Still, it would be best to try and recuperate somewhere, wait until his brain's firing correctly.

No telling who else—what else—might be looking for him.

He doesn't remember, exactly, clawing his way out of the rubble, but it left cuts all over his palms and arms. Must have just started digging. He hit air and sort of flopped there, half his body still under the building, saw firefighters just beginning to dig. Their faces showed their shock at this priest crawling out from what should have been his grave.

They insisted that he absolutely had to visit a hospital. He tried to wave them off but couldn't quite form words through the dust in his throat. They told him the ambulance would be there in a minute, and to wait on the bench. He stared at the big red truck on the curb, realized it was the kind for putting out fires, not one full of paramedics.

Father Abatangelo nodded, took his place on the bench, and slipped away as soon as their backs were turned. Even walked past the ambulance blaring its way down the street.

Then the wandering. Then the woman, when he realized he'd found his way to Gutter Street, his instincts having failed something spectacular. Taste of lemon on his lips.

He tried to warn her. It went poorly.

He touches his chin, the swelling there. How long ago was that? He looks at the city moving around him, the traffic getting heavier. It feels like it was only a few hours ago, last night, two nights at the latest, but he doesn't know. Doesn't know what day it is.

He studies his reflection in the window of a sandwich shop. His hair's still the wrong color. He stares, trying to figure out the trick. The couple inside sipping coffee sees him leering at them from behind the glass and recoils as politely as possible. He turns away.

He reads the street sign, repeats it to himself. Notices his voice scratching its way out.

He remembers that street name. It's time to get inside, anywhere.

There's one place nearby that he knows. He stops walking, squints to make his memory work. Orients himself street-wise and shambles away.

The sewer grate leads Lorelei into some kind of nowhere. Her feet hit the ground and slide. She throws her hands behind her and barely catches herself against the concrete. Water hangs in the air, an invisible mist, carrying an electric smell. Like transistors, but tinged with fire.

She clicks on her flashlight and shines it first at her feet. Black fuzz covers the floor. It looks dry, but she takes a step and her leg zips forward and she crashes to the ground.

She pans the light around the tunnel, at the walls, the ceiling. Everything is covered in the same black fuzz. She covers her hand with the sleeve of her jacket and tests it. Feels like carpet at first, but as soon as she presses down the traction gives and the floor is slippery as oil.

She rises very, very slowly, one hand braced on the wall, the other holding the light toward her feet.

From down the hallway, a slithering.

She lifts the flashlight and points it down into the depths. Very nearly drops it.

The corridor extends farther than seems possible, given the city's architecture, the proximity of the shore. Standing upright, the ceiling touches the top of her head, and it doesn't get any taller. The ground slopes gradually, and the sensation is that of standing at the lip of an echoey cavern, muted and insulated.

The reason for the muting slithers no more than ten yards from her feet. Ropes of hair, squirming over each other like a pit of serpents, dripping some white substance that hardens into clumps in the braids. Busy, very busy, but at what Lorelei can't tell.

The light doesn't seem to affect the hair. Lorelei considers getting closer for a better look, decides against it. She can't look away from the hair, though. Feels a dull fear hidden deep in her stomach, an animal instinct that's not quite getting communicated to her head.

She leans forward, sees the outline of something far down the tunnel that doesn't quite materialize. Perhaps human. Almost certainly not.

No one could be living down here. Jessica, if this was indeed a place she frequented, is long gone or buried.

Lorelei peels her eyes away from the seething mass and reaches up for the lip of the sewer grate. She came down here to locate Jessica, after all. No reason to linger now.

And no matter what it looks like, surely she's not seeing what she thinks she's seeing. She'll get home in a few days and look it up, find out that something like this happens in major cities—maybe something about the water seeping under all that construction.

She gets herself pulled halfway out, black fuzz smearing green on her clothing. A tug on her ankle. She wrenches around, looks down at her leg, at the rope of hair wrapped around it. It twists itself slowly, one way then another. Tentative.

The pressure starts to abate. Lorelei yanks her foot, pulls hard on the concrete.

The tendril snaps back to attention, grabs her ankle again, starts snaking up her leg. Lorelei shouts. Something moves again in the dark. The tendril keeps climbing. Lorelei pulls the gun from her pocket, aims at the hair. Fires.

The gunshot sounds far away. The bullet pings off the wall—little cloud of dust and a divot in the stone.

A noise almost too low to hear grows from down the hallway. Tendrils of hair pluck themselves from the knot and slink toward her.

Lorelei fires again. Empties the clip at the hair, hits it twice. The second hit cuts the tendril off a foot below her leg.

But its friends are coming. They sputter and patter across the ground, raising their own kinetic din against the growing bass roar from the deep. From the raw end of the severed tendril oozes a gray oil. Droplets fly with the writhing.

Lorelei heaves desperately, pulls herself out. She sprawls on her back on the street above.

She makes a perfunctory effort to replace the grate. The bolts are scattered around, un-findable, and she doesn't care. The steel scrapes against the concrete. She gives it a last savage push, wedging it well enough over the opening, and runs.

The spark of fear buried under her stark fascination surfaces, meets open fumes of adrenaline. It burns and rages. She sprints, covers four blocks before realizing she's been hauling ass with a gun in her hand. She stops, shoves the weapon into her jacket pocket. Beneath her panting, something gives. Her adrenaline drains.

She pitches against the nearest storefront and vomits on the sidewalk, keeps vomiting until the fear and panic have faded. A wave of exhaustion hits. Perhaps she'll have the strength to reach her motel. The sun will be coming up soon.

Her jacket bears the smears and smudges from the black fuzz, an oozy green drying into a gray crust. She scratches at the dried patches. They flake off, dissolving in the air and against the sidewalk like cigarette ash.

She makes the motel, barely. Strips off her clothes and flops onto the musty mattress.

Exhaustion hangs wet-wool heavy on her body. She closes her eyes, lets herself drift. They pop back open, spring-loaded. Every vein in her eyeballs scratches her lids when she blinks; she feels she could sleep for days but they won't stay closed.

In the hours between dawn and noon, she blurs off a few times, but jolts awake each time convinced that something is crawling toward her beneath the wallpaper. She turns on the light, tries it that way. It doesn't help.

She dresses and leaves shortly after noon not particularly refreshed. Sunlight like a sandpaper assault. Street teeming with lunch-hour traffic. Lorelei curses her timing, lowers her head, and starts off.

The walk is longer than she thought, and takes even longer because the streets are packed. Sweat drips off her nose. Exhaust fumes. She steps into an intersection prematurely and narrowly dodges a truck.

She swallows, blinks. Going to need to have her head on straight here.

She makes the narrow apartment building. One more thing, then she can get on the interstate and out of this city. Stacy sent her to that sewer and Lorelei needs to know why. Certainly Jessica hadn't been there for some time. It would have been easier for Stacy to make up some other, un-checkable lie, or to send her back to one of the dead ends she'd already hit.

The stairs are even dimmer in the full light of day. The steps creak in a way foreign to her. Not the familiar Florida sagging of humidified wood, the steps feel like they've gone brittle, drying out despite the dankness of the hallway.

It sits all wrong with her.

Light peeks out under the door to Stacy's apartment. Lorelei pounds on it, gives it maybe a half second before pounding again.

The door flies open. A small man in a ski mask raises a knife to Lorelei's neck. The way he breathes, it sounds like he caught himself at the last possible moment.

Lorelei takes a step back. "Sorry, I was looking for— I think I have the wrong door."

She turns to leave. Someone hisses something from inside the apartment. The man grabs Lorelei by the collar and tugs her inside. Bolts the door behind them.

The second man, wearing no mask, sits in a chair angled to look out a crack in the blinds. He has a knife of his own on the table next to him—a diving knife, with some very suggestive serration. His hair is cropped close enough to see scalp. Heavy bags under his sharp eyes.

Lorelei's kingdom for the gun. Except, she didn't have any more bullets; she ran through them in the tunnel, so she left it in the motel room.

But she could have bluffed.

The man by the window puts on a neighborly smile. "Who did you say you were looking for?"

Father Abatangelo finds the apartment with some difficulty. It's been just shy of a decade, he figures, since Hector insisted he return with him, looking to Alan for protection. They both knew, in the aftermath, that they needed something to shield them, in case the beasts returned. Alan's demonstration, toward the end of the initial nightmare fifteen years ago, had seemed effective if particularly dangerous. But by their return visit, Father Abatangelo had already started pursuing the cloth, and Alan's off-brand mysticism was only more off-putting for its efficacy.

Father Abatangelo had to maintain his defenses. Opening the door to Alan's apartment, he wonders how much anyone can do.

Alan's flat was never impressively kempt, but it's a wrecking yard that greets him now. The chair, the big throne of sticky wood whose purpose Father Abatangelo remembers well enough, in flashes and adrenaline snapshots, sits cast onto its side against the far wall. Burnt a little on the bottom. One of the radios is smashed on the floor, still plugged into the surge protector. Two more radios are plugged in there, the other two into an identical surge protector by the next wall. The place is a museum exhibit of home radios through the decades. The refrigerator door hangs open, its former contents strewn across the floor like there was an explosion.

And in the center of the room, a very familiar pendant, with ragged strips of skin turned black and burnt-on at the middle.

Father Abatangelo looks around. The elements all look right, feel like they add up to something definite, something useful. He knows what happened here but can't quite access it.

Blink and flash and he's in the bathroom, breathing hard over the toilet. He swallows and spits, stands laboriously. The bathroom's a disaster, too, but more of the Alan-lives-here variety. He walks back to the living room, limping with both legs—a process of falling forward and catching himself a couple times a second. He steers wide around the pendant, with its burnt skin and implications, and slumps in the corner, under the window. Stares at the chair. Wants to right it, if only to give the appearance of someone straightening up, but he's not getting to his feet again anytime soon.

He looks at the door. No way to tell for sure, but he thinks it's been too long since there were wood and hinges between him and the outside world.

Lorelei takes a seat, uninvited, across the dining table from the second man with the compensatory knife and no mask. The first man doesn't move to stop her. The second man looks her over, amused. Lorelei glances from one to the other, from black polyester to wind-blasted skin. No one says anything for a while.

Lorelei puts her elbows on the table. "So are you gonna shoot me or cut me or what?"

The unmasked man leans back in his chair. "We haven't got any guns."

"Maybe you could start," the first man says, "by telling us what you're doing here?"

"House call. You?"

"Funny, I didn't think Stacy had many friends left. She sure was hard for us to find."

"Somehow I don't think so."

A key turns in the lock. The silence flexes around it. The door opens and a head pokes through. This third man takes in Lorelei and the other two men. Nods.

"Well?" the second man says.

"I—she came up here."

"Yeah."

The new man nods and slips back out, locks the door behind him.

Lorelei smiles. "Well."

The second man shrugs. "So."

"So?"

"We were figuring out what you were doing here."

"I told you. I knocked on the wrong door."

The second man stands and motions to the first to take his chair, keep an eye out the window. He walks to Lorelei, stands over her. Runs his thumbnail along the edge of his knife.

"Now, you know, you're not in the best of positions here. Most times, we probably would have already dealt with this. But," he looks to his partner, who keeps glancing out the window, "we're finding ourselves in a bit of a bind."

"You waiting for someone?"

The second man's expression hardens. He leans forward and touches the tip of the blade just above Lorelei's collarbone. She doesn't flinch. He gets a tired look and pulls the knife away, faces the wall.

Lorelei unclenches her fist, ready for a long-shot swing she decides not to take.

The man turns back to her.

"So," she says. "That other guy's guarding the door? Didn't see him on my way up. Not much of a watch, you ask me."

The man smiles. "He was following you."

Heartbeat. Another.

So they followed her from here, have had someone on her for who knows how long. She didn't see anyone when she went down to Gutter Street. And she was looking. Maybe they saw her go back to her motel room, decided to pick her up in the morning.

Or maybe the masked man is lying to her. It seems like something he'd do.

"I suppose you fellows don't know where Stacy is."

"*There* we go."

"Well?"

He waves around them. "No. We're waiting for her. Need to have a conversation, you know."

"Yeah. I know the feeling."

A frown breaks through the man's carefully held expression. Lorelei watches him, doesn't say anything more. It's a fine line she's trying to walk, between convincing them that she's after Stacy, too, that maybe they can pool their resources—or at least not kill one another—and sounding too much like she's pleading.

She keeps her eyes on the man's chest.

He paces back and forth, letting his indecision show more than he probably thinks. The second man lifts the drapes and leans forward, and for a moment the whole room goes tense. He shakes his head and leans against the wall.

Whoever's down there, it's not Stacy. This seems to tip the scales.

"Okay." The masked man nods. "So she's not here. Any ideas?"

Lorelei nods. "There's a place. Couple of her friends are holed up there. Keeping their heads down."

A glance passes between the two men.

"She told me about it a while ago," Lorelei says. "She's probably there right now."

The man by the window looks to the masked man, shrugs. The masked man nods.

"I don't suppose you could take us there?" Flexing his fingers around the knife, making it look real casual, except it's right in front of Lorelei's face.

"Yeah, okay."

The masked man waves her to her feet, directs his partner to come and frisk her. She holds her arms out to her side, like going through airport security. He doesn't find any weapons, any wallet or identification or money, and Lorelei thinks this is about to be a problem. Instead, she lowers her arms and sees the two men waiting.

She asks them if they know how to get to Gutter Street.

Father Abatangelo wakes after a time, looks around. The light is lower than he remembers, but he can't tell if it's later the same day, or the next, or later still. He feels like he's slept for years. The fog in his head has started to clear. The sight of the room fills the absence he feels with a crawling dread.

The chair. The pendant and skin. The explosion of food. He takes inventory, knows before he's finished what's missing.

There's no body.

It's not a large apartment. Aside from a linen closet and a pantry, there's only the bathroom and the room he's in. Father Abatangelo gets to his feet and checks the remaining spaces. A few mismatched sheets, canned food. No heads or bones or blood.

Father Abatangelo flashes again to the body of the third man, years ago: ribcage open in a scream to the red sky, the metallic smell of unnatural death. He stands easier now, like it was only a bender, something he had to sleep off.

But the memories are becoming clearer, too. He hadn't realized they'd dulled, gone vague. All the years trying not to think about them seemed to pay dividends, but now they're as clear as last week. Clearer, even.

Something is happening. Something like enough to last time, but different. Bigger, maybe. Hector was right—he was being followed. But they didn't have enough time to prepare, to even pretend to know how to fight back. It was on them so fast.

He walks to the chair, places his hand on the armrest. Pauses.

He knows how to fight. Remembers, a little. He frowns. How could he have forgotten? This is more than just the passing of years. And now it's coming back, as though he'd been thinking about it every day since, memorizing the details.

He paces forward, backward, sideways. The carpet doesn't rush up after him; his feet stay where they're supposed to be. He feels for the first time the stinging pain on his hands and arms and chest from the rubble he crawled through. He strips off his shirt to look himself over. Dirt clogs his wounds, blending with the clotting. A few have swollen into angry pink lashes. He prods at one, winces.

If Alan's bathroom is in general cause for hesitation, the shower is a step or two worse. A black ring around the bottom, lime deposits and loose hair. Father Abatangelo notices these in passing. It doesn't slow him down as he steps inside.

Hot water blasts his skin. He yelps, huddles at the back of the tub, and lets the steam build. Eases his feet under the stream, then his shins. The water feels like it's stripping away days, years of dirt and dead skin.

Father Abatangelo gets out of the shower glisteningly awake, aggressively alert. He rocks up and down on the balls of his feet a few times. Wraps a towel around his waist.

The living room is as he left it, but his newfound wakefulness makes it appear darker. What had been details when he first arrived are now the only things drawing his eyes. The pendant sits at the center of the world. If he could position it correctly in his head, he could maybe start to map out the whole thing, maybe, or at least make some progress toward determining what happened here.

It's all connected, certainly. The design of the pendant is perfectly familiar. He touches his fingers to its mirror on his chest. How quickly he's gotten used to the weight. He kept it on in the shower and didn't even notice.

Hector had been heading here. To warn Alan, he claimed, but Hector and Father Abatangelo both knew that wasn't the case. The way Hector said it was enough. He was warning Father Abatangelo that this was what he was going to do—this was how serious a situation they'd found themselves in.

Whatever occultisms Alan had cobbled together had worked at first. Father Abatangelo is not surprised about this. That Alan was capable of what he claimed was never the issue. Clearly, though, it had gone wrong. Could be that Alan had other enemies, other faces to be dodging in the street, but the proximity to Hector's visit, and the presence of the pendant, point to the beast's return Hector spoke of.

Alan had dusted off the chair, looped the pendant over Hector's neck, and performed the same ritual Father Abatangelo had witnessed years ago. Surely it was Hector in the chair. Alan wouldn't take that risk himself. Hector had gone to that place, to see if the beasts had changed, and he brought something back with him.

The absence of bodies, though. Maybe that's the key, a hint that Father Abatangelo can't put into context. If the operation went south, where did the two men go?

He searches the room—the food on the floor, the pendant. There's residue under the food, appearing to at once absorb light and shine. He'll leave that for last. The chair in the corner, the pantry door open from his search.

The linen closet's closed, slats swept shut. Father Abatangelo can't recall if he closed it. He takes a careful step. Something inside the closet shifts, pushing toward the back. Father Abatangelo braces himself, puts his hand on the door.

The door slams open. Father Abatangelo catches it in the elbow, staggers back. The towel flops to the floor. A slim man in sunglasses lunges out. Father Abatangelo reaches for the waistband that's not there, the gun that's buried in the remains of his church.

He resolves to retrieve it if he walks out of here.

The man puts his shoulder to Father Abatangelo's naked stomach. The two men sprawl into the chair. Father Abatangelo goes head-wound woozy. The man rears up, pulls a dirty kitchen knife.

He stops. Tilts his head. Falls away from Father Abatangelo, groaning.

Father Abatangelo sits up. The man is scrawnier than he remembers, and the sunglasses hide much of his face, but the laugh is unmistakably Alan's.

"Shit," Alan says. "I was set to kill you."

Father Abatangelo wheezes to his feet. Alan touches one hand to his sunglasses, checking they're still there, and uses the other to help Father Abatangelo to his feet.

The left side of Alan's face crawls with burns and scabs. The burning runs up his cheekbone and disappears beneath the sunglasses. Father Abatangelo looks around, puts his eyes anywhere but the damage to Alan's face.

Alan smirks. "Looking real pretty, huh?"

"Hector said he was coming around to see you."

"That actually isn't changing the subject, Padre." He up-and-downs the naked priest. "Though, if I could . . ."

Father Abatangelo glances down at himself, curiously unembarrassed, and moves unhurried to the clothes he left in a pile on the recliner. Alan doesn't try to hide that he's watching. Father Abatangelo gets dressed and turns back around.

Alan stares, up-and-downs him again. "In civilian mode, huh?"

"Something like that."

"Man, didn't know you had that anymore."

"I didn't for a long time. Some things have changed."

Alan looks around the trashed apartment. "Tell me about it."

Father Abatangelo sits in the recliner. Alan looks around for a seat and sees the big wooden chair. He shudders, slouches onto the couch instead.

"Well, you might wanna brace yourself," he says, and removes his sunglasses.

CHAPTER SIX

From his back-booth vantage point, Slim watches Asher lean in far closer than necessary to order a drink from the bartender. A blonde, naturally. Slim's faith in Asher's predictability has yet to prove misplaced. The bartender pours Asher a beer. He leans in closer. She pretends not to hear him. Asher visibly raises his voice and the bartender strolls to the other end of the bar.

Slim smiles over the lip of his glass. The beer's gone flat and the flavor doesn't do anything for him anymore, just sits like ash on his tongue, but he still likes the smell. That will probably fade soon enough, but for now he holds the glass under his bottom lip.

A fan bolted to the wall just below the ceiling buzzes above his head. The air moves but doesn't cool. Nobody bothers him, about nursing his drink or anything else. It's a little roadside joint, next door to the single motel room he bought for himself and Asher, no more than two hundred feet from the interstate on-ramp. He made sure Asher stayed in the car when he paid for the room, and they came straight to the bar without going upstairs.

Slim takes a slow sip, pans his eyes around the bar. Someone scoping him from the other end of the room: red flannel and black denim, draft beer and a shot. He's tall and wide, hair scragging out from under a knit cap. The guy holds Slim's eyes long enough to know he's not glancing away, not embarrassed at having been caught. He turns to Asher instead.

Asher's bragging about something to the man two stools over. Slim can't see Asher's face, but the body language of the other person is unimpressed. The man finally looks up, smiles. Red Flannel stands from the other end of the bar, and Asher's audience gives up his stool for him.

Slim tosses back the rest of his beer. Something like the taste he remembers comes briefly through. He carries his glass over to the bar, stopping halfway between Flannel and Asher. Sets it down.

Flannel skirts around him. Glowers down at Asher. Slim watches in the bar mirror. Asher hasn't noticed, but stops talking to finish his drink. The moment hums with static, and the hair on Slim's neck tingles agreeably.

Asher finally notices. "I help you, pal?"

"You talk too much."

"Yeah." Asher twirls in his seat, faces the guy. "I've heard that."

Slim flags the bartender. She's got his and Asher's check ready. He lays enough money on the table that maybe she won't remember their faces, should anybody ask. An irrelevant fantasy, but the gesture feels good.

Flannel leans in close, hisses something to Asher Slim can't quite hear.

Slim leans against the bar, arms to his sides. He slouches down, makes himself look even smaller. "I like this place."

Lolls his head in Flannel's direction. "You know, nice atmosphere. Swell people."

Flannel only gives him a glance. Doesn't take the bait.

Asher stands up.

"Someplace to be?" Flannel says.

"All sorts of places."

Slim searches for the bartender. She's standing discreetly on the other side of the bar, watching, surely, out of the corner of her eye. Probably doesn't want the cops in here if she can help it, but Slim's willing to bet the phone's within arm's reach all the same.

Flannel takes a step forward. Asher plants his fist in a spot just under Flannel's ribcage. Punches out all his air. Flannel slumps onto the bar as Slim pushes off. Flannel wheezes, starts to stand back up. Slim claps his hand on Flannel's back, pushes him back down onto the wood, and leads Asher out the door.

The sun's gone down and the North Carolina humidity's turned from damp blanket to sweet and soft. Asher sways his way through the door and lights a cigarette, breathes deep and lists to one side. He's had more than a few, as he's wont to do after a busy week, and before a busier one.

"Fucking guy, huh?" Asher says. "Yokels, man. Every single time."

Slim doesn't bring up where and how Asher grew up.

"Bubba didn't even see me coming." A big loud draw on the cigarette then whistles out between his teeth. "Walked right into it."

Slim smiles. "I'll give you that much."

They walk around to the back of the bar, Asher breathing out smoke like he's leaking, trailing his fingers along the painted brick. He matches Slim's pace, which is a couple notches slower than natural. Flannel doesn't come out after them. Slim's surprised. He didn't seem the type to lick his wounds quietly. Maybe the bartender talked some sense.

They lean against the back wall, next to the dumpster, and talk about where they're going, the route they'll take. Slim tells Asher honestly, even names the person who told him Lorelei was in New York, poking around after a character named Hector. Hector, of the vague but devout occultism, with just the slightest grasp of things as they really stood.

Oh yes, Slim remembers Hector. He tells Asher about him, broad strokes. Can't hurt now.

The steel door opens and the bartender hoists a jangling trash bag into the dumpster. Slim catches her eyes, smiles. She doesn't smile back. Her glance slides over him like water. The door closes again behind her.

"Surprised that yokel didn't come out swinging," Asher says. "Might've hit him harder than I thought."

Slim shrugs. "Looked to me like you hit him plenty hard."

Asher's pleased enough at this. He looks off at the horizon for a long moment. Slim unbuttons his cuffs, rolls up his sleeves. Flexes his fingers, to make sure the feeling's all there, and waits.

Asher doesn't turn his head. "Know what's the problem with that kinda guy?"

"Hmm?"

"Doesn't think there's anybody could take him down. Been smackin' around little guys all his life, figures he can smack about anybody and not get one back."

"Mmm."

"Think?"

"Sure." Slim puts his palm against the wall, leans closer. "But there's another thing."

"Huh?"

"There's a man—there was a man—who thought he was the end goal. He was the product."

"What I said."

Slim shakes his head. "People get to thinking that they're the *product*. They're not. They're not an achievement in form or perfection. Certainly not special. People are the raw material. He was like a piece of lumber, of iron ore, that thought he was a bridge."

"Dunno I follow."

"People are material. They're what you can *do* something with, if you're trying." Slim does a friendly shoulder-punch, making it seem like this is a slick joke Asher's just not getting. "Can't have the material getting to think it's what you're after in the first place."

"People fight wars for oil, though."

"That's true. Different, though. Oil doesn't get a say in it."

Asher nods at this, more for something to do than to express agreement. He looks to both corners of the building, for Flannel sneaking up on them, and relaxes again. "Dunno what you're talking about, Slim."

"See, it's like this. Say you knew a guy who had, I don't know, this recurring dream." Slim pauses, rubs his lip like he's thinking. He watches Asher's eyes trying not to widen. "You know, same thing, night after night. Kind you probably had when you were a kid. Where you couldn't tell whether a thing was from the dream or if it had happened a week ago."

"Uh, yeah, sure."

"So this guy, right, he's got this dream keeps coming back, except when he wakes up, he doesn't know whether it was a dream or something that happened to him. Maybe he thinks of it in the middle of the day and doesn't remember waking up from it. Can't know then whether it really happened, and he never stops and looks at it long enough to really figure that out. Because it couldn't have happened, right? Why bother trying to remember where it came from?" Slim looks at Asher, who's staring deep at something out in the night. "Know what I mean?"

Asher nods slowly. The philosophical edge has grafted itself onto his beer buzz. He's content to slump and stare and listen.

"Well then." Slim licks his lips. "Say this guy, he finds out too late that there's reason he should have looked a little closer, should've tried to figure this thing out. Definitive proof of the thing, I mean. Well, a fellow might get to feeling pretty foolish then, yeah? Get to thinking that he'd lived with his eyes on the wrong thing. Missed the point."

Asher pushes off the wall and stands straight, thinking he's got the gist. "Yeah, yeah. Sure. Right."

"And suddenly—I mean, picture this guy—he figures out that the dream he's been having since a point he can't remember, about somebody—he can't see his face—slipping into his room at night, with this tiny little needle, he should have known that was real the whole time."

Asher jerks his head around. The momentum almost takes his down. Slim catches him around the small of his back and eases him to his feet. Asher sways and struggles with his balance but a new clarity cuts from his gone-wide eyes.

"Did I tell you—"

"And maybe he can't remember what happens next," Slim says, like he doesn't hear Asher, "and all he can come up with is that the face is a dim blur. But he recognizes it. He recognizes the blur."

Asher tries to run but Slim hasn't taken his hand off the back of his jacket.

Slim slams him back against the wall, drops to a whisper.

"And this guy, by the time he realizes that he's remembering not a dream, exactly, but something else entirely, it's too late for him to do anything about it. And it's only after that that he begins to wonder what the needles were for."

Asher opens his mouth and draws a scream's worth of breath. Slim shoves the edge of his hand in there. Asher bites down, hard. Blood pours out the side of his mouth. Nerve click, bone on bone. Asher pushes hard against Slim, and then his knees buckle. Blood trickles down his throat. He gurgles against it and slumps back, releases Slim's hand.

Slim lifts the hand and drizzles blood on Asher's face. Asher closes his eyes, but it doesn't matter. Human eyes are not watertight.

Asher spits and writhes but tires quickly. "Why me?"

Slim looks around, shrugs. "Who else?"

That's too cold, though. Whatever Slim's feelings for Asher, he did, at least, most of the driving this far. He leans down so his lips are brushing Asher's ear.

"Raw material, remember? Don't worry. Someone might do something with me."

Asher can't answer.

Slim hefts him over his shoulder, feeling refreshed, and flips him into the dumpster. He pulls the gray fishing hat out of his back pocket and pulls it on, slinks back to the motel.

CHAPTER SEVEN

Elijah blinks and blinks and everything's still blurry. The couch under him feels much older than he is. Hair clings to the back of his neck. The taste of dusty eggs smothers his teeth. He hacks a couple breaths and his stomach screams in protest. The room stares at him with its rugs and couches and carpet out of style for decades. It has the feel of someone's crash pad in the woods, but he doesn't think he's seen it before.

A memory kicks up of Slim's sticky blood coating his face. Elijah gasps and pitches over. His gut clenches with raging pain. He's afraid he's about to vomit all over some stranger's carpet, but all that comes out is a quivering dry heave. His body keeps at it until his throat clenches and his diaphragm starts seizing. Then he flops back onto the couch. His gut screeches at his brain. A sticky warmth spreads to his lap.

Elijah looks down at a slow leak of blood in his midsection and feels suddenly and dangerously faint. He leans his head back down, closes his eyes and grinds his teeth until the swimming in his head ratchets down to a mild rocking.

He starts to put it together then.

The memory of Slim and the blood, and that feeling, rocketing from, it seemed, Slim's body, straight through to the back of his skull. He pictures the before. This is the after. Elijah dredges up Asher's proposition, the party, the massacre.

Slim set him up, and he used Asher to do it. Explains the man in the gray fishing hat, why he was being followed when no one should have known where he was. They got him paranoid about being seen and then dangled a way out in front of him.

He looks around the strange living room and remembers getting shot. It all fits. What doesn't fit is where he is, how he got here.

The sound of footsteps at what Elijah figures is the back entrance. He snakes a hand down to his waistband, his pocket, for the gun that's neither his nor there anymore. It was loaded with blanks, and would be empty now anyway, but whoever's out there might not know that.

He closes his eyes to slits, pretending to still be sleeping, and watches the blurry entrance to the kitchen.

A short, skinny man fades into view, like he was always there and Elijah's only now seeing him. The man leans against the doorframe and watches Elijah. His eyebrows go up.

"Morning, Eli," he says.

Elijah tries not to move, not to start. The man knows his name, seems to know he's awake. Could be he's done this a dozen times already, testing Elijah, trying to get inside his head for when he finally came to.

Elijah doesn't move.

"Eli." The man sighs. "Come on, man. I know you're awake."

Elijah returns the sigh, opens his eyes all the way. "The hell you do."

"Breathing's different."

"Uh huh."

"You've been sawing wood in here all day. Now it's quiet as hell, like you don't wanna wake your lady friend."

Elijah looks around the room. Lorelei's not there, of course. It was just an expression.

"Who the hell—" Elijah starts, but now he can see the man's face—the hair that's not a buzz cut anymore, the space beneath his ribs that used to be a beer gut. "Donny."

"You don't sound happy to see me."

"Confused, is all. I don't remember ever getting invited to your—" Elijah looks around "—new place."

"Yeah, all right. We haven't been close." Donny waves at Elijah's oozing midsection. "Still, though. Could be a little grateful."

"What happened?"

"Somebody's looking out for you."

"Yeah, okay."

"Jo brought you by."

Jo?

"And I stitched you up."

Elijah feels a twinge from his gut, and a sinking feeling. He dips his fingers to it, holds them up. "Yeah, super job."

"You fuck." Donny smiles into his chest, shakes his head. "Always were a fuck. Jo'll be back soon. She can put up with your ass, somehow." He turns to the exit. "Beer's in the fridge, old man."

Elijah winces. A beer would actually be nice, but standing's out of the question. Instead, he just lies there and bleeds.

* * *

Donny's pickup is in deceptively non-working order. The steering wheel doesn't turn the tires as far as Jo expects it to. She hopes that mailbox wasn't expensive.

Still, though, this is no neighborhood for attracting attention. The sirens have faded, but she can still hear them through the silence, sense the traffic cop in the bushes off some blind hill waiting to make himself a hero.

She's going not to the abattoir of a house she pulled Elijah from last night, but to his and Lorelei's old place. It's close, though, a couple streets down. She's only been there once or twice, and that more than a year ago. They'd retreated into that house, gradually, until the tension of their lives pinned them together in it. Jo swore after that last time that she wouldn't be going back. She was done with scenes like that, with couples sweating out their whiskey at each other, circling and jabbing like hostile cellmates.

Like they hadn't chosen their living arrangements.

She passes the tiny golf course and the bricked-in subdivision to a slightly older part of town, the early suburbs, and turns down a long street. The streets all have similar names. She remembers this, but it doesn't save her from turning down Trout Court when she wanted Turtle, circling twice just to make sure.

The right street is up next. Jo slows but doesn't turn, looking for cops or anybody obviously watching. Nothing stands out. She circles around the block and comes back, parks just before Turtle.

Anybody watching will spot her walking up like this, but hopefully make less of it, not notice when she slips around the side of the house. She's about to do just that when a fresh-looking wood fence stops her—no padlock on it, but it didn't used to be there. It never did occur to her or Donny that the place might be rented out again, but it should have. It isn't exactly a high-dollar draw, and the university's not far.

Jo dips back to the sidewalk and walks just past the house, does a deliberate double-take, and goes up to the door.

So much for not being seen.

She knocks and gets ready to pretend that she's Lorelei.

A skinny guy in a Florida State sweatshirt opens the door. "Yeah?"

"Uh, yeah, I used to . . . my boyfriend and I used to live here. He said he might've left some of my stuff here when he moved out."

The guy shakes his head. "That was y'all used to live here?"

"Well, him, mostly. I've been, you know, here and there." She tries to inflect it like she's all broken up about the separation, like she spends nights wishing Elijah would call her.

Elijah. It's a funny thought, that.

The guy nods. "Yeah, gotcha. Tell you the truth, guy didn't leave the place looking super great, y'know? But I think there's a bag somewhere in the garage. Here." He steps back, hovers. "You wanna come in?"

"No, I shouldn't."

"All right, hold on."

The guy leaves the door open like a hand on her shoulder. Jo chews the laugh off the inside of her cheek. She hears the door to the garage open, the guy rummaging around in there. The urge to slip through the door and steal something, anything, is strong.

It gives her a second's pause. The nerve of the guy, being civil.

He comes back with a black trash bag showing the protruding corners of not much of anything.

"Here you are. That's what there was when we moved it."

Jo takes the bag. "Yeah. Hey, thanks."

She turns away. The ride to the other house, the hideout, isn't a short one. If the guy had looked into the bag and seen what she wanted, no way would he be handing it over.

"Hey," the guy says from behind, "good luck."

Jo raises a hand and walks back to her car.

The drive south then east winds through fields and along river tributaries. Jo rolls down her window the way she imagines Elijah must have done, breathing in the getaway on the warm breeze.

The air doesn't taste like victory, though, or freedom. Just the sun baking the grass.

She pulls off at an outpost gas station and pins the map to the dash with bent-straight paperclips, gets back on the road. The town the station claimed to be part of isn't on the map. Neither is the next street sign she passes. Could be she missed it by a ways, will have to backtrack. She's sure of it, actually, but then a highway entrance ramp registers with her map, and there's still twenty minutes to drive.

The truck doesn't have global positioning. Donny insists that the cops can track you electronically with what you put in those things. Jo hates to admit that the caution makes perfect sense. Still, it means she'll have a time finding the right house when she gets there. The area, if she remembers right, is even worse than greater Orlando for trying to tell one neighborhood from another.

The turnoff proves her memory correct. She drifts down what seems to be the main street, getting frustrated. A plume of black smoke rises through the still humid afternoon.

She turns toward it, teeth set. Navigates the labyrinthine suburban roads, always turning toward the smoke but never seeming to get any closer, until a street she hadn't noticed leads her around a house she'd swear she's passed twice before and doubles back in front of a company of cops and firefighters.

In the middle of the assembled a squat one-story burns. Bright orange fading to red at the top. Windows burst out, flames licking at the evening air. Something inside the house has already caved in, and in the fluttering light, the glowing wood of the house looks like an impossible-architecture drawing, a painting hung in a metalhead's bedroom.

Jo checks the address, checks again, and does a three-point turn in someone's driveway.

Donny's drinking Pabst in the backyard and Elijah's finally standing. He has to walk in miniature shuffling paces, and with a dipping hunch, but the fabric of the couch has left what feels like a permanent pattern on his skin. Had to get off of it before it assimilated him completely and he became part of the questionable décor.

He steps out front, into a tangle of weeds and low branches dripping Spanish moss. Looking around, there's no way to tell where they are. He has a guess, remembers a similar-looking house someone's mom had—low, wide, with a roof that dips far enough down that he ducks without meaning or needing to, like a man approaching a helicopter—but there's no clues except a three-digit address on the keeling-over mailbox.

His boots have made themselves scarce, so he doesn't go down the dirt driveway to try to situate himself. Donny said Jo was coming back, but he hasn't seen her, has he?

Hasn't seen any sign of her at the house and it's been hours. The past with Donny isn't glowing, but it doesn't seem bad enough to warrant anything as elaborate as what Elijah's started to suspect.

From the back, Donny's voice, muffled.

Elijah comes back in the front door. "What?"

"Don't go poking your head up. You don't wanna be seen." Clink of a can tossed into the bin. "And don't walk around so christing much. I ain't a surgeon by trade, you know."

Elijah slouches out to the back deck and into a chair. Donny's got an eighteen-rack of beer stuffed into a cooler, cardboard going damp and soft, and a plastic fifth of Old Crow. Elijah reaches for the bourbon.

"That's a bad idea, man."

"What about hospitality?" Elijah unscrews the cap. "You going to stop me?"

Donny smiles his way through a long drink. "Hell no. You'd be way less trouble dead."

Elijah's still rubbing the sleep from his eyes when he makes a grab across the table for the keys. He's sitting around the table with Donny and Jo. She plopped them there when she came down from her long shower, testing him. She returned late into the night, Elijah gathers, smelling of fire. Maybe she scrubbed it off before coming down so that he wouldn't smell it, take in particles of the house and get nostalgic.

She had that wrong, though. The house that would pull him by the blood is still standing, rented by some football fanatic, to hear her tell it. But she doesn't know what's hidden under the loose floorboard in the hallway leading to the bedroom. If she did, she'd've hidden the keys away.

Jo snatches them away, just a hair ahead of Elijah's darting hand.

"You said the house, what, burned down?"

"Yes." Jo, already tiring of this conversation. "Damn thing was on fire like you wouldn't believe."

"But did it burn *down*?" Elijah rests his fingertips on the spot on the table where the keys had been. "Like, house gone, welcome to the new scorch mark on an empty lot? Or just like the roof and attic?"

"The fuck does it matter, Eli?" Donny cracks his second beer of the morning. "House burned, man. Can't go back there."

"But did it burn *down*?"

"Eli," Jo says, her voice low, cautious, "is there something you're not telling us?"

Elijah looks from her face to Donny's—from suspicious to already putting it together. Donny wouldn't have missed the coincidence in the timeline between Slim's disappearance and Elijah and Lorelei's quick drop beneath the radar.

Donny holds no soft feelings for Slim. Elijah only belatedly realizes that's not the same as him not paying attention. No way to know just how deep that bad blood runs, how much Slim has been on Donny's mind.

"There are some things in that house," Elijah says, "that I'd like to get my hands on. Things I'll miss."

Jo throws her hands up. "You're not taking my car with that. But feel free to take your own."

"I don't have one."

"Bingo, buddy."

Elijah shakes his head. "I need to get down there."

"You need to tell me why."

Donny cracks his third beer and swallows deep, his empty stomach compensating for his tolerance; he's already teetering a bit. "Hell, Eli. How much was there?"

"A whole lot of sentimental value."

"Fuck sake." Donny sloshes foam onto the table. "Why don't you come out and say it. Not like I don't know. Not like you don't know I know. And Jo, bless you, but it's not like you don't know, either."

Elijah runs his tongue over his teeth. This moment was going to come, he knew it, but the scenes he ran in his head went different. For one, Lorelei was there, and he knew what to say.

Jo stares Donny down. Donny looks away, doesn't care. "We own calendars, Eli. Or at least we know what day it is most times."

Elijah holds down his voice, trying to put an edge into it. "Why don't you tell me exactly what you're thinking?"

"Slim's dead."

"He isn't."

"And you killed him, and then you had to skip town. Stop me if I'm getting this wrong."

"A couple parts of it, actually."

"And then you sent Lori out hell knows where, to sell what you stole. You, brave fucker that you are, stayed behind to wait." Donny sucks down the rest of the beer, crushes it in his hand, and tosses it against the wall. "Tell me I'm wrong."

"You're drunk," Jo says.

"And I'm right."

The two of them lock eyes again. Something passes between them that Elijah can't catch. Gone too long, he doesn't know their mannerisms like he used to. Jo alone he can still read, but life has happened in the interim—he's behind the curve. Best, perhaps, to come partly clean.

"He's not all the way wrong."

Both look to him.

"Lori and I came into possession of some of Slim's things. After he disappeared."

"You mean died," Donny whispers.

Elijah shakes his head. "No. I thought so, but no. And we had some of his things. Lori's got some now. There's some in some other places. Some in the house."

Jo leans forward, as slowly as possible, like Elijah's going to get spooked if she moves too fast. "What, exactly, are you talking about?"

"Shitload of money. Don't know how much, didn't count it. Lori's got some. Some's in the house." He hesitates. "And some Dilaudid. Lori left some of that with me, in case."

Jo nods, looks at the table. "Place was on fire, Eli. It was on fire good. It was gonna come down."

Elijah swallows.

"I didn't *see* it come down."

Three-way silence.

Jo flicks the keys up out of her pocket, clacks them down on the table. "Fuck it. Let's go."

The house hasn't entirely burned down. Jo's heart sinks at the sight of the blackened frame still standing, because she knows what comes next. Elijah looks at her, wide-eyed and still far too pale for comfort.

Jo holds up her hand, waves him to the house. "Fine, go. Just, fast-like, okay?"

Elijah nods and gets out of the car, tries to hide the stutter in his step, which only makes the next wobble more. The poetry of it's almost certainly lost on him.

He makes his way to the edge of the next lot. At least he has the sense to go around to the back, out from under the streetlights, before trying to poke around in the ash.

Jo flexes her hands on the wheel, kills the ignition over her instinct's objections. The night has "quick getaway" written all over it, but a running engine draws more attention. She leaves the keys in. Elijah disappears around the back of the adjacent house.

The shadows on the cul-de-sac shift, coming alive but not showing anything. Jo's had a rough week. She's again outside a house where Elijah doesn't know what he's doing, violence sure as humidity in the air. Doesn't think she's up for rescuing him again.

That night after the party, dragging Elijah sweating and jabbering out the back door and through the side yard of another house and into her car, wasn't long enough ago. He was covered in blood when she found him. His breathing came as a shock. Wiping the blood off him at Donny's place, they couldn't find a source for it.

He's yet to talk about that. She's yet to ask.

The gunshot in his side was a flesh wound. He ought to be up and healthy now, the way it grazed his hipbone, tearing the flesh enough for plenty of blood but not piercing, not breaking or puncturing anything.

Jo's pretty sure she doesn't want to know what happened in that house. First time she'd seen Elijah in a year. Hell of a reunion.

Elijah comes around the corner with something in his hand. The shadows across the street start to move. Jo has to blink hard to be sure, but a man materializes from the stoop. He's dressed in a black sweater, hood back so his face is visible.

Not a good sign.

Elijah beelines toward the car, steady enough to jog, but the other man is faster.

The man passes the car, knocks his knuckles on the hood. "You keep your ass put, sweetheart."

Jo grinds her teeth. Should have brought one of Donny's guns. Even a .22 rifle would be better than sitting in the car with a knife she's in no position to use.

Elijah draws up a few feet from the car. The man positions himself in between. Jo can't see anything in Elijah's hands, just a nylon strap across his chest, for a duffel bag.

The other man's presence means it's unlikely the house hasn't been searched already.

Hell of a reunion.

The man leans back against Jo's door, glances at her, and then back at Elijah. "Well then. You must be Elijah."

"Nah." Elijah's eyebrows arc up, mocking, tempting the violence already thick in the air. "Name's Jimmy. Sorry. Hey, look, wonder if you could give us directions? See, we're looking for my buddy's new house . . ."

The man grunts and pushes off the car door, takes a deliberate step toward Elijah.

Jo grabs the handle and thuds the door open, into the man's back. It only bumps him a few inches, but his sneaker scrapes loose on the sidewalk and he falls to one knee. Jo closes the door and tries to hit him again, but the man slams his palm against it for balance.

Elijah lunges, shoulder down like he's going for a football tackle. He drives the man into the car. Jo hears the door dent under the man's weight. Elijah tries to throw him down. Nothing doing. The man brings his fists up and then down again on Elijah's back.

Elijah gets his footing but the duffel bag slides over, drags him and the man down with it.

Jo cranks the window lever. The man cracks Elijah's head into the door. Jo pulls the knife from the center console and jabs it out the window. The man's shoulder meat gives like cheap steak and the knife takes a couple yanks to free. The man howls.

"Get in the car!" Jo yells.

Elijah finds his feet, woozier than ever.

Jo flicks the lights on, pulls the car around so Elijah's on the passenger side. He at least gets the door open himself and she's driving off before he's fumbled it closed again.

The rearview mirror doesn't show anything for the first few miles. A few miles after that, it convinces Jo that there's no one following. Elijah's got his palm pressed to the blood leaking from his forehead.

"I bet the blood's not even dry from the last time."

Blank stare. "What?"

"The last time you bled in my car?"

"Oh. Yeah." He takes his hand away and wipes it on his jeans. "Ol' Slim, man, he's got more friends than I thought."

Christ. Not this again.

Jo pulls off into a strip-mall parking lot and puts the car in park. Elijah looks around. Jo breathes deep, shuts her eyes.

"We're out here," she says, "away from Donny. If you've got something to say you don't want him to hear, this'd be a good time for it."

"Slim's after me. Thought we covered that."

Jo slaps her hand on the steering wheel. "Don't bullshit me. You wanna tell Donny whatever you think he wants to hear, okay, but not me."

"Slim's not dead."

"Fine." She hisses through her teeth, remembers that Elijah's her friend as she un-gently puts the car in drive.

"Slim's not dead."

"I heard you."

"No. I mean, we—I—shot him, yeah. Couple times. But he's not dead."

Jo nods, stops, shakes her head. "Not sure I follow."

Elijah laughs. He slumps against the door, wheezes a laugh not dissimilar from the sound of strangling.

"Neither do I."

Elijah wakes on the scratchy couch to a muted hissing. Failed whispers. Jo and Donny are not quite getting along in the kitchen.

His head feels clearer than it has in days. The wound on his side is scabbed over and only painful if he touches it. Could be that it wasn't as bad as he thought, but then how to explain the dizziness, the constant need for sleep? His forehead aches where it got hit, and a dull headache's set in just above his eyes, but he finds his feet without any swirling of his surroundings.

". . . and that fucking snake in there, too," comes Donny's voice from the kitchen.

It's about time to move on. Only so many snakes Donny could mean.

Jo storms into the room, makes for the couch. "Oh, you're up. Grab your shit. We're out of here."

Elijah starts to ask for an explanation, but Jo's already snatched the bag he took from the remnants of the hideout and exited through the front door. The air tastes of violence, and Elijah's uncomfortable without a clear sense of its scope. He turns around, looking for his belongings. He has none except the bag. He brushes off his clothes and leaves, down the wooden steps and onto the patchy grass.

Donny's voice suddenly, behind him: "Hey, motherfucker! Wanna talk to you."

Elijah turns, sees Donny standing shirtless in the open door. "Thanks for your hospitality, Donald. It's been lovely."

"I bet." Donny takes the steps in one hop, bounces up on his feet. "You've got some questions to answer. Would've thought that one—" he hooks his head over to Jo, waiting behind the wheel "—would fill me in, but I guess I don't rate it anymore."

"Look, it's none of my business—"

"Nope, no it ain't. But it's some of mine."

Elijah slackens his face like he's lost the thread of the conversation. Donny shines in the sun, booze-glossy and sweating it out. Elijah shrugs, turns toward the car.

Donny hits him from behind. Elijah crashes to the ground halfway between the house and the car, instantly tangled in the branches and crabgrass, wet dirt pressed to his mouth. Elijah expected it, but still can't shake Donny off. There's some iron in those bones.

Donny pushes a knee between Elijah's shoulder blades. "What's in the bag, Eli? Where'd it come from?"

"Like you haven't gone poking around," he says around a mouthful of grit. "Like you don't already think you know."

Donny leans forward, puts more pressure on the knee. He lowers his face to Elijah's ear.

It puts him off balance.

Elijah ducks his head and rolls forward. Donny pitches onto his face, rolling in the grass as Elijah completes the world's clumsiest somersault. Elijah lunges. Donny's to his knees when Elijah's boot finds his shoulder.

Elijah dusts himself off. He looks around for Jo, spots her standing next to the open car door. Donny wheezes.

"If she didn't tell you, I'm not about to," Elijah says. He walks to the car, watching Donny massage his shoulder. "It was in the shoulder because I feel like I owe you a favor."

Donny yells something, but Elijah gets in the car and whatever it is gets lost in the slamming of the door, the grind and clunk as they back out of the rough lot.

Elijah doesn't say anything while Jo eases over the rutted dirt through dense trees toward the highway. This road, focus is important.

Gravel under the wheels, though, Jo's ready to talk.

"What's the beef between you two?" she asks.

"I imagine he doesn't like me showing up and bleeding all over his couch."

"No. Before."

Elijah leans his head against the hot window. He's ducked the conversation thus far, but waking up in the house Donny's mom left him made it inevitable.

"It's something with Slim," she adds. It's not a question.

"Still can't believe he got that nickname to stick."

"Eli."

"But yeah, while back. We were both working at Papa Louie's, yeah? Selling out back of the kitchen. Slim came around one afternoon, took Donny out into the parking lot on a break. I was listening from the dish pit, but it was slow so I went out to see what was up."

The memory clenches in Elijah's gut. Jo glances over impatiently.

"It . . . I don't know if you saw much of Slim then," he says. "You'd kind of dropped away."

"He never did like me."

"Well, he'd gone off the rails. Only way I can describe it. He had this white dress shirt on, sleeves sticking to his arms. With blood. Like he'd cut himself up and down his arms as part of getting dressed. Wasn't the first weird shit, either."

"What happened with Donny?"

"Slim kicked the hell out of him. Was just getting started when I came outside."

Jo shakes her head. "Out back of a pizza place."

"Mmm."

"What'd you do?"

"I watched."

Elijah rides the silence. Drums his fingers on the armrest, scratches at the seatbelt, cracks his knuckles.

Jo frowns at the road. "But now he's pissed because he thinks you might've killed Slim."

"Things change."

"Who pulled the trigger?"

The asphalt hums through the hole of the question.

"Okay, okay." Jo shrugs it off. "But why would Slim go after Donny like that?"

"Some shit went missing—money. Guy named Buddy got arrested, things got tense. Slim thought it looked like Donny."

"Because he didn't even consider it could be you."

The highways jags back east. Elijah finally wonders where they're going. He decides to wait before asking.

ACT TWO

CHAPTER EIGHT

They've spread out along the east coast, the people Slim knows, the people he can call on. Some have been there all along. Some relocated there, staking out the juiciest markets and making supply runs easier.

Interstate 95 feels more like home than Orlando now—plenty of friends, much to do.

Among these people, there exists another layer. A deeper layer, people who know what's coming, know which side of things to be on. These are the useful ones. They know they can either be productive or they can be ground out, left to blow away like dust. They have a future. They trust Slim.

Then there's Rich.

Rich's house on the outskirts of DC feels like the sticks, but the metro station's only a five-minute walk through trees that aren't as thick as they look. It's a façade of isolation. Cars have to weave around for a couple miles to get here from the station, but anybody with a decent set of shoes can be on the move quick enough.

Rich's setup is wonderful, and he's sharp enough to keep his head down and himself out of the spotlight. There's a lot of money to be made where he is, and he's making it. Isn't stingy with kicking in to his friends, either, which goes a long way in his line.

Still, though, three hours after Slim finds the right inter-state off-ramp, Rich is giving him the same look Asher gave him behind the bar in North Carolina. To Rich's credit, he's picked up on enough that he's already giving it before Slim's quite made his move.

"If there's a problem," Rich says, pretending he doesn't know what's coming, "why don't you tell me exactly what it is? My understanding was I've been doing very well here."

Slim spreads his hands to his sides. "Sure, very well. I'm impressed, actually, and I know I'm not the only one."

A smile breaks through several layers of Rich's better judgment. He quickly rights himself.

"And there's no question that you're reliable."

"So," Rich says, "what is it we're talking about here?"

Slim leans back in the rocking chair, runs his fingers along the porch railing. "You know things are changing. There's more to consider than just the flow of narcotics."

"Not for me, there isn't."

"*That's* what we're talking about."

Rich rolls his whole head along with his eyes. "This more of your voodoo shit? You still into that? You want some-body to come cut himself with you, pray to whatever it is you pray to, you're barking up the wrong damn tree." He lowers his voice. "I respect you, yeah? There's no beef here. But that stuff, man, it's not healthy."

Slim smiles. "You misunderstand."

"Yeah?"

"Everything's changing. You're not on the right side of the future."

Rich snorts. "All right, Slim. Get the fuck out. You want to cut me out, fine. There's plenty of people to deal with. Just don't show your face around here again. Don't go fucking with my business. You'll find me less reasonable then."

Slim smiles, doesn't rise. Rich turns around again, eyebrows raised. Slim gives him a shrug.

Rich pulls a knife. "Pretty sure I made myself clear."

Slim sighs dramatic. Rich steps forward and grabs Slim's shirt, hauls him to his feet. Slim lets himself flop limply into Rich. The knife catches him in the arm. Rich twists the blade and steers Slim toward the porch steps.

Slim pushes his arm hard against the blade. Rich's mouth goes wide. The blood wells and spills down Slim's forearm, collecting in the creases of his wrist, the edges of his cuticles. Rich pulls the knife out and lunges.

Slim catches him by the throat before the strike has a chance. "Now, Rich," smearing blood across Rich's forehead, "is that any way to end a partnership?"

The knife clatters to the floor. Rich draws breath to scream. Slim's hand mutes it. The taste of Slim's blood makes Rich recoil as though burned, slamming against the railing and stumbling two feet wide of the front door, into the wall.

Slim picks up the knife. "Now. We were talking about my 'voodoo shit.'"

Rich pukes the blood all over the porch.

"You know who the bosses are. Or, you should. You know I've been trying to tell you."

"I don't buy any of that shit," Rich manages through strings of bile and gore.

"You should. They believe in you." Slim contemplates the knife, like he's talking to it instead of Rich. "They can smell you rotting, you know. We think about it like it comes all at once. Death, I mean. That we're all the way alive until suddenly we're not. But it's not like that, not for them. They can *smell* it happening, the slow decay and the shedding cells, all through a person's life."

The red smear on Rich's forehead rides beads of sweat to his eyes.

"They know full well you're dying, and they see it on a very short timeline. The question isn't anything to do with you, with our ephemeral lives. The question is whether or not they can scrape some sustenance from your bones—whether you have to be alive for them to do it."

Rich tries to stand straight, slumps back against the wall. His breath comes fast and shallow, rasping like a wet rag dragged over concrete.

"You have to serve to be worth life." Slim and the knife come to an understanding and break eye contact. "Now. I've made myself useful. You refuse to. You understand."

Rich's eyes go wide too late. Slim will take his time with this one.

CHAPTER NINE

The motel room above the bar affords an ill view of her apartment building, but Stacy can see the entrance well enough. She's fighting off sleep, hoping to catch a glimpse of whoever's inside, waiting for her, when the tall woman who'd come around asking about Jessica slinks through the front door. Stacy braces her forehead on the windowsill for ten, fifteen minutes, waiting for her to reemerge.

Most likely the woman's poking around again, is about to stumble into something she's not prepared for. Stacy doesn't know exactly what Jessica was into when she split, but she was into something. It would take more than a couple threatening glances to shake Jessica enough to make her run. Maybe Stacy will catch a glimpse of her visitors when they leave, see how they get rid of the woman.

Buy herself some leverage, is the idea. Meet them on neutral ground, in a public place, and do her some negotiating.

Instead, the woman comes out first, walking in long confident strides. Two men file out behind her. Their faces aren't turned up enough for her to get a good look, but Stacy's pretty sure she recognizes one of them from Lucy's Bar, where she used to slum it with Jessica when they didn't want anybody who knew them showing up.

Seems like maybe that strategy didn't work as well as she'd thought.

The three of them turn the corner and cut out of sight. Stacy gets up and leaves, checks that the door's locked behind her.

They've got a head start, but she's pretty sure she knows where they're going.

She hits the street and turns toward Gutter, winding along side streets. The tall woman carried herself well but still smacked of an out-of-towner—she'd be taking main roads, turning at major intersections. She knew enough to track Stacy down, so she'll know she doesn't want to get caught alone on unfamiliar streets, down blind alleys she won't know are blind until she's facing a brick wall. And even if the woman was working with the people hunting Jessica, she'll still want to be on her toes.

Stacy meanders through alleys, taking more care to appear casual than she hopes is necessary. She comes to Gutter Street and pokes her head out, looking for the sewer grate Jessica described. One of the men from her apartment stands half a block away, leaning against a wall and doing a reasonable caricature of a relaxed man killing time.

Stacy inhales, fades back into the alley. The street doesn't get much foot traffic. As much as the lack of passersby will help keep her from drawing attention, it will also surely make it easier for the guy standing guard to hear her.

She leans into the street again. The guy shifts his weight on the wall, lifts his sleeve and scratches at a white gauze bandage on his forearm. He peels up a corner by his elbow and looks under the bandage like he's checking the time.

Stacy scans the street for Jessica's grate, sees it propped up against a boarded-up door. The sewer entrance gapes next to the leaning man.

Stacy crouches and presses her back to the wall of the alley.

A man's scream claws its way up from the sewer. It reaches Stacy, an echo diluted by distance. Shuffle of feet from the man standing guard and indistinct commotion from the mouth of the sewer.

Stacy peeks around again. The guard pulls a long knife. The tall woman drags herself halfway out of the sewer. The guard points the knife at her throat. The tall woman looks at it with some disdain and jabs a finger behind her.

Another scream. Gurgling this time, tearing.

The tall woman pulls herself from the gutter. The guard puts his knife away and draws a gun. He looks to the tall woman, back to the sewer. Takes a breath deep enough for Stacy to see.

The tall woman moves fast. Her hand dips to the guard's belt, comes up with his knife. She jabs it into his neck. He stiffens, goes limp. Blood spurts from his neck. The tall woman yanks free the knife, and the spurt becomes a spray. She drops him to the sidewalk.

Stacy holds her breath, keeps watching. Doesn't dip back into the alley.

The tall woman drags the guard into the gutter and stuffs him down the hole. Another scream, dimmer this time, hollow. The tall woman sprints to the grate and grabs it, but misjudges its weight. She almost pitches over onto the sidewalk trying to lift it and run back at the same time.

Stacy smiles. So there are things the visitor can't do.

The woman heaves the grate into place. Steel grinds concrete into dust. The grate jumps out at her and she has to muscle it back into place. It looks like one of the men is throwing himself against it from down in the sewer.

The tall woman heaves against the grate again and again. She digs one foot and her knee into the asphalt and drives her shoulder into it. Whatever is pushing back stills and the tall woman stands. She takes a step back, holding the dripping knife at her side, waiting.

She wipes the blood off her face.

Stacy dips back into the alley and listens to the tall woman's footsteps scuff around before clicking to the end of the block and fading away.

Stacy has to give it to her: Stacy's hands are shaking, but the tall woman seems rather harder to rattle.

The street sits silent for a minute. Two. Stacy takes some deep breaths. Like they'll help. More like stalling than bracing herself. She exits onto Gutter Street.

It's as empty as it sounded. Stacy looks around, waiting for the movement she's sure is coming. It stands to reason, though, that the tall woman would want to be as far from here as possible, wouldn't be standing around waiting for the worse news to show.

It's just that she's starting to seem like a friend.

Stacy still needs to see what she can see of the gutter from street level. She walks toward it. The location makes sense: street full of nothing but the plywood in the windows, the steel and glass of the buildings. The sewer grate is jammed in very nearly correctly, but two of the corners are stuck outside the concrete.

She dips her head forward. The grate looms a few steps ahead.

A pair of strong hands grips her shoulders.

Stacy whips around, but the hands are ready. They shove her, hard, toward the nearest wall. The curb snags her feet and she gets her face turned, guard up, before she cracks against the brick.

The street goes hazy for a moment. The tall woman's face appears above her, blurred like Stacy's nearsighted.

Stacy." A hand descends, grips Stacy, lifts her to her feet. "We met that time."

Stacy nods, head lolling on her shoulders.

The tall woman lets go, reaches in again when Stacy starts to droop. "Come on. We need to get out of here."

"It was, what, Loretta, yeah?"

A pause, brief but significant. "Lorelei. Come on. You do not want to be here, I don't think."

Stacy's bleeding down the back of her neck, a warm sticky dripping. She's pretty sure she follows Lorelei down the street not from shock or blood loss or punch-drunkenness but because she's starting to seem like the only honest person in Boston.

Stacy follows Lorelei to the hotel, lurks around the corner while she rents the room with money Stacy didn't expect her to have. The stairwell around the back of the building brings her to the second floor. She catches Lorelei at the landing and follows her up one more floor, into a room adjacent to the stairs.

The bolt doesn't catch on the first try. Stacy slams her palm against the door and it clicks, but she hits it again, again, until Lorelei takes her arm and guides her to the mattress. A discomfiting musty smell rises from the sheets to meet her. Stacy knows that neither of them will be rolling down the comforter.

Lorelei stands very still by the window. Something comes out her lips.

"What?"

"I said, it's time you finished your story."

"Not much to finish. Told you about Jessica. Knew her forever. She got in with some people into, I don't know, something."

"Drugs."

"Yeah, probably. I don't know. I had some shit with that when I was younger."

The pause stretches far longer than Stacy intends.

"What?" Lorelei's eyes get sharp. "Busted?"

"Yeah. Not what you're—using, I mean. Charged with intent, so whatever. But yeah, I kept clear of whatever Jessica got into."

"But you were in touch."

"She was my friend."

"Was."

"Certainly fucking seems that way."

Lorelei backs off, turning her suspicion back toward the window. Stacy's a little surprised. From what she saw in her apartment, she'd've thought the woman would be harder to read. Could be what happened on Gutter Street took Lorelei as much by surprise as it took her.

"You want to tell me," Stacy says, thinking it's time to go on the offensive, "what the hell that was I saw on Gutter Street?"

Lorelei snorts. "You didn't see shit."

"What I saw *you* see, then."

"Nope. I mean, yeah, I'd tell you. But I haven't the faintest. I figured at first you sent me there to die, but those guys, they were waiting for you, right? Something didn't add up."

Lorelei scuffs her toe on the baseboard. "Something's very wrong."

"Yeah, no kidding."

The air conditioner kicks into a higher gear. Lorelei shifts back and forth on her feet, doesn't sit. Stacy doesn't know what to say. She wants to know what Lorelei's angle is in all this, what connects her to Jessica, but isn't sure how to go about asking.

She's much more sure that Lorelei wouldn't answer. Not completely, anyway—not honestly.

And there's the question of the welcome-home party waiting for her with knives.

Lorelei looks at her. "Not sure how to ask me, huh?"

"Ask you what?"

"Whether I was with the guys who came for you."

"Well?"

"Nope."

"I admit I'm a little out of my depth here."

Lorelei shrugs. "I'm not after you. You can take that off your mind."

"Yeah," Stacy says, the shape of it coming together. "You're not—I believe that, by the way—but they are. Those guys. There's more than two of them, I'm pretty sure."

"Safe bet."

"They call anybody before you led them there?"

Lorelei shakes her head. "Could've texted, maybe, but no."

"So it's possible they don't know I followed you."

"They wouldn't know that anyway."

Stacy stands, paces to the window. No, they wouldn't know that, but they'd probably put it together. Hell, they might trace it back to why she didn't come home at her usual time and decide that Stacy had been helping Lorelei all along.

And now there's more to it than whatever fresh hell Jessica had summoned. Whatever it was had a definite body count.

Stacy can see the way to cover this. It's simple, elegant. Still, she very much doesn't want to do it. "I can't believe I'm going to say this." She sighs, loud enough that Lorelei looks over. "I just met you."

"What?"

"I was pretty sure you were going to kill me a few minutes ago."

"Uh huh."

"So those people, the men in my apartment, their friends are going to think I was helping you. Whether they know I was there or not. I mean, their guys go, uh, missing, while they're waiting for me to show up? And I hadn't come home yet?"

Lorelei's eyes narrow.

Stacy stares at the industrial green carpet like there's something surprising and a little bit disturbing down there. "I think I want you to stab me."

Lorelei snorts. Stacy looks up, eyebrows raised. Lorelei double-takes. It breaks that Stacy's serious and she starts shaking her head.

"What in the world—?"

"They'll be looking for me, yeah? Well, if I'm in the hospital . . ."

Lorelei sighs. "I haven't got a knife."

Stacy plops hers on the end table. "I'm thinking the shoulder."

Lorelei picks up the knife. "No, you don't want the shoulder. Too many tendons and shit. You'd be laid up for a week." She turns it over in her hand, taps Stacy on the thigh. "Hike up your skirt."

Father Abatangelo drives. Alan's got his sunglasses on again, says he doesn't have a driver's license. That sounds probable enough, except Father Abatangelo hears something in his voice that sounds like a lie. He doesn't press the issue. Sooner they get back to Alan's flat the better, and Alan refuses to talk specifics until they've replaced the broken fifth radio.

They arrive at the pawnshop. Alan declines to go in, just gives Father Abatangelo a description of the kind of unit he's looking for. Father Abatangelo remembers well enough. It's a portable CD player, one of the bulb-shaped ones like he thinks they probably don't make anymore.

Apparently the type of player makes a very distinct sonic difference. It's not the strangest thing Father Abatangelo's heard lately.

Against all expectations, he finds one quick enough. Finds a whole cluster of them, in fact, huddled together on the far end of a shelf alongside newer stereo equipment like they're embarrassed to be there. Father Abatangelo selects the one that looks most like what he remembers of the broken pieces on Alan's floor and carries it to the counter.

Brief moment of panic as he suspects he doesn't have any money. He keeps his eyes down, fumbles out the wallet anyway. Not much in there, but some—enough to pay for last decade's home entertainment.

He gets back to the car, breathing harder than he should. Hands the CD player to Alan. Father Abatangelo starts the car and guides them in what feels like the right direction.

"So. You wanna tell me what the hell happened in there?"

"Language, Father."

"Fuck off." Father Abatangelo twists his hands like the wheel's a throat. His strength is coming back. "Tell me."

Alan shoots him a look like he can't believe what he's hearing and twists the radio dial hard. A burst of synthesized drums, a flash of static, then nothing. Alan shrugs, points at the speakers, and settles back into his chair.

Father Abatangelo does understand the precautions, but fifteen years of insisting Alan's angle is dangerous nonsense might require more dispelling than just Alan's persistence.

Wearing the collar is one thing. Grinding your teeth and diving into the occult, well.

They return in silence. Alan unlocks the door to his apartment, waiting for Father Abatangelo to enter so he can lock it behind him. He flits over to the windowsill in silence and plugs the new device into one of his surge protectors. Father Abatangelo doesn't speak as Alan tinkers with the volume slider, ticking it back and forth with a fingernail, nudging the volume up and down by degrees, standing in no fewer than five distinct spots in the apartment and checking the sound in each.

Father Abatangelo eases himself onto the couch and waits. It takes some time.

Alan sets the slider a final time and stands in the middle of the room, smiling. Father Abatangelo pulls himself from his slump. Alan sits on the arm of the throne, finds rolling tobacco in his pocket and starts to roll a smoke.

Father Abatangelo very nearly asks him for one. It's been almost two decades since his last, but recent events have forced him to revise his own life expectancy. If there's one thing the church and its incumbent readings have impressed upon him, though, it's that imminent death is a poor justification for doing things you said you wouldn't. He's a little appalled at himself that it stuck.

Alan produces a box of matches, strikes one on the buckle of his boot and lights the cigarette. He draws in heavy, exhales. The room takes a pleasantly dark and sticky smell. Father Abatangelo shakes his head.

"So," Alan says. "You wanted to talk."

"I want to know what happened here."

"You know as much as I do, probably." Alan taps ash onto the windowsill. "Hector told you he was coming here, I guess?"

Father Abatangelo nods, swallowing a flinch at Hector's name.

"Well, we did what you figure we did. I put him in the chair, and I did my thing. Like before. You remember."

Father Abatangelo blinks.

"Well, maybe not. But you remember enough, yeah? You remember the feel of it?"

"Yes."

"Yeah, that's about what I figured. I mean, Hector remembered enough that he knew he wanted to come see me. But not all of it, not by a long shot. I'm not sure I do, either." Alan looks at the window like it's about to tell him something. "But it's coming back. I don't know. I think it'll all come back, we give it enough time."

"We might not *have* enough time." Father Abatangelo's voice sounds dry and foreign to his ears, like someone else is saying it, someone he knew once and not well.

Alan nods. "Yeah. So I strapped Hector in and did my thing. And Hector, his eyes opened the way I remember, like he was focused on something far behind me. And then—I have to tell you, I think something's different."

Father Abatangelo doesn't move.

"I can't tell you exactly what happened, but I know the sky outside turned red. Clouds were black. That's ringing bells, yeah?"

"Yes."

"But, *here*, not where Hector was. Where I sent him. Like it's, man. Like it's bleeding over, right?"

A car blasts its tinny horn on the street below. The radios muddle the air.

Father Abatangelo's throat is impossibly dry. "What happened?"

"I was looking out the window at the sky. Next I remember, I heard this sound, like screaming but deep. Very deep. I had this burning on my face and I saw Hector standing over me. He peeled this—" pulling the pendant from his pocket "—off of my face. Put his hand to my neck. Feeling my pulse, you know."

"He thought you were dead."

"Yeah." Alan rivets his gaze on Father Abatangelo. "Yeah, he did. He looked scared. I was talking to him." Alan turns the pendant over in his hand, polishing the bare bits where his skin had been with his fingertips. "I was fucking *talking* to him. He didn't hear a word of it. Took off running down the hallway."

Father Abatangelo waits. Alan doesn't continue, instead takes off his sunglasses and pitches them across the room. The skin around his eyes is curdled, red and peeling. The whites of his eyes have turned an unhealthy purple-black. Pupils wide, gasping at all times for light.

Alan turns his gaze to the ceiling, gives Father Abatangelo far too much of a look at his polluted whites.

"Where did he go?" Father Abatangelo asks, knowing the answer in the marrow.

"Only one way to find out."

Father Abatangelo sits in the very last chair he'd choose. His memories are fuzzy, but he remembers a red sky and black stone and twisting limbs. He remembers that when he and Hector came back there wasn't much for them to say to one another, but Hector's jaw was set and they were both sure they were going to die soon.

The third man, the one who didn't come back, Father Abatangelo still can't remember his name. Can't remember his face.

He remembers his body, though. He won't be forgetting that.

Alan kneels on the floor in front of him. The supplies are arranged carefully within arm's reach: charcoal and candles and a narrow curved knife and various boxes and pouches Father Abatangelo doesn't want to speculate about.

Alan seems dead set on getting it right.

The implication, of course, is: *this time.*

"So where is it you're about to send me?"

Alan looks up from his manic work. "Can't say for sure," he says, like they'd just talked about this. "Another place. This place, but different. I don't know." He looks back down, selects a long piece of black charcoal. "I'm not going to start bullshitting you with dimensions and gateways or whatever, because I don't know."

Father Abatangelo nods.

"The things don't talk, after all."

Alan moves Father Abatangelo's hands into position on the chair's slick armrests. He holds his own hand out, palm-up, and sketches on it with the charcoal. Father Abatangelo follows the lines at first, thinking there must be a hieroglyphic tradition buried in there somewhere, a detectable resemblance between the symbols and what they represent. He thinks he starts to see it, too, but the lines get too numerous, too close together, and he loses what thread he thought he had.

Alan presses the charcoal palm to Father Abatangelo's forehead, keeps it there. Transferring the glyph. He takes the curved knife in his other hand.

"Why is it," Father Abatangelo says, "that I'm the one who has to bleed?"

"You're the one's going." Eye contact. "Ready?"

Father Abatangelo nods. The knife pierces his skin. He feels the touch of the metal but the pain never comes. Instead, a whooshing blast of wet heat and a feeling like falling and rising at once, different pieces of him in different directions.

Father Abatangelo crests and falls flat to a ground of jagged slate. The rock cuts his palms, his face, and this pain does come, in a flood of vague skinned-knee memories and a panic that he's already found himself incapacitated.

He lifts his face, feels dripping down his cheek. Licks his lips. Salty copper.

Off to a great start.

Father Abatangelo rolls onto his back. He's not ready to look around quite yet. He looks at his leg instead, where the knife went in. A dark spot on his jeans, inexplicably scabbed over, already welded to his thigh with clotting, looks pretty insignificant next to the drops falling from his head onto the fabric.

The red sky at the edge of his vision, and the black rock under him, remind him that he hasn't long to linger.

He pushes himself to his feet and looks around. The memories he was still pretty sure he'd made up, powers of suggestion or something, jibe pretty well with the red sky swooping down farther than is natural against the landscape of sharp black rock, with wind-worn arches and monuments that aren't quite familiar but nonetheless ring a distant bell.

Father Abatangelo starts off in the direction he's facing. He's not sure what it is he's looking for, but it's as likely to be there as anywhere else.

A gust of wind rushes over his face, carrying a scent like a transistor radio burning through layers of skin. Like the smell of a formerly lived-in house, it triggers a molecular nostalgia in him, a calling-up of memories that don't quite exist except in the trail they've left behind.

Father Abatangelo sucks in a breath, swallows, but hears neither. The air presses past him. His eardrums pound not with his heartbeat but some foreign rhythm. He wonders whether a person really breathes here at all, or if the body merely goes through the motions out of habit.

This stirs a tingling space where a memory used to be.

No progress to be made mulling things over. It's not what he's here for. He sets his sights on the top of a jagged hill stabbing sideways against the red sky, coming to a fine point. From there, he should be able to see whatever it is he's looking for, if it's nearby.

Father Abatangelo makes it five steps and his brain swirls in his head. Slate catches the side of his foot. He drops to his knees and drags himself back up.

He takes two inaudible breaths and a test step. Wobbles. The footstep doesn't reach his ears; wind seems to flare up around him. He tries another, sliding his foot along the ground instead of raising it, until he finds a good spot.

He remembers something Hector used to say about Florida, how every schoolchild knew a move called the Stingray Shuffle, sliding their feet forward walking into the ocean instead of taking proper steps.

The next foot slides, finds a hold. This is the way to do it.

The ridge he's heading toward seems much farther away.

Stacy's arm itches where the needle was. Drips and nurses and bright antiseptic rooms weren't what she had in mind when she asked Lorelei to cut her, but it does help sell the story. She remembers calling the cops, saying that she'd been mugged, and then nothing but rain on concrete and a chill deep in her spine.

She woke in the ambulance surrounded by blue uniforms and thought she was arrested, then thought she was dead. Balanced between the two possibilities, unsure which was preferable, she noticed the tubes running into needles in her arms, the way her shirt wasn't unbuttoned but cut off her, and remembered the payphone in the alley.

This was not the plan.

It's only the next morning, though. No serious damage, but a not-insignificant loss of blood. Someone's left-behind sweater hangs loose off her shoulders. She hopes the owner didn't die in that hospital. The stitches on her leg burn when she takes a step.

She slips through the heavy glass door and the sun strips the image of outside off her retinas. Stacy blinks away the glare, sees a red sedan, Colorado Jack leaning against the hood. It's Jessica's car. Stacy swallows. Jack opens the door for her. She gets in.

They don't talk until they're on the interstate. The tangle of roads is only vaguely familiar. She wonders just how far across town the ambulance took her.

"Stacy. Long time."

"Hey, Jack. Didn't think we were speaking."

"What did you expect?"

Stacy shrugs. "Pretty much that." She waves her hand between them. "What's this, then?"

"You've been doing good?"

"Yeah, okay."

"Gotta say, you've looked better. What happened?"

Stacy eyes him. "Didn't you ask the nurse?"

"Sure did. Something about how you got mugged, caught a knife in the leg."

"Well."

"What kind of mugger stabs somebody in the leg?"

Stacy tries a smile. "A bad one?"

It's unwise to fuck with Jack, and Stacy almost follows up immediately with the story she has ready, to keep him from getting irritated. If the story were true, though, she'd be reluctant to tell it. She'd want to suss out what Jack knew about Lorelei, where she stood in whatever badness she'd found herself in.

She runs through it in her head, keeps it there. Tries to look natural.

Jack still hasn't responded.

She opens her mouth but he shakes his head and twists the radio dial. Old Springsteen, singing about highways and streetlights and radio stations. The kind of song that always made her nervous. Nearly agoraphobic. All that moving around and no destination in sight, no thank you. Stacy prefers beelines.

Jack couldn't have known that, she reminds herself. And anyway, he doesn't control what's on the radio. Need to keep these jitters under control. Still, she can't help a quick glance at the stereo readout, to make sure it's really a station and not a tape.

Jack pulls off into a hardware store parking lot. They sit, people passing, hauling shopping carts full of plywood and potted plants. Emmylou Harris on the radio now. Stacy needs to remember this station, to avoid it in the future. Jack waits for Emmylou to finish and twists the knob, choking the volume.

He holds up one finger. A shopping-cart man rattles past them to his car. Jack points to the door. They get out.

"So," he says, scrubbing at a pollen smear on the bumper with the pad of his finger, "what happened?"

"Something's up, Jack. Chick was poking around, you know, asking questions."

Jack nods.

"She was looking for Jessica." Stacy tries to pantomime getting distracted by a thought. "Did something happen to Jessica?"

"Dunno. Haven't heard from her in a while. Looking for her, but can't find her yet."

Stacy makes herself nod somberly. At least now it's clear she's being as honest with him as he intends to be with her. He's Colorado Jack, which means he doesn't have to tell people what he knows. The way he's asking questions, tooling around in Jessica's car to try and shake something out of her, means that maybe now neither does she.

"Well, this chick came by, asking about how she wants to talk to Jessica. Says she's a friend of a friend or some shit, but won't get specific. So I'm thinking, maybe a cop, maybe she's got some beef with somebody. Who knows, right? So I stonewall her. Not that I know anything to tell her."

Jack smiles. "It has been a while."

"Right? So I didn't have anything to tell her—I haven't even seen Jessica since I got a job—but this bitch, man, she doesn't believe me. So she starts threatening me with the knife. Decides to cut me, see if that'll make me know something. Dumps me on the fucking street."

"Christ. You know her? I mean, you ever see her before?"

Stacy shakes her head, stares at the asphalt. "No. Talked like she was from fucking Georgia or something. Real slow, you know? Never saw her before."

Jack nods. Stacy waits for him to stop nodding and say something. The moment is a long time coming.

Stacy steps through the coffee-shop door into a cloud of burnt coffee and vanilla syrup. Her pulse throbs against her skull. The beginnings of a panic attack in her chest. She breathes, holds, breathes again. Takes in more of those smells.

She said she'd never come back, is the thing. Out loud, not quietly. To her manager.

The drive-through customer she'd been talking to over the headset had heard, too.

It had been a fairly memorable exit.

The smart bet is that routine turnover has taken care of anybody who might remember her, but Stacy comes in with her head tilted down anyway. Scans the cash register, the espresso machine. Nobody familiar.

A new manager, new cashier. The milk steamer kicks on and Stacy cranes her neck, but she can't see the face behind the machine. She takes a table in the near corner, by the door but with a better view of the counter. Says a vague prayer for anybody not unfriendly.

Meklit steps out from behind the machine, thumps the metal cup of milk on the counter to settle it, and pours slowly, in a turning motion. Slides the paper cup to a fellow in pressed chinos, glances hopelessly at the tip jar.

Stacy takes a deep breath and stands, catches Meklit's eyes.

Meklit starts, glances over toward the back office. Her manager's here, then.

Stacy approaches the counter and leans on it, smiling. "Hey. Long time."

"The hell are you doing here?" Meklit whispers. "This is a pretty bad idea."

"Yeah?" Stacy widens her eyes, pantomiming fear.

Meklit laughs. "Yeah, well, some of us still work here." She hooks her chin over to the door. "Maybe let's meet up a little later? Someplace I won't get fired?"

Stacy nods but doesn't meet her eyes. "Yeah, well. I kinda need a place to stay."

"Right." Meklit's eyes darken. "You mean a place to lay low."

Stacy shrugs. "You doing okay?"

"Yeah, sure. Just, you know," Meklit pulls two espresso-machine levers in time, "climbing that ladder to nowhere."

Stacy smiles too wide.

Meklit peels a house key off the ring that's somehow already in her hand and plinks it on the counter. "You know the address. Just wait there, yeah? It's my only key."

Stacy hits the sidewalk, thumb hooked in her hip pocket, touching the key. She'd kept it together thus far, but with safe haven in sight the impetus to get there swells. Every moment spent on the street is a moment not spent behind a locked door, in an apartment she can trust.

Some shapeless threat lurks around the corner at every intersection, behind every dumpster in every alley. The doors and the shuttered living rooms and the tinted car windows stare at Stacy. She picks up her pace, shoes scraping on concrete, until she makes the familiar apartment building a half-mile away.

She runs up one flight of stairs and down a breezy outdoor corridor and turns the key in the apartment door. She's still not completely sure what she's afraid of. Those guys in her apartment. How they ended up.

And that moment when Lorelei found her staring into the grate.

Stacy whirls into the apartment, slams the door behind her and throws the bolt. She probably hasn't been nearly suspicious enough of Lorelei. She'd been willing to keep her from going back to her apartment, though. Even acted on that suggestion about the knife.

Stacy tells herself she's getting worked up over nothing. That those guys had been looking for Jessica, not her—that things got out of hand.

Still. She's not going back to her apartment.

A shuffling from inside sends Stacy's stomach to her throat. She puts her back to the wall, raises her hands to her face.

Keane rounds the corner from his bedroom, stack of dirty dishes in hand. He catches sight of Stacy, poised to fight. The dishes clatter to the floor.

"Christ, Stacy," he says, one hand to his chest. He crouches after the dishes. "Thought you were Meklit. Fuck, you startled me."

Stacy drops her hands, goes about getting her pulse under control.

"Chrissakes, come in. Sit down." Keane retrieves the plates and drops them in the sink. "Good to see you."

"Sorry to creep around."

They sit across from each other at the table and Stacy gives him the much-abridged version of her week. Keane's frown deepens. As she winds toward the end, he gets up and goes to the cupboard.

"Hey, if you're going to work or something, I don't want to—"

Keane shakes his head, hoists a bottle of gin frosty from the freezer. "Nah, morning shift. Got tomorrow off. Figured, hey, been a long time. Seems you could use a drink."

Stacy accepts a coffee mug of gin. The floral smell brings her back to nights here, a big circle of people shaking off the workday, drinking and telling stories, and the rest.

She wonders why she hasn't been by here.

Except she knows the answer. It's "the rest." It's the people she knew, and Keane and Meklit knew. She wasn't sure where to show her face when she decided to get straight, get out.

So she didn't show it anywhere.

By the time Meklit comes home, an hour later at most, she and Keane are doubled over on the couch, laughing and shouting pieces of the story of how she quit the coffee shop.

Meklit shakes her head. "That didn't take fucking long."

Stacy raises her eyes to her, readies an apology.

Meklit waves it off. "Hell with it. Any clean glasses?"

CHAPTER TEN

Father Abatangelo's sneakers mark a trail up the ridge by the shreds of their soles. He drags and stumbles and scrapes his way up. It's been so long since he looked up that he's certain he must nearly be there, but is equally certain that, should he look, the distance left to travel would ruin him and he would lay himself down on the jagged slate to sleep, to die.

He can't quite remember what Alan's apartment looks like. The general character of the place is vivid enough in impressions, but the particulars blaze and fade out of time. The whole will not present itself. Father Abatangelo keeps at it, grasping for an image of himself sitting comatose in a chair. He's seen it only once, from that side, but that was enough.

He doesn't want to see that again.

The image of Alan's apartment slips past his attention like a trout through hands. Like this place won't let him anchor himself anywhere else, so he has to keep perfectly in this interminable moment.

He keeps his eyes on the next step, the one after that. The wind picks up. He feels this not on his skin but as increased pressure in his ears. The landscape wobbles a bit but he maintains his footing. His skull throbs behind his eyes. The ground starts to level out. He falls to his hands and knees and gasps inaudibly for breath, clenching his eyes shut. Claws the last feet to the top of the ridge.

With the climb over, the prospect of finally seeing what it is he's been climbing toward is freshly terrifying. No telling how long he's been here, or how long he has left. Time to do what you came here to do, old man. He pushes to his feet, looks out.

The red sky's horizon is impossibly far away, though the land between it and his position is dotted with cliffs and peaks at least as high as the ridge. More ragged stone arches. The foreign geography staggers Father Abatangelo. Hector and Alan had never been able to confidently determine where the ritual sent a person, but after his brutal climb, and witnessing the shrieking, violent landscape, the importance of the question hits home.

Which is not to say he has the slightest guess.

Before, he'd only walked around at ground level, scoping and fighting. Somehow he's gone unmolested up the ridge, and this belatedly begins to worry him. Though he knows his sense of time of skewed here, he's nonetheless confident that last time he hadn't walked around nearly this long before the first of the damned tentacles came slithering across the rock.

Father Abatangelo searches for anything that stands out. Catches a twitching at the corners of his vision, which dissipates when he tries to look at it directly. He jerks his head side to side—nothing but black rock and red sky. The silent wind pressure can't be tuned out.

A sub-aural rumbling. He hears it through his feet. Braces himself. Can't find any source for it in the direction it seems to be coming from.

A sliver of blue light blazes through the rocks between him and the next rise. It's not much, but against the rusty air it's blinding. Father Abatangelo watches the light, waiting. For a long moment nothing happens, then another sliver bursts through, then another. The rocks around the light don't seem to be moving, but are somehow suddenly not in the way of the beams.

More twitching at the edge of his sight. Father Abatangelo fights down the urge to turn and look directly. He un-focuses his eyes, hoping whatever's there will present itself to him.

From the base of a ridge, a long black arm uncoils and slithers toward the light bursting out from the ground. Father Abatangelo starts and the tentacle blurs again. He can't believe it could have been there the whole time, without him seeing it. He lets his gaze settle and the tentacle re-materializes. It coils around the light, circling tighter and tighter without touching.

The rumbling again, from behind that same ridge.

Father Abatangelo's bones remember the sound. He hurls himself to the ground, taking cover behind some jags of slate, shredding his forearms on others.

A clutch more tentacles venture out and circle the light, moving quickly, more confidently now. They leave their white crust smeared across the rocks, hair snagged in the clefts. They join the first one, coiling around and piling on each other like a hellish rope coil. Their seething recalls some kind of ant heap.

149

From the ridge, the rumbling grows louder and gives birth to a shaking, dragging sound. Father Abatangelo presses himself to the uneven ground and peeks out above the rock until a mammoth wall of gray leather oozes into view—an oblong body of sagging, hardened hide the size of a city block, pressing itself over the sharp slate without problem. He ducks his head back down.

The dragging sound supplants the silencing blasts of the wind. Another risked glance reveals a yellow eye peeling loose from the leather folds. He ducks down again, with an adrenaline blast born of the certainty that even looking at that eye might alert the beast to his presence.

The blue light pours from the ground in a tight round beam. The tentacles seize and the leather body convulses, tugs itself closer. Cavernous wet smacking sounds, burst of blinding light. The sky flares and Father Abatangelo struggles for breath.

A heave, a settling rumble. Father Abatangelo peeks out to see that the body has flumped down over the light. Eye-first, it looks like. Little tendrils of blue light bleed out along the sides of the impossibly massive body, and the world starts to shimmer, going fuzzy at the edges.

The body seeps down, bit by bit, like it's dripping through a hole. Something he can't be seeing shimmers over its rippling skin—the world as superimposed film strip.

The image resolves: an empty gray room; three chairs, a table; two bodies, leaking black, molding hair from the backs of their necks. A third body, crumpled in the corner, frozen, screaming silently at the ceiling.

Hector's face, unmistakable. Stuck mid-scream.

Father Abatangelo only recoils when another image crashes in to replace it—walls of dank concrete, dripping with some kind of green algae that bleeds black slime. Low ceiling, floor slanting down.

It takes him a moment, but the recognition, like everything else here, is nearly cellular. The tunnel under Gutter Street, nearly unrecognizable in how it's been overrun. The familiar black hair roils atop the green fuzz, under it, coating itself and the attendant white slime in the black goo, which hardens gray and flakes on contact.

Father Abatangelo grips the rock in front of him. More blood as the skin on his hands gives. The leather body churns and the image of the tunnel solidifies. Father Abatangelo is in the tunnel, as is what has to be only a part of the body of the beast, or else its heavily compacted entirety.

His ears pop and he can hear again, a sharp whine against the sudden silence. The air comes damp and cool. He struggles against an incipient cough.

Behind him, the blasted black-and-red landscape. Ahead and around, the tunnel. No clear dividing line but rather a blur. He always seems to be looking at one or the other.

Father Abatangelo stands, confused to find himself upright. The beast's eye materializes in front of him in a massive fold of leather. Sick yellow where the white should be, and an impossibly deep black iris.

Though he's fairly sure he knows better, he detects something like recognition in the way the beast stares at him. The moment hovers, as still as the landscape under the red sky. Father Abatangelo doesn't breathe, can't remember what it's like to.

A tugging in his chest is his only warning. He whirls back to the black slate. The tunnel fades before him, into the distance. His stomach drops, churns. His head throbs again with the wind of that place, then more with the transition.

A sense of vertigo, detached from direction, twists his body against his sense of his physical self. The slate recedes and he draws in breath and jerks forward—

—in the chair in Alan's apartment.

Alan jumps back, tourniquet around his arm, needle empty.

Father Abatangelo hears himself screaming. Doesn't remember starting.

Alan finds his feet before Father Abatangelo catches his breath. "You were gone a long time," Alan says.

Father Abatangelo nods, waits—realizes Alan doesn't know yet what he's seen.

"They're crossing."

Alan blinks, scratches his shoulder. "They're what?" Stops scratching. "You *saw* them?"

"Yeah. Saw one. It was . . . it went to the tunnel. It took me with it."

"Christ." Alan slumps against the wall. "That's new."

"Yeah." Father Abatangelo rubs his hands together. "Yeah, it is."

Alan looks at him, doesn't say anything. Doesn't have to. Something's been knocked loose in Father Abatangelo's head, and he's starting to remember.

Lorelei paces across the street from the apartment complex. She was here not much more than a week ago, when she first hit town. That week stretches behind her, though, and she feels years older than she did the morning she stood at that stoop, confident and working up her game face in case Hector tried to pull one off on her.

That game face has carved its way into a permanent accoutrement. She passed a convenience store on the way to the apartment and the expression that bounced back at her from the window was hard, detached. Waiting for nothing good.

She didn't try to change it. It was kind of nice to see.

She stands across the street from the last address she's got for Hector. She's cycled through his friends and partners and people of a more difficult-to-describe relation. Nobody would cop to having seen him for weeks.

She's posed as a dealer the last few weeks. As an addict, an old friend, once as a long-lost cousin. She figures herself a decent-enough judge of character, an above-average reader of people, but it's led her in a circle. Either she's off about herself in that respect, or truly no one's seen Hector in some time.

The other people she knew from her brief time in the city, she didn't talk to. Nothing to be gained there, then or now.

Jessica was promising. Her ties with Hector were long-standing and seemed not entirely centered on narcotics, but she dropped off the planet days before Lorelei got to town. With good reason, it would seem.

Though after plunging down that sewer grate with Stacy's gentleman callers, it's an odds-on favorite Jessica never got near as far out of town as people seem to think. Lorelei would just as soon not place that bet on herself.

So, one last attempt.

The funds are there for another motel room. What they took off Slim, Lorelei struggles to imagine spending. Her favorite math is breaking down, by the hour, what she made at the hotel, figuring that against the money they waltzed off with after a half-hour's work. She'd've been safely middle-aged by then. Elijah would have probably gotten himself killed riding Slim's wake, and money from those kinds of calculations never piles up quite the way you're hoping it will.

So the money's not an issue, but she can't find a motel with a view of Hector's apartment building. Just stores and other apartments and some upstairs offices. It's loitering then, in this admittedly more inhabited part of town, trying not to draw too much attention while reading the same newspaper for two hours, three.

She leans over, looks at Hector's window. No light, no movement. The mailbox sticker still has his name on it. Nothing moves but the street around her.

She pages to the front of the newspaper for the third time, finally gives up and folds it back and peels off the Entertainment section. A rather vague review of a play, like the reporter maybe hadn't really been there. Raves about a book by someone who lives three blocks from here. An editorial decrying the social implications of this or that techno-gadget, and Lorelei's eyes begin to go dry.

Two men round the corner at the next light. The first is a slight fellow, hunched in on himself in a too-large jacket. The other man is vaguely familiar. He carries himself erect, not in a military manner but nonetheless as someone used to commanding attention. Hands in pockets, shoulders back.

Lorelei blinks. Strike the self-administered buzz cut, pull the gray hair an inch or so longer and stand it up. Add a week's beard and a night or more minus sleep, rub the eyes red and ruin the posture. It's for sure the old man who stumbled into her on Gutter Street.

Except he's not nearly as old as she thought. Once she places the face, the difference is startling. He looks almost as though he's dyed his hair that color. It doesn't belong on his face, his body.

Lorelei leans onto a parking meter, shields her face with a wretched live-music review. The two men don't talk but

154

they're clearly together. The first one, the one she doesn't recognize, hooks his head over to the same building she killed the morning watching. The other, the gray-haired one, nods slightly and follows his mate to the door.

They don't ring the bell. There is one, but the front door's not locked.

Lorelei makes to crumple up the paper, gets in a twist and thinks better of it. She smooths the pages against the coin-op machine she bought it from, folds it over, and stuffs it in her back pocket instead.

She crosses the street and edges into the entrance to Hector's building.

Dirty yellow curtains turn the air to chemical runoff. Dusty air in the apartment, virtually no furniture. Outline of a coffee table in the carpet. Signs of hasty packing, but the apartment's small enough that Father Abatangelo sees there's no luggage.

Hector hadn't said anything about moving, and not that much time had passed. Could be he'd been readying a contingency plan, though

Father Abatangelo somehow doubts it.

Alan strides around the apartment's perimeter, following the right-hand wall like someone trying to escape a maze. He stops back at Father Abatangelo's side, looks to the corners, and takes three careful paces toward the middle of the room.

Father Abatangelo wishes he'd spent a little more time listening to Alan over the last several years. Maybe he'd know the moves, know what to expect. He stands very still and tries not to move, not to make any disturbance.

He's pretty sure he remembers where this is going. Tries to breathe anyway.

Alan shrugs off his backpack and sets out boxes and cloth rolls in a scattered array on the floor. "Okay. Something happened here."

Father Abatangelo holds in his retort.

"I'm going to do something," Alan says.

Father Abatangelo steps toward the door. Keeping watch, he supposes.

Alan takes five transistor radios from his pack. Measures an arm's length from himself to five equidistant points. Each point gets a radio. The radios flick to life under his thumb, already tuned to different stations, set to the same volume. Alan closes his eyes, shifts his head this way and that, gauging the sound. Finally nods.

Father Abatangelo will grant him he's prepped himself. Could be he knows enough what he's doing for this to start making sense.

He pictures a yellow eye underneath a city street, oozing green mold all around.

Making sense is probably optimistic.

Alan's muttering.

Father Abatangelo wonders how long he's been at it.

"Sorry, say again?"

Alan glances to the backpack. "Just that maybe we can figure out where Hector got to. Try to follow him there."

"Is that a good idea?"

Alan shrugs. "Dunno. Not sure what else we might go on. Maybe something'll come up." He looks up again. "Not really an exact science we're doing here."

He settles down again, pulling a few small bundles of dried plants and a jar full of unrecognizable powder from the backpack. String tied around the plants, not rubber bands. No label on the jar, but what looks like letters scratched into the glass, maybe with a paperclip.

Something about those letters rings a bell Father Abatangelo can't quite place. A jolt of cold terror through his veins, then a sound like nervous laughter from his own throat.

"What," he says, "no blood this time?"

Alan's face is serious. "No, we don't want them smelling us, not until we're ready." He opens the jar before Father Abatangelo can pursue that last bit. "Besides, you're a priest, yeah?"

"Yeah. Or, was. Not really sure at the moment."

"Well, sure. But you just seem a little twitchy about blood. Given, you know."

Father Abatangelo takes a second to put it together. "Well, it's—" he almost says *purely symbolic*, catches himself; if transubstantiation falls, who knows how long what little remains of his wall will last, if it even exists anymore. "It's the ritual of the thing, right? It's *supposed* to be intense, to be something we're not cavalier about."

Alan nods. "Yeah. Exactly."

The point is made. His church, Hector's heroin. He puts Alan's occultism next to them, sees that it fits just fine.

Alan dips two fingers into the jar and starts to smear them on the carpet. The substance on his fingers is too dark to be ash and not coarse enough, but it smears in a similar way. Alan holds the jar and his hand as far out from his face as he can while making curving shapes on the carpet.

A hiss of air between Alan's molars. "Of *course* it's carpet."

The shapes he's drawing, curves and swirls, nonetheless begin to cohere into a not-unfamiliar pattern. Father

157

Abatangelo thinks of the pendant around his neck. It's not the same pattern, but there's a family resemblance.

Alan looks around, apparently finds nothing on the ceiling, and strikes a match, holds it to the tip of one of the plant bundles. He holds his hand out flat. Smoke pours off in thick tendrils at first. Then, though the air is still, the smoke suddenly billows, its glowing red point of origin flaring.

Father Abatangelo doesn't see the sigil on the carpet move. He's pretty sure.

Alan's outstretched hand starts to tremble a bit.

The windows darken.

Father Abatangelo holds his breath. Has been for a while. He lets it out slow, silent.

The door slams shut.

Father Abatangelo whirls around. He hadn't heard it open. A tall woman stands now in the doorway, her stealth lost when she entered the room. She gapes, hand on the doorknob.

Alan flinches. Doesn't turn around, but the way his shoulders shift, he's having to hold himself.

The woman opens her mouth. Nothing comes.

In front of her, behind Father Abatangelo, it starts.

Early afternoon light makes a mess of the inside of Stacy's eyes. She's been sleeping, deep for the first time in a lifetime. The light skews her whole plan. With how the apartment's arranged, and the direction the building faces, the amount of light means it must be far later than expected.

Not that she has anywhere particular to be.

She tosses aside a surprising blanket—Keane must have draped it over her—and drags herself up from the couch, into a pulsating headache that nearly sends her back down again. She staggers to the kitchen, toward the smell of un-fresh coffee.

Meklit is slumped at the table. "Morning, dear." Voice lain out in the sun until it cracked.

Stacy does a sound like a collapsing balloon.

"Sounds about right. Coffee in the pot, Alka-Seltzer on top of the fridge."

Coffee over ice, two tablets dissolved in water. Water, then coffee. It helps, but not much.

Meklit lights a cigarette. Stacy holds out two fingers.

"You quit."

"So did you."

"Well." Meklit slides over the pack.

A cloud comes over the sky, chilling the room. Meklit, head in hands, doesn't seem to notice. Stacy lights one of Meklit's smokes. The fizzing from the antacid catches in her throat.

Meklit walks to the window, pushes the shade aside, gasps. Stacy stands and goes to the window. Meklit grabs her by the shoulder, pulls the blinds the rest of the way.

A plume of smoke billows from just far enough away that Stacy's not sure of the distance—three blocks, maybe four. It whips side-to-side over the skyline, its tail indicating a point of origin that Stacy can't pinpoint.

It's black, though. Not like the smoke from a structure fire. This seems chemical, a dark plume blotting out the sun.

Stacy gets her mouth in the shape of a word but the plume breaks off, rockets into the sky in a solid mass. Nothing is left behind. No sirens yet, no indication that anyone but them saw.

Stacy tugs Meklit's sleeve. "Local news?"

"No television." Eyes not leaving the skyline.

"Computer, then?"

Meklit stares a moment more, then drifts to her bedroom. Probably, like Stacy, too tired to consider leaving the apartment, investigating with her own eyes. Which might be best, this neighborhood, and with cops surely on their way.

Meklit returns with a laptop balanced on her palm. She clicks around a bit, shrugs. "Nothing about a fire or whatever."

The sky darkens again, beyond normal cloud cover, the way the sky will turn yellow before a tornado. It only lasts a moment.

Stacy blinks. Must be her hangover fucking with her. Still, it takes Meklit tugging on her shirt for Stacy to pull her eyes from the sky.

Lorelei sneaks the door open as quietly as she can. Nothing moves in the apartment. She smiles, easing into the idea of something finally going her way. Then she sees how the light's not coming through the windows, and how the flame leaps from a bundle of plants in a crouching man's hand. Some insane symbol, a circle twirling into itself, smudged on the carpet in some kind of ash, twists wildly like a trapped animal, and the door slips from her hand.

The slam brings around the head of the gray-haired man. The one she recognizes. His face is calmer than it was in the alley, but there's tension beneath his composure.

Lorelei hears hissing from the crouching man, but not words. The gray-haired man surges forward while she tries to get out of the room. He shoves her flat against the wall, presses the meat of his forearm over her mouth.

The far wall begins to move.

The gray-haired man leans in, eyes peeking over his elbow, voice a rasp. "Not a word. Not a move. Nothing."

Lorelei's hand drifts toward her pocket, to the gun there, but she doesn't have any bullets left and this seems a bad time for bluffing. She nods instead.

The crouching man weaves back and forth on his knees, holds out a hand. Lorelei doesn't know if he's been holding it out the whole time. It's shaking hard, waving too fast and wide to be neurological. More like they're on a boat that's about to turn over and he can't handle the waves.

The apartment is perfectly still, though, except for the smoke pouring thicker now from the plants clutched by the crouching man. It moves as though in a wind Lorelei can't feel, collecting heavier in the corners of the room. Lorelei watches the heaviest part billow up, spreading across the ceiling, and realizes the smoke isn't being blown by anything at all.

It's tracing the outline of the apartment.

The crouching man dips his chest toward the carpet and takes a deep breath. The gray-haired man drops his hand from Lorelei's mouth. The crouching man jumps to his feet, holds the bundle of burning plant away from him, and waves it in a slow circle. Smoke hangs like a pencil tracing on the air.

The gray-haired man turns and squints at the carpet sigil, like he can't quite tell if it's moving.

Lorelei can tell just fine. It's squirming in place like a pile of snakes.

The gray-haired man leans forward, hisses, "Alan."

Alan shakes his head, once, hard.

Lorelei's more interested in the wall.

Above and to the sides of the curtained window, the wall undulates. The smoke is too thick along the bottom of the wall to tell what's going on there. She watches it. It's darker than dark; light dies inches before touching it.

Sudden night falls outside, bleeds through the curtains, makes the window disappear. The smoke rockets in a plumed sheet toward the ceiling, cresting in a wave over Alan's head, before diving back down again, into the burning bundle. The bundle glows. Alan waves it slowly back and forth, sending a ripple through the cresting smoke and down the sheet of it in front of the wall. The ripple widens, starts to sketch the outline of vague shapes.

The shapes sharpen, become a room, chairs.

Lorelei blinks, but it's still there—a mural in the smoke.

The gray-haired man isn't keeping her from running anymore, but she can't get the message to her legs.

The lines in the smoke shimmer and double and are suddenly three-dimensional and creeping toward Lorelei. New walls spread around her. Chairs and a wide table appear. Three faceless shadows emerge, one slumped in a chair, the other against the wall.

It's a second room, carved from the smoke and layered atop the one they're standing in.

Lorelei can't make out anything distinguishing about the figures. The quivering blast of breath from the gray-haired man's mouth says that he can.

Alan maintains his position for long heartbeats before finally straightening up and holding the glowing bundle out in front of him. He waves it twice and takes a step, twice and takes a step.

Preparing the way for himself, looks like.

He does this, wave by step by wave, until his body is pressed against the far wall. He continues to walk in place, and the smoke-room moves as though he were walking forward in real space.

Blood rushes to Lorelei's head. The room blurs. Both rooms do.

She steadies herself. Alan crouches next to the smoke body in the chair. His face twitches. Lips compressed, eyes narrow. He looks to the gray-haired man. No words. He runs a hand along the top of the body's head. Lorelei's starting to suspect that he's touching more than smoke.

Alan's hand finds something protruding from the back of the figure's skull. Lorelei couldn't make it out even if she squinted, doesn't want to try.

The lines of the shadow furniture start to blur. A little light peeks through. Alan notices but keeps his hand on the head. Turns and sprints toward the wall where Lorelei is standing, the not-room whirling around him like a film being rewound, fading back into wisps and puffs. Alan crashes into the wall.

Sunlight creeps back into the dim room, but less than seems right. Less than there was outside, before Lorelei climbed the stairs to the apartment.

The gray-haired man reaches out, but Alan waves off his support. He's looking over the apartment, searching for something that's not there anymore.

The gray-haired man retracts his hand. "You know where he is?"

"Yeah." Alan frowns. "But it's not him anymore."

"No kidding."

"No, I mean, I don't know if he's dead. But it's not *him*." He turns his head. "First thing, though. We have a guest."

Lorelei remembers to bring her guard up again, too late for it to matter.

"So. What in the world brings you here, Lorelei?"

Hector is a cog in a machine. He knows it, can feel it now. But soon he won't be able to feel anything at all, ever again.

He has all his answers, or at least the ones to the big-picture questions. The movements of the beasts have become clear in this room that used to look like the inside of a police station. With the tightening in his limbs, the incredible pressure in the back of his head, the illusion has faded. He sits in a cramped room, wallpapered in the beast's mold, which he now understands is not a consequence but a requisite of their presence. A part of their body. Perhaps fungal limb, perhaps symbiosis.

The beasts don't think in those biological terms.

They do think, though. Their thoughts burn into his brain as the connection grows closer, promising to eventually drive his own mental processes to the margins. And the thoughts do not come in words, but impulses that he has to translate.

The translation is becoming easier, his old language more foreign.

Beast thought-impressions are redolent with hunger, terrifying in scope. They think in terms of networks, of incorporation and assimilation. Perhaps *they* is the incorrect pronoun, if such things still have any meaning. Hector has no way of knowing if their separate bodies are distinct entities, and not nodes of some horrifyingly immense being.

The small answers still elude him: how exactly he got to this building, what they did to him when he thought the woman pinned rotting yet writhing to the opposite wall was a cop, the man her sergeant. But with time he has developed the feeling that they never mattered, were the wrong questions entirely.

The beasts are reaching. Hector feels their ambition like a burning in his stomach, a wave crushing him from inside and out. He is becoming part of them, a piece of their project.

Whether this knowledge is part of his being integrated, or whether the beasts, in some incomprehensible, parasitic magnanimity, have let him know, he cannot say, but he suspects that it is nothing more than the chemical changes erupting in his brain, mirrored by the softening of his skin. But he understands their project, now.

They had thought that the key to the beasts, their lifeforce, was the same thing that made the symbolic manifest in their presence, that lent solidity to Tony's prayers and efficacy to Alan's occult symbolism. They'd thought the beasts were meaning machines. What presumption! What simple apocalyptic misunderstanding. Only now, at the end, does Hector understand.

It is exactly the opposite. The beasts hunger for flesh. They are meat machines.

They traffic in the symbolic, and have for longer than they would have allowed themselves to think, because the symbolic roots itself in the meat of the human brain. Only the brain can deliver the rest of the meat—the bleeding organism—into the beasts' influence.

Once the human body is tied into the greater system by the dexterous hair, its mental faculties are stripped away. Hector can feel it starting to happen. When it is complete, he will be in the same condition as the two other people in the room.

He knows what they are, can feel what has happened to them. They live despite their desiccation, twitching, pinned in place by hair that isn't hair at all but alive. Giving up to the beasts their bodies, so that the beasts might propagate themselves, receiving in return that life which the beasts have stolen from them in the first place.

They are vassals, hosts.

Fifteen years are the business of a moment here. Hector remembers everything like it is happening now: how they found the clock, Alan's curiosity. The tendrils of the beasts—scouts to the current invasion force. The beasts must then work on a timeline beyond Hector's ken, both longer and faster than any natural creature. The old encounter and the new catastrophe are one continuous motion to them. The time between nearly doesn't exist.

And he remembers, now. Tony—Father Abatangelo— had been working on a city-mapping project. For a community college course. Christ. To preserve the history of Boston, those areas subject to new development, erasure of the past. He'd enlisted their help, Hector and the third man. He still can't remember that last name. Understands now that the body, seemingly destroyed when they found it in the beasts' realm, has by now become so absorbed into the beasts that it would be unrecognizable as a corpse.

That man has no name now, in the truest sense.

By the time they found Alan, asked him for help, the process had gathered inertia. Nothing they could do.

And they had the nerve to believe they had won. To take a decade and a half as assurance of their triumph, as though that length of time could possibly matter.

He knows better now. They had scraped the symbols into the walls of the tunnel, burned a length of hair, still matted into a tentacle after being severed, and sealed the entrance.

All they had done was close a door. They'd had no way to lock it.

So now Hector sits in this room. He can't move but for the involuntary convulsions. They started as spasms, disconnected from each other and coming in no discernible sequence, but have developed into what he understands to be the rhythm of his new masters.

The foulest heartbeat, the throb of the end of the world.

A wave of hair flows down the wall, lubricated by its accompanying mold. Twists itself into a limb and joins its fellows at the back of his neck.

He would scream, but the pain doesn't feel like pain anymore. He has no frame of reference.

Pulse accelerates, external. Skin grows slippery. The room blinks away. No place, no person, no feeling but the inexorable throb of the beasts forcing themselves deeper into the world through him.

The pressure in the back of his head reaches a breaking point, an intensity beyond which he surely cannot endure. The break comes, and warmth washes over him and he no longer needs endurance, no longer needs at all.

CHAPTER ELEVEN

Highways twist and turn, and the interchanges bleed into each other, brief moments when the roads are all one, winding together, a directionless pause before scattering off again. For those moments, you're focused on the signs more than the road, with the concrete edging up in your peripheral vision.

Slim holds the steering wheel, rides back onto the highway. He rolls down the window, breathes in asphalt and exhaust. Something is changing. He can smell it. It's making him salivate. Every strip of highway brings him closer.

And then he crosses the Massachusetts state line.

It's already starting.

He doesn't know how he knows it, but somehow he does, in his bones. Or, more likely, in his blood. The air is different and the car seems to drive itself, delivering Slim to the city.

His new blood seethes pleasantly. When he first transcended, bleeding out from the Sirkos' gunshots in a dead man's pawnshop, it was a sharp scratching pain on the insides of his veins. Burning. But with time, a settling has obtained. His body and the intruder have made their peace, and what's left in place of the burning is a boundless, floating energy. He sleeps an hour at a time, pacing around between. His senses seem heightened even as his sense of self fades, becoming a story he tells himself.

To keep on course, yes. To remember where he's come from, where he's headed.

He feels bodies bustling around him the way he imagines a dog might smell a person through a wall. Deeper and deeper into the city shadow presences build and stack until a solid wall of them borders every block. He breathes deep. The smell of the air has changed, become organic.

And below, building, the smell of static and burnt hair and something somehow empty, like even while breathing in he's always already done smelling it.

He swings the car around corners and through intersections, without recourse to signs or context, following that smell.

It's the smell of the goal, the smell of transcendence.

The smell of his new flesh.

CHAPTER TWELVE

Lorelei stumbles behind Alan. Father Abatangelo tries not to let her fall behind him, has to stutter-step a few times, change his pace. It's irritating, until he dimly remembers where he saw her last, the state he was in.

There's a lot of it going around.

She makes it to the car but doesn't seem to see it. Father Abatangelo's hand hovers by her head, wanting to ease her in with a gentle version of the cop-car shove, but she floats in without impact. He gets in the passenger side.

Alan's in the driver's seat, waiting, staring out the windshield.

Father Abatangelo clears his throat. "You can drive?"

Alan snaps to like he'd been thinking about errands he had to run. Puts the car in gear.

Lorelei, in the backseat, doesn't move.

Eyes in the rearview, watching for signs she's paying attention, Father Abatangelo whispers, "How did you know her name?"

Alan looks at him, shrugs. His hands shake a bit on the wheel. He clamps down. "I don't know. It just came. Soon as I was leaving."

Father Abatangelo considers this. As soon as he was leaving. Leaving the place he wasn't really in, the place that wasn't a place by any definition he can conjure. Which resonates with certain teachings he'd just as soon it didn't.

They don't seem to be of any help here, anyway.

He doesn't ask Alan where they're going. Talking right now could be dangerous, and, from the whiteness he sees between the joints of Alan's fingers, his driving is danger enough.

They pass the turn to Alan's apartment and keep going, turn the other way, then back in their original direction, through neighborhoods Father Abatangelo doesn't know. The streets are narrow enough he can't stop bracing for a collision, imaging someone popping out from between parked cars.

They turn onto the freeway and his muscles shake themselves relaxed. They take an exit and slow past a warehouse, on the water.

Father Abatangelo glances to the warehouse, to Lorelei, to Alan. Tries to will his bad feeling directly into Alan's skull. Either it works or Alan wasn't planning on stopping anyway. They drive alongside the freeway until they're past the city limit. Stop at a Travelodge that's seen better days. Alan shuffles inside, no sunglasses to hide the burns around his eyes.

Father Abatangelo gets out of the car. Lorelei remains still a moment, staring straight ahead. She starts, like she just heard the car door slam, and misses the door handle, thumps her shoulder against her door. She finds it, tries again. Child-safety locks. Because of course Alan would think of that.

Father Abatangelo pops the handle on his side, eases the door open.

Lorelei's breaks for the road, stops and wheels around instead. Stands a couple inches from violence. He can as well as see the inside of her head. She's hovering between escape and wanting to fight, unsure which will work best. Maybe biding her time to see what happens.

He waits on his guard for her to settle on the latter. It's only when she does that he even thinks about how this might look from the Travelodge office, how bad it could have been if he'd had to stop her from running.

He doesn't turn and look, though. Isn't quite that confident.

Lorelei slumps momentarily then pulls herself back up. "Quite a party you kids were having. Sorry to interrupt."

Father Abatangelo smiles. Her swagger, laid thick over pure fear, sounds just like Hector.

"What *were* y'all doing, anyway? If you don't mind my asking. Being abducted and all."

"We didn't. We didn't abduct you."

"Can I leave?"

Father Abatangelo doesn't answer.

"Well then."

"Would you rather we left you there?"

Lorelei's silence is pointed. They watch each other refuse to speak until Alan shuffles out of the office, key card in hand, and toward a first-floor room. Father Abatangelo doesn't move. Holds his hand out for Lorelei: after you. Lorelei sighs, starts walking. Father Abatangelo follows close behind.

The room smells like old bad dreams, all molding carpet and ancient curtains. Alan fiddles with the thermostat, gets a blast of hot air from the unit instead of the cold he wants. Twists a knob, stands back. A revving like an impressive car, then a child's whine. The unit hums itself back into silence.

Lorelei drags a chair over right next to the door.

Alan cocks his head. "You're not going to want to run. We're not a threat, you know. Just we might have some stuff to talk about."

Father Abatangelo comes in, a couple beats late: "Sorry, think the air conditioning's out. Not our finest accommodations, but I do hope they'll suffice."

"You want to talk," Lorelei says, engaging Alan, "go ahead and talk."

Alan sits on the bed, sneaking him a baffled look. "Well, to start with, I'm Alan. My unsociable friend is Father Abatangelo."

"Tony," he corrects, knowing it won't stick. First thing everyone remembers is the cloth.

"Don't think it's the first time a priest was involved in kidnapping," Lorelei says.

"I *used* to be." Father Abatangelo pauses. "A priest, I mean, not the other."

"For fuck's sake." Alan shoots him another look. "Sorry for the blasphemy."

"It wasn't. Blasphemy is when—"

"Anyway. I'm sure you have some questions."

Some complicated business happens under Lorelei's face. Too many muscles pulled in too many directions by too many things; she can't decide on an expression. "A couple. First: Can I leave?"

Father Abatangelo looks at Alan.

Alan nods. "Yeah."

Lorelei gets to her feet, turns toward the door.

"But not right now."

She stops, hand on the knob. Looks back to gauge how serious Alan is and sits slowly back down.

"Okay." Alan settles in. "I'm sure you have questions about what you walked into. That's fine. We'll answer them. But first, I need to know what led you to that apartment in the first place."

"I was on my way to visit a friend of mine."

"What's your friend's name?"

Lorelei tilts her head, doesn't answer.

"Well. What led you there that *isn't* bullshit?"

"Jessica. My friend's name is Jessica."

Father Abatangelo catches Alan's glance, doesn't know what to do with it.

"Well, I was looking for Jessica. I figured Hector might know where to find her."

Alan doesn't look over this time. Father Abatangelo feels his own face go as pale as Alan's. Lorelei looks from one to the other.

"You wouldn't happen to know Hector, would you?" Lorelei's voice goes sugar-sweet. Her eyes are steady, pinpointing Alan first, then Father Abatangelo, who's wondering exactly who it is they've checked into a nondescript room with, under one of Alan's fake names.

Every sound from the ancient wood of Meklit's apartment sends a jolt through Stacy's spine, followed by a pulsing flare from her hangover headache. She settles her forehead into her hand. The vein in her temple throbs against her palm.

She shifts again, breathes.

Meklit stands over the stove, pan-frying something that smells like grease. Stacy watches her back, the way she doesn't step to the side to switch pans or reach for a spatula, but rather sways at the waist, feet planted.

Meklit slops and scrapes scorched hash browns onto two plates, shakes salt and squirts ketchup. Slides one plate to Stacy and refills both their coffee mugs.

The steam from Stacy's mug and the grease glinting on her fork promise some degree of revitalization. Along with the Alka-Seltzer, a multi-course cure. She eats and sips. The new coffee is sweet, some mixture from the silver pot on the stove and sugar Meklit did something strenuous to with a spoon. Tan head floating on top, bitter and sweet. She says it's Cuban.

Meklit's woken up enough to get fancy, and the life's coming back to Stacy by the minute. They finish eating. The coffee's churning its way through Stacy's blood and it feels good. She stands, tries to insist on doing the dishes. Meklit waves her off but Stacy gets her fingertips under Meklit's plate and spins to the sink.

The front door booms against the hallway wall and echoes closed again.

Stacy drops the plate. It bounces off her foot, shatters.

Keane stumbles through the hall, falling twice to his knees on the way to the kitchen. He reaches out a hand to brace himself on the table but catches it too low and sends it skittering. He goes down, taking the far chair with him.

His shirt is soaked through. The dampness on his back isn't water, Stacy doesn't think, but Meklit gets to him before she can say anything.

Meklit jerks back with red-stained palms, smacks her hipbone on the counter. Her hands fly to her face, stop an inch away. She stares at them, dripping.

Keane works his hands under him, slips and flops onto his back. A sound not unlike a death rattle scrapes from his throat, but another shallow breath follows. The back of his head thumps against the linoleum.

Stacy kneels next to him and braces his head with one hand. He trembles under her touch. He doesn't move in any intentional way, but his body shakes and his eyes, trying to keep focus on her, drift to the sides and snap back.

She leans in, not sure if she's helping or not. His eyes don't seem to be focusing now, and she feels heat dripping from his collar onto her hands.

"Keane. Come on, man. Stay with me." Stacy waves to Meklit. "Call a damned ambulance, yeah?"

Keane's hand jabs up, grabs her by the shirt. "Smoke."

"What?" Stacy leans down.

"Smoke."

His eyes trail to the side like he's following something walking behind her, toward the door. She glances behind, all around the room. Nothing but the displaced table and broken chair, Meklit clutching a phone to her head.

Keane tugs on her shirt again and falls back.

Stacy leans back in, waiting for him to say more. He stares out the window, eyes widening even as his lips seem to narrow to a point.

Meklit shouts the address into the phone, compensating for imagined static interference.

Stacy keeps watching as Keane goes still but for his shaking. Her mind sees smoke spurt from some building down the street, thicken and break away.

* * *

The man called Father Abatangelo doesn't talk much, just sits on the mattress and leans back against the headboard, straightening up when she or Alan say something that catches his attention. Only actually talks when Alan pitches the conversation his way. Lorelei reads that as Alan being in charge of things, but somehow she can't get that impression to stick.

She tries to keep part of her attention directed to Father Abatangelo, to keep track of his reactions, but it's tough enough keeping track of what exactly Alan is talking about.

"You understand," Alan says.

"Sure, yeah," Lorelei says. "I mean, I follow as far as there's something in the sewer under Gutter Street."

Alan slaps his hands on his thighs. "That's as far as you've got?"

"That's about as far as I follow you." Lorelei looks to Father Abatangelo, finds him inscrutable. "The rest sounds like you've spent a lot of nights in the weird parts of the library."

Alan damn near smiles. "I did at that. Most of it's from elsewhere, though. Harder sources to pin down."

"Well, far be it for me to question your occult credentials."

Alan bristles. "You *saw* them."

"I saw *it*."

"Whatever. Them. It. Fine. You saw what you saw, though, and now you're playing the skeptic. I wonder whether you know exactly how much of a shit-storm you've stepped into."

Father Abatangelo's eyes slip out of focus, like he sees something in the wall behind her that's of critical interest.

"Well," Lorelei says, "I saw something. I'd hoped you were going to explain it to me."

"I've been trying to—"

"Yeah, bang-up job."

Alan stares at his feet. Father Abatangelo glances fast between the two of them, returning his eyes to whatever was so interesting on the street-side wall.

"Well," Alan says, "maybe pay some fucking attention."

Lorelei gets to her feet. Enough is enough. She's starting to feel like a cow strolling toward a slaughterhouse on the good word of men with hammers.

Alan springs to his feet, inserts himself between her and the door.

Lorelei sticks her hand in her pocket, points the gun at Alan without removing it.

Alan looks to Father Abatangelo. "Well, Tony, I don't suppose you bothered to fucking frisk her?"

Lorelei hears Father Abatangelo's shrug in the rustling of his shirt behind her.

"Though," Alan says, tracking slowly back, "if she had bullets in that gun, I suspect she'd've put one in you back at the apartment. And probably one in me, on the way out." A surface-level smile spreads across his cheeks. "I'm right, right?"

Lorelei narrows her eyes anyway, pulls the trigger. The hammer clicks empty. Alan smiles. She pulls a couple more empty clicks at him, still can't get him to flinch. She sits down on the bed.

They know where she stands in terms of firepower—probably have since they started this conference. Maybe waiting patiently, letting them think she's given up, will reveal a way out.

That, or there's the off-chance the two crackpots will have answers for her.

Alan settles into her vacated chair. "Look, I'm just trying to get you out of a jackpot."

"For shit's sake." Father Abatangelo says. "Don't bullshit her."

His voice surprises Lorelei. Alan flicks his eyes toward him.

"Seriously. Who are we trying to kid? She's in it, and she's in it hard. Tell it to her like that."

Lorelei faces Alan expectantly. Borderline innocent. Pretending, at the very least, like the last hour or so didn't happen, that she's here of her own free will.

Alan meets her stare. Doesn't seem eager to go back over things. "Remember how I said that the things move in a way that doesn't make sense? How they get from place to place?"

Lorelei nods.

"It has to do with people. Like, they can approach a person more easily than they can an empty building. Some people, they get close to them, and it sort of changes them."

"Changes."

"Yeah." Alan looks to Father Abatangelo. "Tony, how many times have you been out of the city since it happened? In the last fifteen years?"

Father Abatangelo's face goes hard. He shakes his head.

"Ever try?"

An equally curt nod.

"But?"

"Something wouldn't let me. I don't know. I got out into the suburbs, and it was as though I suddenly realized I didn't want to go, or I'd forgotten something I meant to do

179

back home. Wasn't until I got back that I remembered how badly I wanted to leave."

Lorelei snorts. "So you decided not to go on a trip. Not that unusual."

"I did that six times."

Alan sits back in his chair and crosses his arms, trying not to look too triumphant and failing. Lorelei can feel him watching her expression. She tries to keep her muscles perfectly still, to give him nothing. She's gotten better at it over the last couple weeks.

Then her phone buzzes in her pocket like a fourth person in the room. She pulls it out, sees Elijah's name, and reels from a rush of vertigo. He knows not to text while she's doing this. Something must be wrong. Someone found the suburban hideout, or the man in the fishing hat came back. Something.

She clicks the phone on, reads the message:

Code Red, meet me there.

She can't keep the expression off her face this time. Alan leans into a question she doesn't hear.

"I have to go. Now."

CHAPTER THIRTEEN

Air hisses into the brakes and the bus stops and shudders and finally rocks into silence. Elijah presses himself against his seat and pries the duffel bag from between his legs. It's big enough for the overhead rack but he's not letting it out of reach.

Ash clings to the stubborn parts of his fingers, from scraping off the scorched top layer of cash after Jo dropped him at the bus station.

The guy in the seat next to him gives him a strained look, doesn't like the way Elijah's elbow digs into his ribs. Elijah looks to the bag and back and offers an apologetic shrug. The bag, held on end on his lap, droops over and covers his face.

The man sighs dramatically and heads to the front of the bus.

Elijah gets off last. Boots on concrete and a kink in his back. The sun bleeds pink over Fayetteville. Exhaust and rubber, vending-machine food and sweat. Eighty minutes until the bus leaves again for Raleigh. He asks a guy hanging around outside the station for directions to a coffee shop.

The guy, dressed in a jacket made for another season, in some other climate, shifts foot-to-foot. "Coffee?"

"Yeah, coffee. Like, a coffee shop nearby?"

"Coffee." Head cocked to the side. "Oh, coffee. Yeah." He points in a direction and Elijah walks three blocks to a coffee shop shaped like an old convenience store. They've added a speaker box to the prescription drive-through, through which an employee leans, dangling his company cap in hand. Elijah tries to duck eye contact, anything that'd tip the guy off that he's about to interrupt him.

Ten minutes later, Elijah's halfway through what smells like a pretty decent cup of coffee, but he can't seem to register the taste. Hands starting to shake. The shop is empty except for the lone worker, who hung around the counter for a couple minutes until it was clear Elijah, staring into his paper cup, wasn't going to bother him.

The air conditioner hums. No conversation, no people breathing his air. No pressing of body heat and swallowing sounds and the creak of other people's fidgeting.

He'd just as soon not get back on that bus.

Another sip of coffee, a glance at his watch. Hand shaking a little worse now. He presses his palm to the steel table. The caffeine grates against his crowd-worn nerves; he feels it in his fingers, but he doesn't want to reach Raleigh groggy.

He puts down the last of the coffee and strolls back to the bus station. The guy in the jacket's still there. He watches Elijah until he gets in front of the right bus. Elijah rolls back on his feet, up on his toes. Cracks his back. Still fifteen minutes to departure, and then another seventy to Raleigh. He looks around for a phone booth. The husk of one sits rusting and peeling just around the corner, long-severed cord jutting out from its casing.

Elijah takes out his cell phone. He and Lorelei had promised to avoid using them for anything like this, especially anything logistical. Always use a payphone in case of emergency, and maybe mutter a little bit, keep some deniability against any unwanted ears on the line.

But replaying the last week, Elijah's pretty sure this is an emergency beyond what they'd anticipated.

Less than a day in the city and Slim's head flares electric, a tingling blast in some reptilian lobe near the back of his skull. The heavy smoke swings away from the water. He whispers to himself that this is surely a coincidence, leans against the car like he's going to sit and watch the smoke drift.

He chuckles over this, fires up the car and drives toward the plume.

A run-down apartment complex. Slim's guess: service-industry workers, two or three to a one-bedroom and the rent's still too high. He's spent no mean amount of time in like neighborhoods. Strange to be here without thought of making money, of hitting up local dealers, shaking hands or slitting throats or maybe both. Today, however, he's got a higher prize than money on his mind.

Slim parks and feeds quarters into a meter a few blocks down the road. The smoke plume's gone, broken off and rocketing away. Traffic's light, but still too heavy to get a read on which car might be carrying people from that apartment building.

Doesn't matter. Slim scuffs his heel on the concrete and strolls down the road, looking for something he can't name but will know when it comes.

A man staggers out onto the street in front of him. His trajectory puts him heading roughly from the same place as the smoke. Slim slows his pace a touch. The man's not doing well, looks like. He moves like he's new to walking, but won't be able to start again if he stops to gather himself.

He's likely involved. Slim plays the odds.

The man, young, dressed in black slacks and long black shirt—a restaurant uniform—staggers his way up a series of streets Slim wouldn't have thought led anywhere. They don't, really, except the man turns at the right moment, the right alley, and weaves a course roughly parallel to the road Slim had been walking down, only going in the other direction.

The man heads for another apartment building. If not for the different view of the shore, it could have been the first one Slim saw. His quarry slumps against the wall next to the door, slides along it, and continues inside the building.

Slim has to grant the man that he's dealing well with a situation for which he couldn't possibly be equipped. He strolls to the doorway and presses his hand against the part of the wall the man had leaned against. The feeling in the back of his head is still there, but not any more than it was. He focuses. The electric throb's off in the distance, like his head's a few miles away, broadcasting the feeling to him.

The doorway. The smoke. The bloodied man. Must have been he stumbled on something, and it's taking him apart. No point in following him any farther.

What he's seen will probably take care of him without any help from Slim.

The tingling buzzes him around, points him down a different road. He follows, keeping his twitching feet as close to a leisurely stroll as he can. The soles of his sneakers make little scratching sounds with the vibrating of his body.

Apartments, docks, the underside of the freeway. Slim drives for hours, tracking the tingling as best he can on Boston's convoluted roads. He feels it in a straight line, but can't drive in one. Passes a used-car dealership and pulls into a motel where the freeway dips down.

The inside of his skull hisses, tuning the channel closer, closer.

A few cars in the motel lot. Bored attendant watching the office television out of the corner of his eye. Slim circles around the back, the sides, keeps clear of the office. Stalks past each door. Listening. Waiting.

Quick shocks in his fingertips outside room thirty-two. He presses them to the wood. The feeling rolls up his arm, settles in his chest.

He presses his ear to the door, pulls back before he has a chance to hear anything. No point. This is the one.

He takes a step back, rears up to kick the door. Thinks twice. Shifts to the window.

The paramedics don't ask if Stacy is Keane's wife or sister or what, the way she thought they would from movies. They just wave her to a tiny space to the left of the stretcher. She tries to shift her weight off her knees, but the rocking of the ambulance threatens to send her tumbling over Keane's shirtless body.

She thinks *body* without meaning to, wonders if that's right.

The medics watch her, to see if she's going to be a problem. Meklit's headlights bob behind them, in the ambulance's wake. Every turn, Stacy thinks Meklit's lost them, until the Honda comes whipping around the corner, trying to avoid slipping too far back and getting caught in the normal flow of cars.

Keane doesn't move, hasn't since the kitchen floor. Stacy reminds herself to breathe and tries not to get any of his blood on herself. It's pooling around Keane, gathering and dripping off the sterile paper in rivulets. The medics have slowed the flow. From what Stacy could gather, they couldn't quite figure out where so much of it had come from.

The medic to her left hooks his head down to Keane. "You're sure he's not hemophiliac?"

Stacy blinks. "Yeah. No. I don't think so, anyway."

But they're not listening, are busy adjusting his position on the stretcher. He rocks with each jostle from the road, eyes not quite closed, until his spine seizes stiff. Stacy thinks she's imagining it. Then he thrashes to one side and back again.

Splash of blood down the front of her skirt. Not imagining it after all.

The medics curse and lunge and pin his shoulders to the stretcher, work a tongue depressor between his teeth like he's having a seizure. Keane whips his head side to side, like he doesn't know he could just bite through it. The medic keeps it steady.

Keane settles down again. The medic pulls the depressor from his mouth real slow. Keane arches his back as it comes out. Blood flicks everywhere, and Stacy doesn't have enough room to recoil.

The ambulance screeches and rocks to a stop in front of the hospital. Stacy's not ready, slams against the wall. The medics snap the stretcher up, slide it onto the waiting gurney.

The driver comes around back. He sees Stacy still kneeling on the floor and touching her head, and holds out a hand to help her down. Feet on concrete, she doesn't listen to whatever concern comes out of his mouth, just nods until he goes away. She saw Keane to the hospital, but she's not going inside.

Meklit comes sailing across the lot. "Is he—" She up-and-downs Stacy. "The fuck happened?"

Stacy looks down at herself. Her skirt hangs close, folding in on itself around the drying blood. Her sweatshirt and the back of her hands are spattered. Meklit pulls a bandanna from her purse and wipes it across Stacy's face. It comes away red. Meklit frowns, goes to clean off the rest.

Stacy waves her off. "I'll get it myself."

Meklit goes to put the bandanna back in her purse, catches herself, crumples it into a ball with the blood to the inside before putting it away. "The hell happened in there?"

Stacy tells her about Keane waking, his thrashing around. She can't think how to talk about the way the blood gathered on the stretcher, how it looked wrong. She makes a swirling motion with her hand instead.

"Come on. Let's go," Meklit says.

Stacy looks to the sliding hospital doors, feels a pit growing under her feet, one that will only grow and swallow her if she walks through those doors. It's strange. She's never been afraid of hospitals or doctors before, not even as a kid.

She looks down at her clothing, starts to get a sense of context after the last couple days, of who might be watching if she were to walk into the hospital.

"No," she says, waving at her face. "Lemme get the rest of this off of me."

Meklit storms off toward the doors. Stacy stuffs her hands in her sweatshirt pockets like she's looking for a tissue to wipe her face, until Meklit goes inside. The driver curses from the ambulance and Stacy slinks off, not looking back to see if Meklit's watching through the window.

Father Abatangelo lets go of Lorelei's arm. She needs to hang about a while longer, learn how to protect herself, but she gives him a murderer's glare. He puts his hands up and takes a step back, and the window bursts in.

A withered-looking man—basketball shorts, white undershirt streaked with dried blood—steps through the window into the room. Sneakers crunch shattered glass into the industrial carpet. Gray fishing hat pulled down over sunken eyes. Scars and scabs roping up his arms, shaped like some kind of alien lettering.

By the time Father Abatangelo notices the tingling in the air, Alan is out of his seat, shoulder dropped and charging. The man twists around without even seeming to move, throwing Alan with his own momentum. Alan's shoulder slams against the door. He slumps down, wind knocked out of him.

Lorelei backs away. "The fuck? Slim?"

Slim's face cracks and twists into something resembling a smile, like the muscles are working independently and with limited communication.

Father Abatangelo means to move. He really does.

The tingling in the air gets worse. Light bleeds into itself. The room becomes a shadow and Slim's teeth glisten.

Lorelei groans. She pulls the gun, holds it at her side.

Alan pushes himself halfway up. His arm gives out and he falls back to the floor.

Slim draws himself up straight, the center of light in the room. He bounces his legs in turn, rubs his fingers together. He seems to vibrate. His savage broken smile widens.

Alan hurls himself about Slim's waist. Slim cracks his elbow down on his skull and Alan drops. His face catches Slim's sneaker coming up. Wet crunch and a splash of blood. He rolls into the corner and lays still.

Lorelei feints with the gun. Slim takes the bait and Lorelei comes in with the heel of her other hand. Gets a snap from Slim's ribcage. He shrugs and flicks his elbow, and Lorelei's against the wall, bleeding from her nose, looking around like she got hit by a ghost.

Father Abatangelo thinks maybe she did. His legs won't move. His lungs will not inflate.

Slim walks over to him, doffs his fishing hat and fakes a swing. Father Abatangelo flinches. The man holds his fist in the air, uncurls its fingers in a flirtatious wave.

Father Abatangelo's eyes widen.

Slim looks around. Is about to speak, seems like, but instead drives an elbow into Father Abatangelo's diaphragm. He gasps for air, blurry shadows and shapes in his vision, and goes down. The bed behind him breaks his fall.

Slim takes a little bow. "Well now. Hello, y'all."

Lorelei finds her feet. Father Abatangelo watches Slim bury his fist in her stomach. She doubles over like she's praying at the foot of the bed.

"That any way to greet your old friend?" Slim holds his hands out at his sides.

Lorelei spits blood through her teeth. It doesn't even hit his shoes.

"The other two of you, well, I figure you're the people I was feeling, yeah?"

The air gets staticky, twitches and sputters. Father Abatangelo braces himself against the spinning in his head. A long needle mark inside Slim's left elbow glows in the preternaturally dimming light, shining like the answer to everything.

"What have you done?" Father Abatangelo says, sound catching in his dry throat.

Slim pirouettes triumphantly. "Ah, he can speak! Yes, what have I done? You know, don't you? Surely you're not as close to things as I can feel without it crossing your minds?"

Alan wheezes from his corner. Lorelei bleeds from hers.

"I don't know," says Father Abatangelo. "You seem familiar."

"I bet I do. Yeah, you've seen me before, but not in this skin."

Alan pulls himself up. "Look at his fucking arm!"

Father Abatangelo stares at the glowing scar through wavy air. Slim seems to be the only thing in the room reflecting light.

It's like one of the beasts, on the other side. But that's impossible.

"That can't—who in the hell would—"

Slim's smile carves fissures into his cheeks. "Me, for one. And others like me. We are fucking legion, as the man says, and we're coming."

"What? Why?"

That fucking smile.

"I mean, what could you possibly want?"

"He wants," Alan wheezes, "to fuck with the balance."

The man forces a laugh through his nose. "There's no balance. It's always been tipping, and we've decided we wanna be on the side it tips when it tips final."

Alan shakes his head, can't seem to even find words.

Father Abatangelo realizes what the man's talking about, what he's shot into his arm. How he could feel them, find them this fast. "You know—"

"Don't." Slim shakes his head. "Don't try. My die's cast, Father Fucker, and I'm not even here to kill you. I'm here to let you know that I will, one day soon."

The words are barely out of his mouth before he yanks a box cutter from his waistband, gets a little spurt of blood from high up on Alan's shoulder. Slim smiles and all but curtseys. Twists his hand a little more. Sends Alan gasping to the floor.

A distant smash—the glass from the narrow bathroom window—and Father Abatangelo finally notices that Lorelei's left the room. Slim tugs his fishing hat low over his eyes and leaves the box cutter in Alan's shoulder, unlocking the door and exiting, sliding it shut again over a jingle of broken glass.

Blood ticks onto the carpet from between Alan's fingers.

Father Abatangelo sees in Alan's eyes the same feeling he's surely wearing on his face.

This is far, far worse than could have been expected.

Vertigo hits. Father Abatangelo puts a hand to his brow and raw panic takes hold.

Elijah slides his driver's license across the table to the motel clerk. The clerk glances at it, and then to the computer. Elijah's heart skips, but the clerk just scrolls a bit and scratches Elijah's name in the ledger by hand.

For not the first time, Elijah curses that friend of Lorelei's who said he could get them fake IDs and then couldn't, far too late for them to find another source. He worries the computer might put his name in some database. He doesn't know, has no idea how these things work. Can't begin to guess, for example, whether a list on a motel computer might be checked against a list of wanted persons.

And he doesn't even know whether he's a wanted person. Or by whom.

The clerk slides the key card across the slick counter and goes back to watching the little television set in a corner of the ceiling. Elijah takes the key and slides it in his pocket, doesn't walk outside too quickly.

A hooded jacket slouched over in front of the ice machine contorts itself, reveals a face. Gaunt, glassy look.

"Hey fuck, man." The head jerks. "No ice."

Elijah keeps his head forward. Tries his best to look less than friendly.

"Hear me, fuck?" The sweatshirt sprouts legs and takes a step. He curses endlessly. Turns, curses some more, punches the machine.

Elijah finds his room and inserts the card key. The LED in the handle doesn't blink green. He tries again, pushes when it stays dim. Nothing. One more time—the lock wheezes open.

The room, nonsmoking, reeks of cigarettes. Sheets the color of thin cheap whiskey, television bolted to a hardware-store stand. Air conditioning works, though, and that's enough.

Elijah deposits himself gingerly on the bed. His phone blinks at him when he pulls it out. So Leon remembers him and will admit to it. He sends a text, gets a response. Asks for a twelve-pack, too, while Leon's at it.

The television's got all sorts of exotic channels. Maybe that's where the money saved from ten years of not buying new sheets was funneled.

The news flashes images of thousands, tens of thousand, flooding a public square in Egypt. Signs and fists held high. A voiceover about a camel attack, tear gas. People still in the square the next day, as the sun goes down, their blood and rage and confidence. They've held their ground and are surging triumphant. Elijah's hands twitch. He tries to imagine that strength but can only really conjure the crush of people. Feels a twisting in his stomach, the pinprick echo of a panic attack.

He finds instead a station broadcasting old football games, the player's uniforms baggy with the decades in between, picture grainy from tape transfer. He slumps back onto the bed, listening to dead announcers call plays no one remembers. Sheets like heaven against his skin and he realizes the sleep he got on the bus wasn't, not really. Props himself up straighter to avoid greeting Leon blurry-eyed. Moves to the chair instead.

The chair's uncomfortable enough and the ancient football game drones. A knock at the door in the third quarter. Elijah looks out the peephole at the back of Leon's head, scoping the parking lot. Elijah turns the bolt and opens the door, lets him in.

Leon slings a twelver onto the table, some label Elijah doesn't recognize, and takes the chair Elijah'd been using. Elijah peels back cardboard and cracks a can, gulps without pausing to taste it.

"Liquor store down the street, you know."

Elijah shrugs. "Didn't much feel like making the town."

Leon snorts. "This ain't exactly the town." He points to the beer. Elijah hands him a can. They sit and swig.

After a while, Elijah grabs another round. "And the other?"

Leon stares with some concentration at the top of his can. "Was wondering if that's what you meant. If you remembered the code and all. All those numbers, y'know."

"Yeah. And, yeah. Pretty sure I do."

"Well. Can't be too careful."

Elijah nods like this has some apparent meaning. "So, what then?"

"Thing I oughta tell you, maybe." Leon tips his can back, swishes beer through his teeth. "About an old friend of ours. You know?"

Elijah does.

"Anyway, got word he might be stopping by a little while ago. Couple days, a week? Went to see Rich. Remember Rich?"

"Yeah." Cold pit growing in Elijah's stomach.

"Well, you can stop."

That hangs there. Elijah offers Leon another beer. Leon shakes his head. Somewhere through the walls, somebody yells at a television or a spouse. The air conditioner drones.

"And no one's heard from Asher in a while now."

Elijah covers his mouth with his beer. "Asher? From Orlando?"

"Yeah." Eyes narrowing like maybe he hears something in Elijah's voice. "Was supposed to come up here a few days ago. Nobody can raise him."

"Slim, then?"

"Who else? So, you understand I'd be a little nervous. About the other, I mean. The package."

Elijah shrugs. "I'm not a cop."

"Not what I meant."

"I'm not on real friendly terms with old Slim, either."

"I heard somebody shot him."

Elijah stares.

"Thought maybe somebody'd like another shot at him."

"Maybe they would."

Leon looks like he's about to answer. Instead he gets up and walks out of the room.

Elijah shuts his eyes. He can hear the car door opening, slamming, footsteps returning to the door. He lets Leon back in.

"Take credit cards?" Elijah says, not reaching for the bundle of paper until he's paid for it.

A glimmer of a smile from Leon. "Cash business, baby."

They make the exchange and Leon goes to leave.

He turns back at the door. "Goes to show, can't trust a guy who makes up his own sonofabitching nickname."

Leon's gone. Elijah unwraps the paper, finds a chubby little .38. He takes the box from the paper and clicks open the cylinder, remembers Lorelei's uncle with his old shotguns saying if you needed more than two rounds, you didn't deserve to kill anything.

This one holds five.

Elijah's not sure that helps his odds much.

CHAPTER FOURTEEN

The scope of the thing breaks over Father Abatangelo in waves, crashing and pausing to clarify itself before washing backward into significance, to leave a breath before the next crest. A loose networks of kids—former kids, forever-kids—across the long stretch of land between here and the other ocean. People like the man in the fishing hat, the dead-eyed figure with blood on his hands, Hell's own fury in his blood, looking across endless space at each other. Narcotics first, probably, or maybe music or maybe both, but soon enough their network came to this, to now.

They're animals praying to the slaughterhouse. Trees singing wildfire ecstasy. Children embracing the logic of self-immolation as though death were a purely hypothetical question, something to be hoisted high on twin pillars of novelty and ritual. The pure cold knowledge of their own deaths will never come to temper their lusts, or will come too late.

The savagery in the man's eyes lingers in Father Abatangelo's vision, the afterimage of a flashbulb. In the shadow of the flash, his hope crumbles and his faith stutters like the lie it has always been.

What salvation, from not monsters but their acolytes?

He begins a prayer and trembling lets it turn to ash on his tongue.

The man called himself Slim and the end is fucking nigh.

Father Abatangelo scolds himself for his apocalypticism. He chokes on nothing and remembers to breathe. Peels himself from the wall, grabs the bag that's been waiting for him on the top shelf of Alan's closet for days and empties it into the backpack he took from Alan's car.

His old gun, salvaged from the ruins of his church. A new box of ammunition. Douay-Rheims Bible and the rosary and the old heathen pendant.

A straight razor. A few dozen dollars.

He heads off toward a huge mirrored building whose name he used to know. Stops outside to check his face in its reflection. Not too bad. Eyes a bit distant, hair unwashed, but maybe no one will notice.

He slings the duffel bag over his shoulder. There's a desk, a receptionist, but Father Abatangelo slams his feet on the marble with a confidence he doesn't remotely feel and the man's head doesn't turn. The elevator comes and swallows him, ascends just as quickly past floors of offices. He watches the numbers climb as high as they know how.

Alan was calling an ambulance when he stumbled out the door. Nothing he could do there. From the way Alan was dripping everywhere, maybe the same goes for the ambulance.

The woman, Lorelei, was in the wind.

Father Abatangelo grinds his teeth. And they thought they could help her. They didn't know what was going on any more than she did. Maybe less.

It hit him looking in Slim's eyes, even before the man said *we*. The sense of something large—and beyond that, human. The calm set of his face and the manic twitching in his arms, the way the air in the motel room vibrated.

Alan had thought that other people had seen the beasts, maybe even gotten away from them. It had made sense. Why should they be the only ones with those particular memories?

Neither of them had considered the possibility that the beasts had worshipers.

The elevator tops out, dings open. Father Abatangelo weaves through hallway intersections, trying to look like he has a reason to be there. Security cameras poorly disguised as light fixtures bounce back a blurred reflection of the top of his head.

He finds the roof-access stairwell. Stiff hinges have kept the latch from catching. He shoves it open and eases it back, almost shut.

He'd gotten the feeling, gasping back into the world in Alan's apartment, that he'd remembered everything. Those first days, years ago, all the way through the gory ending—the third man who never returned, the sliding of the world back into normalcy. He'd even remembered the slipping-away of that time, the way the world he came back to smoothed out the jags of those memories until only the shape remained, hulking and ghostly.

He doesn't trust the feeling anymore. What he remembered has a sharp edge to it, a high-definition vividness that makes him cringe. The suspicion that he doesn't remember as much as he thought he did.

Like the feeling of everything becoming clear was the product of some chemical reaction set off by black rock and red sky.

But the clarity had done its trick. Slim didn't track them down, didn't get their location from anyone. There was no one to get it from. He'd felt them, felt *him*, and it was only tearing through the motel-room door and down that sidewalk that Father Abatangelo realized that he'd let his priestly camouflage drop. Flashed his ass to any tentacled bastard trying to sniff him out.

The memories, real or not, had something to do with it.

And so now, stepping onto the roof of the building, he carries with him texts and amulets of both varieties. The sacred and the profane. Or: of this world and the other.

The crucifix and that melted, serpentine pendant.

He takes up a spot in the shade of a hulking heat vent, crouching with his bag on his lap. The sun casts his shadow long in front of him. He can see the way he came, the motel out by the freeway impossibly near.

He doesn't much think this will help. He's out of better ideas.

The faith that's not in him anymore, not even by pretense, he thinks he needs it.

He takes the razor from the bag, sets it on his knee. Opens the Bible on his other. Wraps the cord of the pendant around his wrist so that it rests atop the vein.

He rolls up his left sleeve and turns the top of his forearm toward himself and picks up the razor in his right hand.

He got the idea from the man called Slim. Perhaps it will lend him some shelter.

If he can't keep the faith in his heart, he will carve it into his skin.

Slim died. Lorelei saw it. But he's not dead. The corner of Alan's little leather notebook digs into her palm as she runs.

Tough face though she put up, she'd listened to the two men talking to her in the motel room. Sometimes people will try harder if they think they can't get you to listen, tip their hands more than they intend.

Alan and Father Abatangelo had certainly done that.

There'd been no time to press her advantage, though, if that's what it was. Just a moment to grab the notebook Alan had been glancing at when he dove at Slim, before wrapping a towel around her fist to punch her way out the bathroom window.

She doesn't turn toward the parking lot, doesn't approach the front of the building at all. The hedges around the back of the motel are about waist-high. She hops over and crouches down, making for the other side of the elevated freeway.

She's not sure exactly how to get back to her motel room, but it doesn't matter. She's not going back there, not with Slim sniffing around town.

She makes the other side of the freeway and traces it to an ancient-looking factory with a couple old cars in the lot. A rusted pickup looks promising—break-into-able, hot-wire-able—but she wants better mileage. Not that she couldn't afford to refill, but she can't risk running dry on some stretch of freeway. Doesn't want to have to risk sitting still at all.

A little sedan looks newer, like maybe its parts are less likely to fall off. Lorelei leans against it, dips her head forward so her hair covers her looking around for anybody watching her. She tries to remember through the years someone explaining to her the best way to break into a car without smashing the windows, but it's not coming back.

She runs a hand over the door handle for a couple minutes, trying to jog her memory. Nothing. She tugs at the handle. Unlocked.

Figures.

She hops in the passenger side and scrambles over the gearshift into the driver's seat, gets her hands ready to tear at the paneling, to get at the wiring, but her breath is coming shallow. The building in front of her shimmers as though behind a summer sidewalk. She takes her hands off the paneling, presses them against the wheel. Her lungs don't want that much air at first, seem nervous about the wait between breaths, but she gets them, eventually, to cooperate.

The world shifts down a gear. She only notices the slamming of her pulse against the inside of her skull when it begins to recede.

She remembers the unlocked door and checks the visor pocket—no television luck. Next she pops the tank. There's a spare set of keys nestled next to the gas cap. She smiles. It sends a pulse of pain through her nose. Water springs to her eyes and her ears ring and she guns the engine before whatever's next hits her.

The freeway comes up fast but traffic's barely moving. She drums her hands on the wheel, trying to will a space between the cars, belatedly realizing that depending on when the real owner of her new ride gets off work, she might not be ten miles away before the cops are looking for the plate number.

Nothing to be done, though. Even if she wanted to get off the interstate, work her way around, the next exit's not in sight yet.

She plays Elijah's voicemail, but it's what she expected. North Carolina payphone number, code-red. They'd agreed to use payphones to call each others' cells. As a precaution. Wiretapping seems such a quaint concern now.

She pulls her cell out, sends Elijah a text. Hopes he won't panic at the further breach of protocol.

Panic, though, is pretty well called for.

And their arranged meeting place in North Carolina, they'd picked it because they knew people there, and those people were far enough away they might not get to asking questions about Slim's death.

But Slim's not dead.

She suggests a town in coastal Virginia, asks if he has a car, and puts down her phone in time to narrowly avoid slamming into a brake-lit Cadillac. She rocks hard against the seat. Grinds her teeth. Opens Alan's notebook and pins it upright behind the steering wheel.

It'll give her something to do besides twitch.

A couple pages in, several cars blast their horns at her. She barely notices.

#

The walk to the subway station takes forever. Stacy's not accustomed to the part of town the hospital occupies, and misses the street on her first couple tries. Finally manages to triangulate her way to the station and crams herself in the corner of a subway car.

The stop she thinks is Meklit's is actually one past, so she's walking again. Grateful, if she's honest, for the chance to get her blood pumping. Keane's thrashing about in the ambulance remains in front of her eyes like the afterimage of the sun.

She hits Meklit's block and everything has promptly gone to hell. Keane as coal-mine canary.

The blood on the concrete catches the light in such a way that Stacy doesn't know what it is until she squints, blocks out the glare. Then she moves to the nearest wall and stands perfectly still.

A bug-man sees her anyway and swoops in. Sunlight glints off his black riot helmet, white letters spray-painted on his Kevlar chest.

Stacy puts her hands up, gets pulled from and slammed back into the wall.

The cop hisses something like a question.

Stacy, taking a guess: "I'm staying with my friend, right there." Points at the building to her left.

The building the squad's shutting down is a half-block to her right. The honest answer, for the first and last time in Stacy's life, is the one that gets the law's hands off her shoulders.

A deep sound from the other building. The cop flinches, catches himself from turning toward it.

"Well," he says after briefly hesitating, a little clearer now that he's decided against laying into her, "get on, then. Can't stay here."

The wind catches the smoke coming off the top of the building and whips it down in front of the doorway. It carries the honest smells of burning wood and insulation, sheetrock and asbestos. Organic and chemical smoke doing a number on whatever lungs are present. Not the phantom smoke from earlier.

The cop lets Stacy go and she backs away. A body-shape makes it halfway through the fog before the other bug-men lift their rifles and pop him flat to the ground.

Stacy whips around, away from the newest body, like she hasn't seen anything. She expects to meet concrete soon, regardless.

Her feet find the door to Meklit's building and she doesn't look back, doesn't question it until she's gotten up to the first landing. She listens for heavy boots behind her. None come. There is a window in front of her, though. She peers through, watches armored bodies sieve through alleys and into a tightening circle around the building.

From her new angle, she can picture the smoke she and Meklit were watching not long ago. It had come from directly behind the burning building. Like maybe they're related. Like that smoke caused this smoke.

She shudders, imagining a slow, slow predator, inching toward the smell of Keane's blood.

A third-story window shatters in the burning building. Smoke pours out. A phalanx of bug-men form up at the door, boots stamping on the recently felled man. They plow through the open front door, two in the front holding up transparent shields.

That thumping again, deeper, long enough that it can't be simple impact. Something breathing, moving.

Stacy tears herself from the window and runs to Meklit's apartment. Triple-checks the deadbolt.

Gunfire filtering through the afternoon. Memory of Keane, stumbling through the door, covered in water that wasn't water. Red stains seeping into the fabric of her clothing, the ridges of her fingertips.

She paces jittery around the kitchen but can't find a place she wants to sit. Can't decide whether she should stay, if she wants to be here when Meklit comes back.

She sits crouched under the table in the corner with her knees propped up. It comes up just past her head.

The highway again. The wheel under Elijah's hand lends a bit more feeling of control. The revolver in the glove compartment doesn't hurt, either. Miles of roads, unfamiliar this far north, but identical to wherever. Highway signs for the same five restaurants and three gas stations grow from the flat distance and blow past like dim reminders of a home planet.

The car hits an uneven patch near some construction project. Elijah clenches the wheel, touchier in the vehicle he paid cash for than if he'd followed his first instinct and tried to steal one. He didn't, though, for the same reason he's hanging out in the right lane, doing exactly three miles over the speed limit. Fast enough to not look like he's hiding something, slow enough to not be an easy notch in some highway patrol ticket book.

The beer last night didn't get him drunk, just whipped through his fraying nerves, kept dragging him from sleep. Something about the way the asphalt sends vibrations up through the car reminds him of lying in the stiff motel sheets.

He's held off thus far but finally caves, reaches into the center console and pulls one of the bottles from the duffel bag. Puts a pill between his molars. A chalky bitterness hits the back of his throat and he thinks twice about biting down.

Dry swallowing proves tough enough, but he at least doesn't have to pull over to heave.

The radio plays a couple dull songs before the Dilaudid hits his blood. Asphalt vibrations turn from irritant to salve. The old feeling—road beneath his wheels, gas enough in the car to get anywhere—floods in, and then some. Who knew that what you needed to scratch a wanderlust itch came childproof-bottled, pressed and stamped.

He thinks about some of the characters he'd seen out back of Papa Louie's with crumpled bills in their hands, eyes looking always behind, trying hard not to scratch. He starts to understand them. It's not ideal. He doesn't know how it'll affect him with his newfound insomnia. Still, what was quickly becoming a panic attack curls back up into itself in his chest, contracts until it's gone.

The road stretches, newly clean and golden, out to the town Lorelei named. He has to return to the well once, manages to swallow faster this time.

He arrives in a haze, a smile growing sore on his face, and circles town looking for a place to hold out. The highway dumps him by the coast, near the kind of waterfront hotel on the other side of an invisible money line, where you start to pay for how small the place is. Better to keep away from the crowded coast, and the ocean takes away one direction of escape.

Elijah winds through town. The property values take a while to start descending, but when they do, they slide fast. The problem with the shore is the buildings are all too close together, the visibility too high. The problem now is finding a place at all.

He does, though—an old white house, paint clinging to the wood in ragged strips, wooden vacancy sign hanging off a post planted in the yard. The bored old woman inside is willing to take cash. He unloads in the room and considers sleep but he's not tired. He stashes the revolver in the back corner of the closet, on the top shelf, and leaves, locking the door behind him. Blood still warm from his little driving aid.

He pushes down the urge to go back to the room for another dose. He walks until he doesn't feel like it anymore. Sun creeping out from behind an afternoon storm cloud. Salt on the wind. He's crossed the invisible barrier between seaside and not.

He scuffs at the concrete under his boots. It doesn't feel all that much different, any richer. Still would never have gotten here a year ago, two months ago even, not on a dishwasher's wages. A lifetime ago, talking to Lorelei, planning what to do about Slim, that situation soon to came to a head. Slim would figure out where his missing inventory had gone. They wanted so badly to get out from under everything.

They have, of course. Gotten out from under.

And found themselves spread over the east coast, something un-nameable and violent—incomprehensible, inevitable—stalking toward them.

He blinks twice, lets the worry ride the last of the opium wave into the distance. Slips his hand into his shirt pocket for the third dose he'd accidentally pulled from the bottle, forgotten he put there. Gets the wave cresting again.

It's a nice enough day for a walk to the shore, but then he remembers what he was told about Rich and Asher. Their disappearances aren't much of a mystery.

Which means Slim is heading north, toward Lorelei.

If Slim has heard that Elijah's not dead, he could be heading back south; if he's picked up Lorelei's trail, he'll know exactly where to go.

Elijah heads back to the room, walking until he tires, feeling like he's preparing for an inevitable emergency.

Fingers gone numb. Can't afford the attention of going on all fours, can't quite stand up straight. Only numb the fingers on the one hand, a desperate tingling above that— bone-level itching.

Slim's box cutter certainly hit a nerve, an artery. Alan's wondering where he's seen the man before. A guess, yes.

Not a memory. Which is worrisome.

He probably ran in the same circles as Alan, as Hector—heck, as Father Abatangelo, back before. Or he knew those crews. Hard to get a read on the man's age through the darkening eye sockets, the mania trembling its way to the surface and breaking through his skin.

Alan's vision is not as good as it was an hour ago. Shock. Blood loss. Something else, too.

He staggers up the street, away from the building where he'd done the ritual and met Lorelei. The sidewalk sprouts a few people but they're all going the other direction. They see him from the front, their eyebrows rising.

Turns and stumbles down an alley and away with the jacket, the shirt. Itching underneath pronounced but indistinct. Certainly this is some maneuver of Slim's, some ritual. The exposed skin moves too much, seems to be coming loose. Turning green at the far edges of the wound, black around the punctured flesh.

Somewhere along the line he lost his backpack full of supplies. In the trunk of the car—the car he left, stumbled away from, not checking to see if one of the other parties in the room had taken it. Just stumbled off, heading roughly north with no particular destination—exactly the sort of move he'd cautioned Hector about so many times, so long ago. No planning. Just adrenaline.

Adrenaline and blood.

He looks around the alley, unsure exactly where he is. Dumpster to his left, shielding him from the street. Another alley to his right, old buildings built close. Sliver of sun creeping its way between the rooftops, lighting up a little strip of sidewalk.

And now footsteps, coming down the alley. Too loud for how far away they sound.

A rush to the head. Alan gathers himself, rises to run, but settles back as his muscles hit critical tension. He can see the blood, after all, on him, around him.

Slim, a surgeon with that box cutter. It's unlikely in any case that Alan will be leaving this alley. Might as well see who or what's walking over.

The footsteps grow closer, not louder. Which doesn't make sense. Alan tilts his head, listens harder, but that's what he hears.

The feet that come around the corner are just feet. Worn black work boots, yellow socks impervious to washing. Jean cuffs over that, rolled up a half-inch.

Whatever's dripping into those cuffs, though, from above, it's rather distinctive.

Black. Viscous. Smacking against the denim, spattering and drying where it lands. It turns the color of cigarette ash and flakes away into the wind.

Alan watches one drop, two, three. The way the texture of the goop changes, flakes, seems familiar. He tries to tilt his head up, see the face that belongs to those boots. Creaks and whimpers and gets a clear view, but nothing quite registers—just blind terror and vague nostalgia.

A familiar face and no shortage of that black fluid. Its features are sunken and far past sickly. Jutting cheekbones, yellow-gray skin, brow ridge like a continent set adrift.

And the hairline.

Alan blinks. There's too much hair until there's none at all—a swirling mess of ropy tendrils that resolve to something very like hair, but growing into the head instead of out.

The figure tilts its head, and when it does, the hair moves first. Like marionette strings. Like faraway tentacles.

"Hector." Alan slumps forward, fingers brushing the boots.

A drop of the black liquid splats burning and tingling on the back of Alan's hand. He digs his fingers into Hector's boots. Hector doesn't move. Alan twists his head up and looks into his eyes.

Rotting pits. Organic matter far past dead, decomposing in advance of the rest of him. Purple and black and seething somewhere deep, like maggots under the skin of a spoiled avocado.

What used to be Hector bends down suddenly, from the waist, like a machine. Strong hands on Alan's shoulders, digging into his collarbone. Alan gets hauled to his feet in a dizzy jerk and his feet barely touch the floor. A stench surrounds Hector like burnt steel, calcified flesh.

Alan's throat struggles between needing air and shutting out the reeking putrescence.

Hector pulls him closer. Creak and crack of Alan's collarbone giving. Colors float between Alan and Hector and the world goes black at the edges.

Alan pushes his head forward the little he can. "You were right."

The other face blinks, part of the eyeballs clumping to their lids.

"Hector, you were right."

And the tentacles slide, marking slimy trails down Hector's face. The sense of Hector being controlled finally hits Alan in full, and the beast holding both of them shoves its appendages through Alan's gaping lips, slithering wet down his throat, hairs catching on his canines and molars. His last scream doesn't make it past the seething mass.

CHAPTER FIFTEEN

The morning sun puts a hard edge on the world. Cars lined with glimmering razors, building corners like a television with the contrast turned up too high. Elijah grimaces, fiddles with the car's radio like this will fix it.

Nothing doing, but he knows more of Slim's stash would help. And he can feel in his blood exactly how far down he'd ride that train. One more, just this time, just to take the edge off, and soon enough he won't be leaving bed without a taste, unless it's to the back door of whatever Papa Louie's translates to in Virginia.

No, better to grind his teeth and let the sunlight scrape raw the back of his skull, and keep his eyes open against the glare for Lorelei.

A text message first thing this morning, meant to be last night. She's ditched the ride by now. She'll be walking into town, toward the address he sent her. He's the only driver on the road. Everyone's heading for the coast and here he is, cruising the other way.

Through the heat shimmering off the asphalt he sees her narrow silhouette approaching like a silver-screen gunsling-

211

er. It grows, takes on features, shimmers in his rearview. His hyper-sensitized shoulders, stiff from days on the highway and sleepless motel nights, whine their way through a very illegal U-turn. He pulls over a dozen paces ahead of her and leans over, pops the passenger door.

She draws even, her hand set back on her hip, gripping her pistol.

Something tugs at Elijah's chest but he turns it into a smile.

She sees his face and sighs, takes her hand off the gun and gets in. She's talking before the door's even slammed, about a sewer grate leading to a passageway underneath Boston where something brutal and efficient lives, and the people sucked into its orbit.

He doesn't talk, just lets her go. Reaches across the gear-shift to palm her thigh. She gives him a smile around the next piece of her story.

He drives them back to the motel and shows her to the room. Even flourishes the door open for her. And she's still talking.

And he's still listening.

A couple things start falling into place in the back of his mind. The necessary pieces for the puzzle he's been at since she left—about Slim and Asher and blood.

The door doesn't quite latch. Shoving it closed, he hears Lorelei tell about seeing Slim only days ago, in a motel room full of death.

His first thought is whether that room looked much like this one.

His second is how exactly she got out alive.

He lets his hand rest on the door, then on his forehead, and Lorelei starts to tell him about a notebook she took off a man who is almost certainly dead from blood loss or something worse, and his head starts spinning. Rituals and monsters and some kind of landscape made of jagged slate.

Turning around, Elijah doesn't find any not-bolted-down furniture to barricade the door with, sets his body there instead. Lorelei's about to say something, to continue the conversation, but she looks down at Elijah and he looks up at her and something happens on her face as he feels it happen on his. She sits down beside him. His arms find their way around her before he knows it's happening and they slump easily into one another.

It's a funny thing. He's never seen his wife collapse like this. But he's never seen her as hard and focused as she was a moment ago. Makes him wonder whether he's changed, too. How the days they spent together before gunning for Slim might be the last those two people existed.

When they've held each other awhile, caught their breaths, he does what little he can to fill her in.

"Rich?" she asks. "And even Asher? What the hell."

"I don't know. Like he's cleaning house, you know?"

"Yeah. Okay. If he's into . . . whatever he's into, then whoever's not has got to go, right?"

Elijah nods like he's thought of this as well. But there's only two people he can think of.

"Oh, fuck me."

Lorelei nuzzles into him. "Yeah."

"So," he says. "I guess we're not heading to Boston." He says it in a tone that says, absent this development, they'd be burning rubber toward the city, to do the big hero thing. That they'd be scouring this Alan guy's notebook for information on the way, hoping they can do the right thing.

With Jo, though, and Donny, and how alive they still are despite knowing Slim, it's like that choice has been wrenched from them.

It's a relief. Let the city burn while they step into a different fire, one no one sees coming, and maybe get out with their few remaining friends.

Stacy thumps awake against the underside of the table. The day sounds bright outside. She's not sure at first whether it's the same day or a new one until she pulls herself out from under the table. She sees Meklit face down on the recliner in the living room, with the footrest up and leaned all the way back. She pulls herself up, has to stretch out some kinks.

Approaching upright, vertebrae cracking in protest, Stacy watches Meklit turn and meet her eyes.

Meklit's face doesn't move. Stacy stands still. Meklit's eyes sharpen in disgust.

Stacy looks around to gather her things. She hasn't any.

Meklit rolls over onto her back. "He's okay, you know."

Stacy nods like she knows what she's talking about.

"Keane. He's all right."

"Yeah, I know."

Meklit ratchets the footrest down, rocks upright. "No, you don't. You fucking bailed." Shakes her head, not even angry, not really. "No surprise. Just, he was real happy to see you."

There's a scene brewing, one Stacy can't stick around for. "Look, I—"

"Yeah." The look Meklit gives isn't suspicious. Like she knows Stacy didn't have anything to do with what happened but might know what did, and is too tired to try to find out.

When she's right, she's right.

"Hey, why don't I go down and see him?"

"No." Meklit wipes at her eyes. "He couldn't see you. Not doing quite that good."

Stacy hovers a moment and then puts the door between her and Meklit.

There's only so many times she can leave like this. At least she doesn't intend on coming back.

She caves and looks behind on her way out at the besieged building. Nothing but yellow police tape, brown blood-stains on the concrete. It occurs to her she didn't ask what was wrong with Keane. Maybe it doesn't matter. Maybe she brought it upon him by showing up here.

She looks back over her shoulder at the last place she knew she could run to in the city, disappearing into the distance, and takes the subway to her apartment.

Walking up the stairs carefully, quietly, she's not sure whether she's paid the rent for the month. Or what day it is. Her key works, though, and she hasn't gotten a phone call. She turns the key in the lock, remembering her intention toward stealth too late. She jumps back from the door, nudges it open with her foot. Nobody there.

She looks around, inhaling familiar air. What to do now. She's certainly fired from the old woman's corner store. She shakes her head. Paces. Doesn't know what to do with herself, where next month's rent will come from.

There's really only one option. She's known it for a while, she thinks, but didn't want to admit that her running and hiding, that the knife wound she took from that tall woman, was all leading her along the same old circle, only backward.

When Colorado Jack picked her up outside the hospital, she feared he thought she was involved with whatever Jessica had gotten into. Or, more likely, had gotten away with.

But if he still thought so, she wouldn't be walking around, wouldn't be able to reach into her pocket for a cell phone and scroll to his number.

Certainly she wouldn't be doing the very last thing she ever intended to, putting on a level but friendly tone, asking, "Hey, Jack, what's the action?"

Fifteen years like the blink of an eye. What Father Abatangelo had mostly managed to forget bleeds over the intervening years, the forgotten burning bright as the rest dims to a poorly recollected dream.

His drying blood in the evening light like a second skin. Darker where he's made the cuts, lighter where it's dripped. An ornate crucifix. A crude Madonna.

An arrow down the back of his left hand for Saint Sebastian, preparation for war. A steaming coal grill for Saint Lawrence, patron of the poor, in memory of his lost congregation. Saint Jude's club, for Father Abatangelo's certainly lost cause.

Shallow cuts are the key, to emblazon the symbols in the flesh without severing anything crucial. Still, his head starts swimming as he readies the final cut.

He holds his hand steady for a delicate final touch, skin giving like wrapping paper under the razor, only beginning to hurt moments after the flesh has been parted. A crown, intricate and bejeweled, rays of light sparking off it. For the Coronation of Mary.

Memory of the rosary dredged up by that Mystery, of huddling underground to be buried, rosary in hand, a single nauseous yellow eye staring and staring.

He pulls the razor away and admires his handiwork in the instant before his thin blood spreads too much to make it out. He leans back against the air conditioning vent, gathering himself. Feels a rising in his chest, a purely spiritual pressure. As though his faith only needed some physical room in order to retake its place in his body.

The sun begins to set over the buildings down the street. Father Abatangelo puts his feet flat on the rough rooftop and rises, shaking. Spreads his arms, dripping blood on the weatherproof tiles. Remembers something he said to Hector not very long ago, in his rectory, about how his congregation couldn't afford salvation. It was an off-the-cuff comment, trying to meet Hector on his own terms, but the beasts haven't come for him here. Truth is, he didn't expect to make it anywhere near the end of this private little act of restoration without the hairy tentacles slithering up onto the roof.

He looks over the gleaming high-rise buildings around him. They're catching the last sunlight in a postcard way, tentacle-free and majestic, and very nonthreatening except in size. A rare visit to the winning side of the gentrification line.

He smiles to himself. Another thing Hector was right about. Which draws him again toward the clock under the road.

Father Abatangelo crouches down and unzips Alan's backpack. He spreads out the supplies, trying to remember exactly how Alan did it, hoping that it will work doing it to himself.

He smudges the wet black ash onto the brush. The smell of the stuff brings him back to the black-and-red waste, as always. He draws the circle around him on the ground, carefully chalks the sigil on his palm. Presses his palm to his forehead, the symbol already running in rivulets of blood. Jabs the tip of the knife into his leg.

He tries to brace himself for the rush. Fails. Comes down on the jagged slate as breathless as ever, flailing for balance, for air, tearing his hands on the rock, struggling to get his wind in the hissing vacuum.

He finds his feet as before. Remembering the moves isn't helping him stay oriented, but it does cut down on the panic.

He comes to the narrow cliff, where he last saw the beast moving, and starts the long descent. The blood on his hands renders slick the razor handholds.

By the time his feet hit more level ground, the devastated world blurs more intensely. The bleeding-away of sound ceases to throw him. Pulse pounding in his temple, shoes slipping and jamming against rock until he remembers to shuffle them forward. He strips off the sodden rag of his shirt, feels twinges from scabs tearing.

Finally the hole—the portal. He breathes deep, hopes Hector was as right as he'd thought he was, and steps in.

The sharp black ground and red sky fizzle and fade, replaced by the dim tunnel under the sewer grate on Gutter Street. He's right at the entrance this time, like the portal shifts where it appears on the other side.

Father Abatangelo's breath sounds right but his footstep comes at him as though from a distance. He frowns, looks down. His toe has dug out a rivet in a thick carpet of the black mold residue. It's the same substance as before, but with growth has started moving in waves, like it's taking sleeping breaths.

He glances behind. The concrete wall shimmers and bends, the city side of the portal holding steady.

One of their endless arguments, fifteen years ago, after they'd exhausted their failure to figure out the nature of the beasts and the purpose of the clock and what the hell they were supposed to do, was about where they went under the sigil. Whoever stayed behind could attest that their bodies remained lying there, eyes flitting back and forth like they were dreaming, but they'd never remember that when they came back from the beasts' realm.

Now, having taken the portal to the same city from which he left, where is Father Abatangelo really? In the tunnel, or under the red sky?

He looks up from the ditch his toe dug, already filling itself, and forgets the question. He sees hair riding up and down the walls, coalescing into tentacles, plastered to the walls by slimy white mold, none of the concrete showing through—a new construct supplanting the architecture by sheer organic density.

Down the shaft, the sodden mold grows until the passage is only a few feet high. Air's too humid—there's wetness on Father Abatangelo's face. Feels dark, wrong.

Thrumming comes through the floor, deep, subtle. Lazy drumming on timpani—a low, heavy heartbeat.

And movement, a kind he can't track.

A scream from down the hallway like the death of an entire world racks his bones. Father Abatangelo spasms his way up the ladder, impeded only by his efforts to keep his feet from the portal.

Up onto the street and it's still only dusk. He steps faster than he should. The residue on his feet doesn't catch on the concrete. It semi-dries and flakes away, leaving his feet millimeters above the ground. He crashes down, rolls across the street. Stops on his back, staring at the very real bloodstain streaked along the asphalt.

He grabs the edge of an empty newspaper vending machine and pulls himself up. A man comes around the corner and shrieks, hands jumping to his chest, and runs the other way.

So he's visible, present not merely in ritual but in flesh. Father Abatangelo looks himself over in a window—shirtless, covered in his own blood, and surely emanating every sort of otherworldly odor.

He looks around, sees no one else. The sound from the tunnel grows, echoing.

He remembers how the tentacles wove their way into open cuts, the way Hector's shadow was sprouting them from its head. The way, fifteen years ago, the third man's corpse seemed to be growing them.

Of all the memories that have come flooding back, he'd give every one of them to remember that man's name.

But the blood is still wet where he tore off his shirt.

Father Abatangelo rummages again through Alan's bag and finds a long length of rubber tubing, for use as a tourniquet. A little dried spatter where some forgotten junkie's shaking hands tore their skin too much. He walks to the lone car on the block, parallel-parked in a reserved space in front of a little corner store, and pries the gas panel open with Alan's pliers. He feeds the tube in as far as he can, puts his lips to the rubber and sucks until his mouth and throat blaze.

He gags, and the gas runs clear out of the tube and over Father Abatangelo's head. He comes near to passing out from the burning pain, manages to aim the bloody runoff toward the sewer grate.

He takes the rosary from his pocket and wraps it around his wrist, strips off his jeans and holds them to soak up the last of the siphon.

Nothing to produce fire, though. A laugh of pure delirium pushes and coughs its way through his swelling throat. But the car door's open and the cigarette lighter doesn't need the engine running.

A silent countdown starts, a race between the pop of the lighter's little black plastic handle and his own consciousness. For a teetering moment the world starts going black, but the sound of the lighter ejecting brings him around just enough. He takes it and grinds the edge of it into his palm, stings himself awake.

Now he'll find out if Hector was right. Hector said the clock was the key to the balance, but it could be activated by blood, led to slip its watch and unleash the beasts. It stands to reason it could be turned off.

Father Abatangelo sets the burning steel tip to the stream of gas.

Nothing happens.

He turns the jeans in his hand until he finds a dry spot. Sets the lighter to it, gets a smolder going. Sets the little flame near the runoff. Perfect blue fire runs down, underneath the street.

He follows it.

What looks like mold isn't, judging by the way it takes to the flame. The gas couldn't have spread even a tenth as far, not with the slow way it was trickling down. But the opening he saw down there is already ablaze, the tunnel acting like a furnace, driving every organic part of him back.

There is a part of him that isn't organic, though, and Father Abatangelo tears the ancient pendant from around his neck and clutches it in one hand, the rosary and flaming jeans in the other, and, wordlessly thumbing the beads—the right prayers playing purely on memory—sprints as hard as he can down the tunnel across the squishing, burning floor.

The dull roar he heard before, that which owned his dreams more nights than not, escalates a couple octaves, somewhere between a mechanical screech and a lion's roar. Father Abatangelo's bones shake with it.

The wad of what used to be jeans blazes in the same hand as the pagan pendant. He gathers his legs and makes a final lunge forward before touching it to his chest.

Flames lick and catch on his gasoline skin. His momentum carries him deeper into the tunnel. Hair peels from the wall and slimes together, reaching but never quite touching him. He spots a splayed body along the wall with a face he's seen before, but now the tentacle pressing through the front of the skull has been joined by a few of its friends. Skin's peeled back around the puncture wounds, letting yellowed bone taste the foul air.

The head turns, eyes bulging and dissolving. The drumming sound comes now from its mouth.

And the heat on his chest reaches his shoulders.

In the eruption of gasoline and righteous fury, he sees the clock grinding already to a halt before the untouched white mold catches, sends the world away in a concussive blast he feels between his ears but never hears.

In the space between his eyelid catching the signal to blink and trying to slam down flesh that isn't there anymore—has already turned to vapor—he feels something click: time moving sideways—a return to some instinctive balance, before his bones join the assembled kindling in scouring the walls and the surface of the clock.

* * *

More rolling highway, tiresome the way Lorelei promised herself a restless lifetime ago it would never become. Elijah's slumped in the passenger seat, his body heat somehow soothing. In the new morning light, though, something happens to her vision when she glances indirectly at him. Nothing dramatic—an occasional fluttering. Like heat rising off the motel parking lot when they left. She sees it out of the corners of her eyes, while checking the mirror or simply flicking to her husband's face.

It's disconcerting enough that she draws back, especially paired with the way he doesn't seem to sleep.

Not that she could in good conscience mention it to him, not after the trip she's had.

It's not just her eyes. She's always sort of appreciated, even as it annoyed her, his tendency to maintain a constant contact, despite his embarrassment at anything resembling too public a display of affection. But over the last eight hours, he's just as often stared at the wall like he's not completely aware she's there.

For the first time, she's not sure where he's coming from. And it doesn't not scare her.

They roll the highway up underneath the car, returning to zero. Back the way they came. The look in Elijah's eyes as he told her about the missing guys in North Carolina, and the only conclusion they could draw about Jo, was argument enough.

Donny, she'd just as soon let Slim have.

Hector's theories, recorded in Alan's book, take on a truer ring. She'd seen the subterranean hallway, the outlines of the stone clock he thought was central. It certainly appeared so. Not so far-fetched then, his idea that there might be a group of people who've thrown in with the beasts.

Desperation, nihilism, whatever. She gets that. The months before she and Elijah hit Slim, she'd've been hard pressed herself to say no to the idea of drowning the world in monsters and fire.

But they'd had their moment, soon after, and she's loath to let it go.

A few more miles and Elijah looks over, opens his mouth. "I didn't mention something."

It's been this way since morning, each only breaking the silence to fill in further blanks.

"That party, I mean." Gesturing at his torso.

"Where you got shot."

"Yeah, but right after."

"Thought you passed out."

"But there was something. It slips my mind, you know? But Slim did something, with his blood."

Lorelei blinks, glances at Elijah. Sees the shimmering. She can't decide if she thinks it's because of something with her, or something different about him.

"He, yeah. Cut himself. Put it in my eyes."

Lorelei jerks her head over. "He put the knife . . .?"

"His blood. Hand on my forehead—" he pantomimes "—and just dripping, you know?"

The brakes whine when Lorelei slows for traffic. "And then?"

Shrug. "Dunno. Fuzzy, blurring. But, like things were coming apart." He shudders, whispers. "Like his blood did something to my brain."

His tone chills the next few miles into silence. She finds herself not scoffing at his description of something being done to his brain, is inclined to take him at face value. A new strain scrapes his throat. He's gone quiet.

They make the nerve-racking drive through Atlanta and three more hours to Valdosta, and then the state line blurs past. They talk occasionally, discussing details they might have overlooked. Elijah pages through Alan's journal, face like a mathematician on the verge of making his career.

They pull off on the Florida side of the border and Elijah pays for a motel room with bills from the duffel bag. The clerk offers a wake-up call but they know they won't sleep.

CHAPTER SIXTEEN

Elijah can feel the tension vibrating off Lorelei. She's not driving anymore and seems not to know what to do with herself. Her legs cross and uncross. Her fingernails scratch at the ridged vinyl seatbelt.

Faint salt tang creeps through the cracked windows as the highway edges close to the ocean. They take an off-ramp to a surface road, to a dirt one, and Donny's place rears up. Lorelei goes suddenly still.

Donny comes outside before they can exit the car. Shirt-less, shotgun level with his waist. Eyes wide, hunched over in a wounded sort of way.

"Hey," Elijah says loudly, sensing Lorelei moving out to the right. "We come in fucking peace, man."

Donny holds him in his sights for a second then swivels to Lorelei. "Back." Donny jerks the gun toward the car. "Don't get fancy on me, Lori."

She makes a halfhearted show of holding up her hands and drags her feet back to the car. Stalling all the way, but Donny never drops his aim.

She sighs and leans against the car. "Better?"

"A little. Sticking point's y'all're still here."

Elijah holds his hands out to his sides, turns side-to-side. "Not much elsewhere for us to go, Donathan."

Donny's not so worked up he doesn't cringe at the mock name. Which is something. He racks one into the shotgun. The racking's for show, and the shell that'd been ready plops into the dirt next to him. Elijah stiffens anyway.

"So. Maybe you wanna tell me why you're here."

"Maybe we wanna do it sitting down inside," Lorelei says.

Elijah winces. It's not how he would have handled it. Not how Lorelei would have handled it a month ago. Donny nods, though, relaxes his aim without quite taking the shotgun off them.

They file into the little house. Elijah smells the mildew and flashes on bleeding, on being vulnerable. He wants to hit someone to clear the feeling but follows Lorelei instead.

They take places around the yellowing plastic kitchen table, Elijah sitting where Jo sat forever ago, guarding her keys none too effectively. The others sit directly across from each other, like the three of them are leaving space for a fourth person.

Donny leans his chair back on two legs, props the barrel of his shotgun on the table's edge. "Okay, so. Why don't you tell it to me?"

Lorelei waits for Elijah, like his old relationship will come in handy here. Donny rolls his head in Elijah's direction.

Elijah clenches his teeth, sets his elbows on the table. "Slim's cleaning house."

Donny snorts.

"Okay, don't believe me. Heard from Asher lately?"

"We're not exactly close."

"Fair. Rich, then? Or Leon? Or, you know, anybody from the old crew?" Elijah watches the barrel of the gun waver. He lifts his hands like he's about to emphasize a point and brings them down hard against the edge of the table instead. The other end pops up, sending the barrel into the air. He braces in advance of the ceiling-bound shot he's expecting.

Donny surprises him, has his finger off the trigger. Is at least that much smarter than Elijah thought.

Lorelei ducks down and moves around the table. She presses her pistol to Donny's head. "So help me."

Donny looks to Elijah, betrayed. Hesitates. Reaches down and sets the gun on the linoleum. Elijah jerks his head to the side. Donny slides the gun across the room with his foot, away from the three of them.

"Well then," Lorelei says. "I think we were about to talk about something like civilized fucking adults."

Donny sneers but takes his seat quietly.

"What we're doing here," Lorelei says, "is partly making sure you're alive. We've done that, for better or worse. So: Where's Jo?"

Donny glances at Elijah. "Ask hubby."

Elijah braces himself for a violent flurry out of Lorelei but her voice only gets quieter. Takes on a razor edge, tries its best to cut Donny.

"Don't feed me fucking riddles, Donny. I've had a week."

Donny looks again to Elijah, this time like maybe he can rewind whatever's started happening here.

"I don't know where Jo is," Elijah says. "I haven't seen her since she drove me to the Greyhound station."

"Funny. I didn't for a while, either." Donny watches Elijah's face. "Jesus. Could've sworn it was you."

Lorelei clears her throat.

"She's in the hospital. I only found out a couple days ago. Something's seriously, weirdly wrong."

Elijah leans forward. "Wrong how?"

"Come on. Let's go see for yourself."

After few seconds and an unresolved pissing match over whether Donny should be allowed to drive himself, Elijah follows Lorelei following Donny out the door, into the scrub lawn. Donny twirls his keys on his finger, happy about something. Elijah walks to the driver's side of his car, Lorelei and Donny to the other.

Donny turns and says something to Lorelei. Her shoulders tense. He laughs enough for Elijah to hear and shakes his head.

Lorelei's on him before he takes a step. The car door catches the back of his head and he's down. Lorelei stands over him. Doesn't look to Elijah.

Elijah smiles to himself. This will be over soon and they'll have an easier time for it.

But Lorelei's not done. She crouches, gets hold of Donny's shirt and lays into him. By the time Elijah gets around the car, Donny's bleeding from his nose and mouth, trying to keep his hands in the way of Lorelei's fists. The frustration of the last week vents through her hands. All the people she couldn't strike at, everything that didn't make sense, Donny's paying for all of it.

And Elijah's going to stand here and watch him get battered, for the second time in seven months.

But something slides across Lorelei's scowl. Her hands move faster, a little jerky. Eyes wide, though somehow still dark. A shifting feeling calls Elijah back to that living room with Asher and Slim, where the world tore itself into component parts that somehow clung together—that feeling creeps back while watching Lorelei, deep down by the base of his skull.

She leans in close to Donny. He's resisting less and less. Elijah's feet are moving before his mind is. Fingers hook into the collar of Lorelei's tee-shirt, pull her spinning to her feet. He slams his knuckles into the jawbone of her face gone wrong.

She reels against the car and Elijah's heart drops through his shoes. But there's no other way to be sure.

Lorelei's stunned enough that she doesn't stop the second blow, can't keep Elijah from dragging her toward the trunk. He gets it open, thinks the bungee cord in the back might be a good idea, but he won't be able to keep this up for long.

He shoves her face-first into the trunk. It seems like the way least likely to hurt her.

She lands and doubles up on herself, expecting further violence. Elijah fishes a spool of twine out from next to the wheel well and ropes her hands together as fast as he can.

Trickle of blood from the bruise growing just below Lorelei's lips, and it's high time to close the trunk.

Her voice, calling his name—a small echo before the trunk slams shut.

Donny gapes from the dirt.

Elijah makes a show of dusting himself off, like this was the culmination of some plan. "Fuck it. Ride with me." He points toward the passenger side.

Donny doesn't move.

Elijah lets his eyes narrow. He takes a step toward Donny.

Donny gets up and into the car in record time.

Stacy puts her hand flat on the apartment door before knocking. The text back from Jack was a little cryptic.

Didn't sound quite like him. Wasn't sarcastic, for one, and was pretty brief, which has never quite been his style. Still, things must've changed a little since she left.

The building's peeling paint and dead lights are classic him, though. That at least gives her the courage to knock.

From inside: "It's open."

Not Jack's usual paranoid caution. But things change. And there aren't too many other entries on her list of places to go. She eases the door open.

The smell doesn't hit her until the door's closed behind her. Once she's finished gasping through the copper-and-mold air, she sees that all of Jack's instincts are gone now.

The first thing she sees is a very not-Jack man sprawled in the moth-eaten recliner Jack was always so protective of. Soiled white undershirt, baggy basketball shorts. Goatee like a bloated parasite. Something on his arms—scars or tattoos or something.

Stacy squints and a smile spreads over the man's gaunt face. Looks like he's shaking in place, like a film reel rattling in its groove. So many individual twitches and tics that there isn't a baseline for comparison, no part of him that's still.

And Jack. The breath rushes out of Stacy even as she opens her mouth. The man in the chair doesn't move. A second man on the floor is only barely recognizable, Jack's cool, hard mouth twisted into a surfeit of expression foreign to it. Ribs reach out from flayed flesh into the air, grasping for the man with the goatee, for another body to live in. A malignant tumor of blood has spread asymmetrically over the carpet, already gone brown at the edges.

The gash runs throat to pelvis. Stacy sees more of Jack than she ever wanted to.

An insistent tapping from the armchair. Blood drips down the lounging man's arm too fast to be transfer from Jack, beating something like a heartbeat into the dead-still room.

She steadies herself, stands up straighter.

The man's mouth only pushes the smile further. He shifts in the seat, leans his head on his knuckles. "Hello, Stacy."

"Don't believe we've met." Voice steadier than she expected.

"They call me Slim."

"Do they now?'

Something passes behind Slim's eyes. "Now, who have you been talking to?"

Stacy looks behind, at all the people not there.

Slim stands, smears a long bloody handprint across the arm of Jack's recliner. At this, everything else hits Stacy in the stomach. Her gut wants to fold over on itself. She shakes and sweats with the sudden effort it takes to stay upright.

"Well," Slim, still twitching but striding steadily toward her, "much as I'd love to stay and chat."

Stacy steps to the side to let him pass. He tilts his head at her, smiling like she should know what's about to happen.

"Could be you're not as scary as you think you are, Tiny."

"Slim. And there're some things you haven't seen."

She smiles. "I've seen a lot this week." She's not sure what she's stalling for, unless it's for Slim to give in to blood loss and keel over.

He doesn't. Pulls his shoulders in a circle and cracks his back instead. "I was wondering who kept texting Jack, you know. Nobody who'd been paying attention the last couple days."

"We had an appointment."

"And you don't look like you really have anything to do with this." He frowns. "You ever know a woman named Lorelei?"

Stacy shakes her head, but can feel the blood draining from her face, giving her away.

"Of course," Slim says, snaking a hand around to the back of her neck faster than she can see. "This is her fault then. You don't seem like you were even involved."

Stacy opens her mouth to agree but nothing comes out. Slim heaves her across the room. She crashes into the dresser.

"But, dear, certain sacrifices must be made." His shadow covers her.

Stacy gasps for breath. Her neck is sticky where he touched her. A stinging sets in as the blood air-dries. Slim reaches down, wriggles his fingers into her mouth.

"You wanna tell me why you just clocked your wife in the face?"

The parking lot bakes in the sun. Elijah parks at the far edge, which is empty. The walk to the building feels like a heroic journey.

"Not really," Elijah says, not looking over.

"Yeah. Well, fuck, man." Donny passes his hand down his face. "I mean, your fucking wife, man."

"You sound disappointed in me, Donny. Didn't think your opinion of me could get any lower."

"There's certain things, is all."

Elijah looks at him, sees some kind of assessment happening. "You didn't complain much. And I think she may have been about to kill you."

"Could have just been an honest ass-kicking between folks."

Elijah doesn't mention how not that long ago, Donny would've been making up some story about what really happened, so it wouldn't have been him getting knocked around by a woman.

"Will it make you feel better if I told you I'm pretty sure I had a good reason?"

Donny's spit splats on the yellow curb.

"Okay. Well, will it make this conversation stop if I say that?"

Donny probably nods, but the doors are already whooshing open. Elijah slows so Donny can lead the way, which he does, past a reception desk that takes his nod and head-tilt toward Elijah as good enough. They head down a hallway, into an elevator, and Elijah realizes Donny's been here more than once. Which clashes a bit with what he'd pictured. He should maybe give Donny a bit more credit.

His expression, reflected in the elevator door, would seem to confirm this. Then they're at the fourth-floor ICU and he gets Donny's back again.

He badly does not want to go into the room Donny stops in front of.

The door's glass is just clear enough to think you can see through. Can't, though. It's a lovely touch, one Elijah'd like to not ruin. But then Donny's opening the door, holding it for Elijah. Pure hospital smell wafts out, lemon antiseptic and sweat. Elijah steps inside.

Jo's in the bed, tubes running from her body, beeping monitor, the whole bit. She looks like a hospital patient, but something's wrong.

Elijah looks to Donny. Donny points to her face. Elijah leans down then jerks back. Jo's eyes are peeled wide open, pupils hugely dilated. There's a greenish tint to the whites, something moving underneath the irises.

Elijah shakes his head. "What the fuck? What happened?"

"Dunno. Doctors don't seem to, either. Here, look." He tilts one drip bag so the light plays off it, lets it go. Takes hold of another, does the same, and nods. "Only sometimes, yeah, but here."

Elijah observes the bag. The fluid's clear, but as Donny tilts it, something moves, same as her irises.

"What the hell?" Elijah reaches for the tube to pull it from her arm.

Donny catches his wrist. "The fuck are you doing?"

"What? Pulling it out."

"It's not the bag, man. It's her."

Elijah looks from the bag to Jo's arm. The fluid's clearly going in, not out.

"It's way after they put one in, when its about to be replaced." Donny forces Elijah's arm back to his side. "Back-blood, maybe. Like when someone shoots up?"

"I don't think that's how drips work."

"Fuck it, something like that, anyway. You only notice it when they've been there awhile. They're not like that when they come."

Elijah doesn't ask how many times Donny has been here to have figured out a pattern. He doesn't say anything, just looks at the irises squirming, at the way Jo's not moving that makes him think she's holding her breath, waiting to jump out and surprise someone.

He can't get out of the room fast enough.

Donny follows, stepping quick to catch up. "What do you think?"

"Think we have to talk to Lorelei."

* * *

The voices come through the walls. Jo twists her head around to the room she's in, to the window no light's coming through. She's not sure how long she's been there, but has the feeling that she went to leave a little while ago and came back, like she forgot something.

The walls are an aging gray. Rough shape of a motel or an office or something. She steps out into the hallway, with its darkened fluorescent lights set at intervals, and looks back into the room.

Not a motel or an office. A hospital.

She looks around in wonder and starts slowly walking. The floor doesn't give under her, the ceilings haven't started to sag or crumble. But the walls are covered in a thick layer of dust and filth, like the place has been abandoned for years.

She runs a finger through the grime. It feels light but gritty, like turmeric. Her finger leaves a groove, flaking gray like ash. She rubs the substance between her fingers, dimly aware that she should be recoiling, entranced instead.

The grime turns from looking sticky to flaking between her fingers, the same way as on the wall. Her fingers start to stick to one another. She cringes and spins, searching for a clean place to wipe her fingers. Doesn't find one. Clenches her jaw and wipes them on her jeans, doesn't look at the stain left behind.

There's no one in the hall. A reception desk comes up on the left, then a plastic door. She circles around and wanders, steps falling quicker and quicker. Rooms and doors and ceiling tiles whip past. Something moves in the corner of her vision. She snaps her head around but can't catch it. Movement to the other side; misses that, too.

It doesn't slow her walking one bit.

The flickering ramps up. The walls blink in the very little light. Jo sees a corner coming and then she's around it, like she's jumped forward on a videotape. Like her surroundings are moving too fast for her to process, or her mind's firing too erratically for her to notice the interstitial moments.

The rooms pass, identical to one another, shadows creeping and diving when she's not looking. Somehow she knows when she's come back around to the room she started in. She's drawn here, finds herself back with no particular memory of telling her legs to bring her here.

The voices bleed through again, insistent. They sound familiar, like a couple of old friends, but too distorted to place. Then they start to fade, like intangible people walking away, through the walls.

Jo looks over the room, wondering what she came back in here for.

From down the hall, a rumbling, like something massive approaching. The wrongness of the building paralyzes her and she waits.

The building has the rough shape of a motel or an office or something.

She steps into the hallway, looks back into the room.

Not a motel or an office. A hospital.

It's been forever since Lorelei heard Donny ask why Elijah had gone after her, and the trunk's been getting smaller. If only she'd heard his answer. Might put her situation in context.

But that's bullshit. She knows exactly why he moved on her, if not why at that moment.

She's known since watching him on the freeway. While she was gone he got close to the beasts and something happened. Poisoned him, the way it did Slim. The way Slim did to himself. No way to know if he even knows it, but she should have.

The relief of seeing him again, though, made her close her eyes to it. Which got her stuffed in the trunk, bleeding, it feels like, from at least one part of her face.

She's got her guard up, though, now. Hand around her pistol, waiting for the first crack of light when it opens.

It takes a lifetime and a half, but footsteps finally approach. They're the first she's heard. She gathers Elijah parked at the edge of the lot, where nobody was going to walk by. Smart.

Means it's a big lot, too. Which narrows down their location by precious little.

The footsteps stop just outside with a jangling of keys. Lorelei braces herself as best she can with her muscles cramping. The key scrapes the lock, finally finds purchase.

Lorelei jabs the barrel of the pistol through the first sliver of sunlight. Metal hits bone. A shout, the sound of a body hitting the asphalt. The trunk rocks all the way open.

Lorelei steps out, leading with the gun, trying to hide the stiffness in her legs.

Elijah's sprawled on the parking lot, clutching his face. Donny takes a couple steps back, hands up in surrender.

Lorelei makes a show of cracking her neck, stretching herself vertical. Playing the moment, the way Elijah's bleeding through his fingers. She takes a step forward, nudges him with her foot. Jerks the gun in the universal sign for *stand the fuck up.*

He does.

"You didn't take her gun?" Donny says quietly, like that way he won't startle her into murder.

"Didn't think of it." Elijah stands still and bleeds at her.

"Our Eli might not be quite himself at the moment," Lorelei says. She nods to Donny, hoping he'll catch on.

He just shrugs. "Dunno, sounds about what I'd expect, if I'm honest."

She shakes her head. "Well, lover. Probably time to disarm yourself."

Elijah presses his palm to his jaw, pulls it away to root through his pocket. Along with a cell phone and a wallet and a keyring, he pulls out a revolver and plunks it on the ground.

Lorelei smiles, shoves the pile behind her with her foot. "Donny, be a dear?"

He looks at her with a very blank face.

She moves the gun toward Elijah. "Hold his hands back, I mean." When Donny doesn't move, she adds, "Or, you know, I could finish killing you."

It gets his attention. She switches the gun to her left hand, so her body shields it from anybody watching inside the hospital.

Lorelei steps back, reaches into the trunk and finds with blind fingers the bag she was holding when Elijah deposited her there. The pendant, tucked behind the last page of Alan's notebook, wrapped in tissue paper and held in place by time, slips into her hand.

She takes a menacing step toward Elijah. He doesn't flinch. It slows her a bit; could be he's gotten clever.

"Just need to see something." She lets the tissue fall from one side, which she presses to his forehead.

A second, two.

Elijah barely reacts. A whisper of steam drifts from the pendant across the air between them. His pulse comes weakly through the metal. She presses down harder and pulls it away. It leaves a slight indentation in his skin, a tan discoloration where the twisting metal symbol touched him.

Not at all what she'd expected from reading Alan's notebook.

"Okay then." Elijah jerks his arms free of Donny. "I read the book, too. Let's see."

He snatches the pendant from her. The gun hangs in her hands, so much dead weight she doesn't think to lift. Elijah steps forward; she steps back, hits the bumper of the car just below her ass.

He's less gentle with the pendant-on-forehead routine than she was. Like this is her fault.

Her head rocks back under his hand. She holds her breath, thinking maybe she's had this thing backward all along.

But, staring at his face twisting itself, hardening into something foreign, there's nothing but that same wisp of steam—maybe a little heavier.

Elijah drops his hand and steps back. Turns the pendant over.

Lorelei straightens up, wanting to swing at him again but not really sure about it.

"Huh," Elijah says.

"Yeah. Was that what happened there?"

"Uh huh."

"Hmm. Me too."

Elijah smiles a little, the way he will when he doesn't want to. Donny looks from him to her, his face a blank.

"Guess we both read that book."

"Oh," Elijah says. "You need to see something. Bring the bag."

She grabs Alan's bag, not letting him out of her line of sight.

The two of them stroll down the hospital halls in front of Donny like they're not both bleeding. Like this is the aftermath to some wholesome bonding moment.

It's not a total surprise, but their dysfunctional little love story usually took place in something like this world.

Something's changed. He gets that.

What he doesn't get is what the hell it was. It's not like they're leaning their heads on each other's shoulders, but Lorelei's hand brushes Elijah's while they're waiting for the elevator, and Elijah gives Lorelei this schoolboy smile. Neither feels the nurse scoping them or wonders how far Donny's credit with her will go.

Elijah and his fucking schoolboy smile.

It's not what got Donny's ass kicked by a bleeding-through-his-shirt Slim a year and change ago, but he figures it's not quite unrelated, either.

Both are pretty solidly Elijah's fault.

Lorelei seems to be taking charge, though. Donny's pretty grateful for that, given the alternative. She pulls ahead, then seems to realize that she's the one person who *doesn't* know where they're going, and lets Elijah go in front.

Donny waits for Elijah to fuck up the directions, having only been through once. He doesn't, though, and they arrive at Jo's bed. Donny closes the door behind them, hoping nobody's tipped security or whichever doctor's in charge. He watches Elijah take Lorelei through the same couple of moves he took him, pointing out Jo's eyes, tilting the first bag in the sunlight, then the second.

Lorelei nods, taking it in stride. Doesn't ask anything, just traces her hands down the tube to Jo's skin and back up again, like she'll be able to detect the problem by touch.

"Huh," she says. "Remember how Hector cropped up in that book? How he kept himself from getting noticed by those things?"

"Yeah, and the priest."

"Uh huh." She shakes her head. "But I don't think we're gonna make a convincing Catholic out of Jo. Even if she woke up."

Elijah snorts at that and Lorelei smiles. She opens the bag and rifles around inside.

Donny looks back and forth between them, waiting for any of this to start making sense. "Anyone feel like filling me in?"

"Not really," Elijah says.

Lorelei flashes warning eyes at him. "It would take a long time, Don. Trust us."

As though she lived through a completely different last couple of hours than he did.

She pulls a slender plastic package from the bag, peels it open, and takes out a hypodermic needle. The ampule comes next.

Donny's stomach clenches. Rush of blood to the face. He's never been good with needles. The irony's not lost on him.

Lorelei fits the two pieces together and motions to Elijah. He pulls a yellow prescription bottle from his pocket. She produces a lighter from the bag. Footsteps approach, and they all freeze until the person passes the door, turns a corner, and fades away. Lorelei looks around a minute, dumps tongue depressors out of a metal cup, to use the cup as a spoon.

Donny at last steps forward. "No fucking way. Are you insane?"

Elijah's hands on his chest, pushing him back. "Stand the fuck back. Just wait."

"You don't think they've got her on painkillers, Eli? You think they just sort of *forgot* that? At a hospital?"

While Lorelei crushes two pills in the cup with the bottom of the lighter, Elijah's eyes track over to the IV bags hanging next to Jo. Donny holds still, watches the wheels turn, hoping for Elijah to come to his senses.

Instead, Elijah tilts his head toward him. "That weirdness ever happen with the saline?"

Donny shakes his head. "What?"

"The saline. Look." Elijah points to the stand. "Three bags. Say one's saline, the other's painkiller, the third's whatever medicine they're trying now, right?"

"No idea. Sure, why not." Donny tries to sound noncommittal, like he's not giving his approval for whatever's about to happen.

Lorelei sets the lighter's flame to the bottom of the cup.

"So," Elijah says, "does what you showed me ever happen to what's *not* the painkiller?"

Donny wants badly to tell him, yes, it does, but whatever that conjures might be worse. "I honestly have no idea," he says. "Could be, maybe not. Shits are all clear, you know?"

Lorelei lets the flame die and sets the cup on the counter. Sucks on her fingers where the metal got hot.

Donny tenses in place, ready to stop them.

Lorelei looks to Elijah. He nods. Donny moves toward her.

She raises her hand, steps back. "Easy, Donny. Hey, Eli, show him what we're thinking, yeah?"

Elijah nods and motions toward Jo. Donny turns his head. Realizes his mistake when Elijah slams his palms into Donny's shoulders and drives him back against the wall.

Lorelei pulls her belt through the loops in her jeans. Donny thrashes against Elijah, manages to land a knee in his stomach. Elijah droops, but works his forearm up, presses it across Donny's throat.

Donny gasps for breath. The forearm lifts, but not all the way. He can either breathe or move. He decides to breathe, immediately hates himself for it as Lorelei uses her belt as a tourniquet and pumps the opiate needle into the only person in the room he cares about.

Elijah pushes off the wall and away from him, hands held high to say, let's all be reasonable here.

Donny nods, straightens his shirt. Swings the sloppiest haymaker this side of reality, but manages to twist his lead foot and load his weight behind it. Elijah's not expecting it. Knuckles on jawbone—Elijah stumbles, falls.

Donny moves toward Lorelei but she doesn't budge. Hands at her side, she fixes him with a look that makes him drop his hands and step back.

At least he remembers to move toward the door and not Elijah.

Elijah pulls himself to his feet, eyes slashing at Donny.

Something wet splatters to the floor. They all look for the source. Donny catches sight of the liquid seeping under Jo's bed.

He points. The couple looks. The bag fell from the stand in the fracas, and now bleeds its contents onto the floor. They watch the clear liquid spread and spread. It slows eventually, having gone as far as it can, and its edges turn black, gray tint spreading and fading toward Jo.

Donny looks from the tainted spilled fluid to the IV rack to Jo. Her skin moves, not her body, not anything made of bone. Donny blinks and it happens again, like something's writhing under her skin.

He opens his mouth, but Lorelei and Elijah are already dashing to her side. Donny sidles up between them. Jo's skin writhes. The tube running into her arms darkens, swims.

Donny grabs Elijah by the shoulder. "What the fuck did you do?"

"I don't know." Voice dull, distant. "Worked in New York."

"What? You cured someone with a fix? Is that what you think is wrong with her?" He's got more questions ready but they don't get past his lips. The Sirkos aren't listening. He follows their eyes back to Jo, forgets his own train of thought.

She rolls back and forth on the bed and then stills. The drip goes straight black. Her eyes stretch wider and from their corners oozes a green sludge.

When she starts seizing, it's almost a relief.

Lorelei drags Elijah to the door. He catches on and they both flee.

Donny presses his hand to Jo's forehead, looking over his shoulder for anyone at the door. No way they can stay here long, and Jo's got the mother of all fevers.

The gunk from her eyes touches the edge of his hand. He recoils. He can't leave her here.

He's going to leave her here.

He's sure the clerk is going to stop him on the way out but no one does. The sliding doors release him into the garish sun.

The Sirkos' car is gone. Of course.

245

CHAPTER SEVENTEEN

Slim doesn't remember the names of the streets he's walked. His feet ache. He hasn't felt sore or tired or hungry in so long that he experiences terror before he's able to decode the feeling. This city, alive and buzzing with promise when he arrived, grows colder to him by the moment. He can't feel the press of bodies, can't hear their heartbeats behind the walls, ready for harvest. The smell of flesh and electricity replaced by tawdry asphalt and exhaust, concrete and dirt.

It feels like the girl in the apartment took something out of him, more than the blood he used. But that's not it. It's something both deeper and external—a shift in the air, and in his bones.

It's left him drained, stumbling.

He takes side streets and alleys to avoid the crush of people who'd certainly take issue with his appearance. The car's gone, left wherever he last parked it, a location lost in the haze that took over the last couple weeks. He wouldn't be able to find his way back to it even if he did know where it was.

He's increasingly unsure about a lot of things. The scene with Elijah at the house party, the set-up Asher put together, it feels like the last thing he consciously did, like in the intervening period he's been on a track, flailing his way not unenthusiastically through a predetermined set of events. Twinge of regret about Asher, but it had to be done.

Or it felt like it had to be done. He thinks he stands by it, though, regrettable though it may have been.

The feeling of the masters in his veins was, until an hour ago, an irresistible thrumming throughout his body. More than he had hoped for. The world was changing, a precarious balance he loathed finally coming apart, the masters surging forward into the world in ways he couldn't have imagined.

The others, around the country, had described the feeling to him, always only days before he lost contact with them. The experience had exceeded all their descriptions. It could only have been a sign of a new world forming.

There had been a reaching, and he had been its fingertip. Now it's pulled back.

He saw the effects of the push, the new balance: hallucinations, lost time. The masters melding with the minds of men seamlessly, ingeniously. This new art, now a drab retreat.

He should have killed that fucking priest.

He's convinced it was him. There's nothing he's more sure of. The look in the priest's eyes in the motel room, when Slim dispatched the other man—the one who all his senses told him was the threat he'd tracked—was more traumatized than anything. The look of a person so beyond his depth that he'd spend the rest of his life staggering around, half-connecting with the world around him, while all the while half-convinced that none of it was real.

And yet.

There will be another moment, another push. Slim hasn't been told this but he is certain of it. Other clocks, or something new. For now, though, the flesh weighs, the muscles burn.

His head grows heavy and he begins to worry that he'll lose consciousness right here, bleeding on the sidewalk.

A street sign finally jogs a memory. He only needs to walk another five or six blocks.

He almost doesn't make it. By the time he's climbing the steps, he has to drag himself up by the handrail. A man meets him at the door.

Slim points. "Need to get inside."

The man nods. The set of his face is familiar, something Slim only recently lost.

"Of course. Sit awhile, though, first."

Slim slumps against the wall in the shade of the awning. The man eases himself down, hand on Slim's shoulder, and crouches on the balls of his feet until Slim slips into a dark sleep.

Elijah skids out of the hospital parking lot and drives too fast for four miles before the man in the backseat throws off the blanket and sits up. Puts a knife to Lorelei's throat in the passenger seat.

The car nearly leaves the road.

Elijah steps on the brake, but the man clucks his tongue, shifts the knife so the point's just above Lorelei's jugular.

"I wouldn't," he says. "Not if you're attached to your wife. Or your upholstery."

"Who said she's my wife?"

"Don't fuck with me, Elijah."

"What should I—"

"Get back up to the limit, please. And not over. If we get pulled over, we are all going to die."

Elijah obliges. Silence until the needle hits fifty-five. The man relaxes the knife, sets it flat against Lorelei's throat.

"So," she says, soft so her neck won't move, "what can we do for you?"

The man smiles in the rearview. It's a familiar smile, muscles moving independently, like he's trying out the expression for the very first time. Apart from his knife hand, his body shakes and twitches. The sleeves of his dark blue Oxford shirt are further darkened in places, patterns close to the skin and clotting.

"Slim," Elijah says. "Slim sent you."

The man's smile widens. "Not quite. I know the man, though. Let's say we work together."

Lorelei grimaces. "Put the knife away and we won't shoot you, too."

"Shoot me? Whatever you did to Slim, it wasn't that crude. And I'm not going to risk finding out what it was before I'm ready."

"Did? What we did to Slim?"

"What did I say about bullshit? You know as well as I do that we won't be seeing him for a long time. Now, if you don't mind, shut the fuck up and head toward the coast."

They ride in silence, Elijah watching both the road and the mirror, Lorelei watching the knife. The man watches everything with darting glances.

Near the coast, the man opens his mouth to say something and slumps forward. The knife moves maybe an inch from her throat.

It's enough.

Lorelei brings her arm around and down on the man's wrist. Pins the blade to the cup holder. Elijah stamps down on the brake, praying no one's behind them. The man's face slams into Lorelei's headrest and he rebounds into his seat.

He blinks dumbly. Anger, then surprise, seeping into pain like he's never been hurt before. Blood pours down his face. He puts his hand to the small gash in his forehead and screeches.

The knife rattles in the cup holder. The man yanks his hand free and is out the door, sprinting across the rumble strips and into the trees before Elijah can make a move.

He doesn't even think about pursuit, just gets back into his lane and drives.

"Do you think he was on the level about Slim?" Lorelei asks once they've both caught their breath.

"I don't want to find out."

Stacy slams into consciousness, slumped against a bathtub. She can smell that she's vomited. She reaches, eyes closed, to the faucet and turns it on. Avoids looking at what's in the tub, to maybe keep her stomach still a moment.

She turns away as the water gets going, finds a completely foreign bathroom. One bulb of four is lit over the sink, a stiff and cracked vinyl toilet seat cover. She's never been here before.

Before confusion can set in, she sees her own bloody footprints leading from the next room and up to the tub. It all comes back.

Jack. The other man.

She rummages in the medicine cabinet and finds a straight razor. Holds it out in front of her like a totem and stalks out of the room.

Jack's where she left him. The other man, Slim, is gone. She paces the apartment carefully, jabbing the razor into the closet before looking, hauling the mattress off its frame rather than peek under the bed.

No one there.

She licks her lips and gags. Tongues crusted-over teeth. Tastes copper.

Back to the bathroom. She sees herself in the mirror and has to vomit again in the tub.

She collects herself as best she can and returns to the sink. Doesn't look this time at the drying blood across the lower half of her face, collecting in the corners of her mouth and between her teeth.

Jack has a plastic cup full of toothbrushes in the cabinet. Apparently was a freak for dental hygiene. She wouldn't have guessed. Would rather have assumed that anything of the sort in his place was to be avoided for health reasons, but she no longer cares. She grabs the first toothbrush she can find, slathers toothpaste on it, and scrubs at her teeth.

At first the bristles just slide over the crusted blood. Must have been a while, if the blood has managed to dry inside her mouth.

The toothbrush finally works its way in, dislodges the first meaty flake from her teeth. She spits a chunky pink. Shuts her eyes and brushes harder.

Long minutes and endless gagging later, she scrubs her face and spits and turns off the water in the tub.

Time to get the hell out of Dodge, for good, and hopefully not too late.

Her clothes are a lost cause. She strips and stuffs them in the oven, twists the dial.

251

Jack was not a large man, but the clothes she ferrets out from the closet hang loose. She stuffs yards of flannel shirt into the waistband of baggy jeans. Hopes she looks relaxed, not criminal.

This had been her last resort. Nothing so bad as crawling back to Jack. The ultimate indignity. But Slim has at least done her the favor of convincing her that calling on her father is now conceivable.

There is nothing in this town but death.

She heads to the Greyhound station, toward a ticket to Minnesota and an awkward reunion.

She won't be calling ahead.

By the time Lorelei shows him the *Globe* story, they've driven all night and the rest of the next day, paid for a trailer in Nebraska with cash, and before sleeping, hung twisted icons in every corner and smeared charcoal on the walls.

Lorelei drives to the mall and buys radios. They keep a bottle of Dilaudid on the coffee table in case they feel something coming.

The last owner left a bible in a half-broken side table. Elijah puts it under a cushion and doesn't leave the rough couch for two days.

Lorelei glances over her shoulder at him. "Look at this."

Elijah groans, nauseated and shaking. He doesn't feel like he's getting any better.

"Seriously." She waits. "Oh, fucksake." She carries the laptop over to him.

Florida man, between the ages of twenty-five and thirty-five, found dead in Boston alleyway. Unintelligible carvings on his arms and torso. Torture and murder suspected, due to the number and varying age of the cuts, though police have no comment.

Elijah doesn't read any further. "Well. That's one less thing to worry about."

Lorelei nods. She puts the laptop on the coffee table and sits on the floor, back against the couch, head resting near Elijah's. "Still," she says, "there's more of him. More of them."

It's the third time today they've traced this territory. Lorelei wants to get started on gathering people, finding anyone who might know anything and setting out to strike at the beasts and their lackeys.

Elijah wants to never go outside ever again. The thought of going into some house, some bar, meeting up with a person and guessing at their motives, sets his anxiety to raging.

The panic attack he dampened with pills on the highway has surged back, never killed but having retreated to gather strength.

"We don't know if there's anyone out there anymore. If it will even help."

"The people who died," Lorelei says. "Always alone, right? Or mostly. Nothing in the book about a group."

"But it *does* say that it had been getting worse. And even that wasn't as bad as now."

"Had to have been Slim and those people. Had to be. Setting things loose, fucking up—"

"'The *balance*.' Yeah, I've read it. Maybe it's restored, then. Maybe things are back to normal."

"That's kind of what I'm afraid of."

"Then don't go chasing after it."

"I don't think you're hearing me." Lorelei swallows. "They fought it, right? The priest with his dogma, the guy with the radios. I mean, even Hector's narcotics worked. See?"

"Nope." Trying hard not to.

"When's the last time you saw prayer change anything in the world?"

Elijah grinds his teeth. "So, what, that stuff works because the things are there?"

"I don't know. What else?" She points to the pendant hanging on the front door. "Even that thing. We both saw what it could do."

"Yeah."

"Could be we can use it against them."

"Could be."

She sounds like she wants to push it further but catches herself. Elijah rolls over, traces his fingers down her shoulder and laces them between hers. She grips his hand, rolls her head to rest against him.

Outside, an argument between geese. They stay still, trying to sleep and waiting.

ACT THREE

CHAPTER EIGHTEEN

The Minister takes his time. The roads in the middle of the country lend themselves to a constant, gradual increase in speed, but he's loath to invite investigation. It's a long drive from Los Angeles. No particular reason not to let it stretch.

His destination, he knows, is somewhere in the Midwest. Beyond that he can't be sure. But the surest way to throw himself off the scent is to rush it, to force a trajectory where none presents itself.

His business in LA is done. That provides enough solace to make a patient man of him.

The beasts almost never get that far west. Or, they didn't used to. The Minister hopes it isn't the start of a trend.

It makes LA off-limits for him, too, for a while—probably forever. Not a huge loss. He can't really stand that city, has never found the version they're always shooting and project-ing onto big screens—wide lawns and swimming pools and clever conversation in the hills.

His experience has always been of this flat, sun-bleached place, strip malls and parking lots and somebody pushed up against a bad-news wall. Not unlike the rest of the country.

But those other parts, they're not pretending quite so much. Not in the same way. They think that they're the kind of small town where things don't happen, not bad ones. Where someone like the Minister has no business visiting.

They'd be mad, of course, if they knew. But they'd be misplacing their anger, shooting it his way instead of at what he came to clean up, at the problem they don't know is sweeping through their towns like a deep black plague. It encourages the tendency toward subtlety he's been honing for longer than he cares to think.

An interchange headed north presents itself. He feels it, deep in his bones. It's almost with regret he turns away from where the couple's holed up. He knows the Sirkos are in a trailer park in Nebraska because a recently-departed acquaintance in LA knew, and he knows too that they've been close enough to things to warrant a little of his attention.

First thing's first, though. A couple more motel room and a couple more days on the road, and he'll cross the Minnesota state line.

He breathes deep.

Time to get to business.

Stacy drags her apron off the top of the passenger seat and slams the door of her father's car. Shuffles along the patchy grass to the front door. Screen hanging by one hinge. Low television drone that means her father's home, on the couch. Wishing he was drinking, by the sunlight still hanging around, but not wishing for long.

She hates him more when he's sober.

Not like he's ever raised a hand to her or anything. She knew she was safe enough coming back to Minnesota. Safe in the physical sense.

The six months she's been here, though, she's felt the town eating at her. At who she thought she was, back east.

She kicks aside the screen and opens the door and the old man's not in the living room but right in front of her, at the kitchen table. Someone sitting across from him, long, narrow face and a limp brown suit like an old-time traveling salesman.

"Stacers," her father says, not watching for her wince. "Looks like one of those job applications paid off."

She hasn't been filing those applications, has been pulling names off office park signs on the drive home, to recite to him.

The other man nods. "After a fashion." Fixes his eyes on Stacy. "Your resume was referred to me by a recruiter. I assume you sent it to him." The man raises his eyebrows, a clear enough message.

Stacy ignores it, shakes her head. "Nope."

"Well." The man finishes the Coors in front of him and tips it to her father in thanks, all without breaking eye contact with Stacy. "Perhaps it was referred to us by one of your prospective employers." He dips his head to the old man. A sidebar: "We have standing agreements with local employers. If they have more qualified candidates than openings, they refer the remainder to us. For a fee, of course."

Her father grins big. "See, Stace? Told you. Just keep on plugging, it'll come. Hell, my first job after college—"

"Think maybe I ought to hear what the man has to say, huh?"

"Sure, sure." He cracks his beer and hauls himself creaking from the chair and heads to the living room.

Stacy nods to the front door. "Out front, maybe?"

"If you think we need privacy, yes."

"Like Jack didn't send you here."

"Jack?"

"Jack, yeah. Colorado Jack." Her voice fades to the tense whisper she's been holding back for months. "Don't fuck with me."

"I'm not."

"And you say you don't know who Jack is."

"I didn't say that. And you know he didn't."

Stacy waits.

"He couldn't." The man sighs. "He's dead. You know it. I know it. So if you'd like to talk out front, okay, but you should know I know more than you think, and you're not going to be able to lie to me."

"I didn't hear about Jack. Whatever else I feel about him, that's too bad."

The man raises his eyebrows. Isn't buying it.

"All right then." She holds the door until he walks through.

Back into the sunlight then. The place she's working, a quarter of the tables are outside. Being the new girl, she gets to work them—two-tops mostly, for the languorously paced. Time off, she prefers indoors.

The man doesn't seem to mind the glare. "I expect you're expecting some exposition, yeah? Some big story about why I'm here."

"It had occurred to me you might explain yourself."

"Stands to reason."

They stare at each other.

"Well?" Stacy tries more confidence than she feels. It sounds hollow.

"I think you maybe know more than I do."

"I don't know shit." The words are coming and Stacy can't help it. "If this is about what happened to Jack, you can go ahead and get out the pliers and the blowtorch if you want, because I don't know. I stumbled in on the aftermath. Everything, the last few months I was out in Boston, I was getting there right when it finished. I have no fucking idea what happened, and a few months later, you know, I don't think I want to know. Something real bad went down." She swallows, reins it in. "Far as I'm concerned, it's over. If it ever happened."

The man leans against the porch railing and smiles more authentic than she expects, like he knows what she's feeling and is glad to hear it. Like he's here to help.

She steels herself.

"I get why you'd want to think that," he says. "But you know—if you stop to really think about it, let yourself feel what you're feeling—you know it's not true."

The bottom falls out of the world exactly the way she thought she could balance against. She clenches her teeth.

"But I do know what happened," he says.

"Lotta people did."

"Dead people, yes?"

She stares.

"I'm not dead."

She nods. Yes, this is true. The moment stretches until her aliveness becomes the only thing that matters.

"Okay. Come with me, if you would. Unless you have pressing business with your dad?"

Stacy looks behind the man into the house. Peeling paint

and dying grass and her father's self-satisfied presence po-
lice-procedural noise seeping out of the small house.

"Nothing in particular. You've got a car?"

"Parked around back."

Stacy nods. "You have a name?"

"You know, that almost never comes up. Minister Jim."

She stands in place, waiting for him to smile or shrug or
acknowledge the fake name.

"All right," she says. "Lead the way."

The joint the Minister staked out has a locals-only vibe. Buried in a neighborhood just near enough to Minneapolis for
people to make the commute, and just far enough no one's
dropping in unless they live in this direction.

Stacy looks around, trying not to advertise how she's not
making eye contact. Scopes the surroundings in the same
fashion, so that maybe he won't know she doesn't know
the area.

It tells him he picked the right place heading from the
interstate off-ramp. Entering a city like that, smaller and
smaller circles, you get to see the lines between neighborhoods, the places that are like a different country to someone living a half-mile away.

You make yourself a denizen of the between places.

He pulls off in front of the bar, pulls around to the parking in the back. Watches Stacy double-take, wonders how
she didn't see the parking from the street.

"Well, here we are."

She looks at him, then to the back of the bar. Unbuckles
her seat belt, crosses her arms.

He opens his door, has to walk around to get hers. She
gets out, though, follows him at what he assumes is a kni-

feable distance, probably thinking this will give him pause, make him think about how dangerous she is. Really, though, it's letting him note her instincts, figure out how quick she might be. So far, so good.

And he's not particularly worried about his own death anymore. In the improbable event she gets the drop on him, he expects he'll be able to relax, ease himself into it.

They come in out of the sun. Men's and women's restrooms on the right, kitchen smelling of Old Bay on the left. He watches her face, notices as she recognizes the scent. Good.

Through the hall and into the barroom. Couple of crusty regulars at the end of the bar, one more at a table in the corner. Stacy checks them all and isn't obvious about it.

They take a table alone by the window in front of the bar.

"You want anything?"

Stacy thinks a second, shakes her head. "I'm okay."

"You sure?" He turns to the cocktail waitress pulling up to their table. "Well, I'd like a Bud."

"And for the lady?"

The Minister turns to her.

"Maker's rocks, please."

The Minister makes an approving face as the waitress walks away.

Stacy shrugs. "Didn't see me as a whiskey girl?"

"Didn't think you wanted anything."

"Didn't wanna drink alone."

They sit in silence until their drinks come. The Minister pays cash from his wallet, which he tips toward him so Stacy can't see how much is in there. She'll have questions enough as it is.

He waves off the change. The waitress grunts thanks

and walks away. Stacy puts her glass to her lips and pulls it through her teeth. That tremble happening in her hand, it's the first definite sign the Minister's had that she's at all shaken up. It's more than nothing, but not much.

He wonders how she got that steady. Most people, after the things she saw, wouldn't hold a glass with one hand for a year. Maybe ever.

But the far-away hard thing happening in her eyes says she's filing him in the category of things that happened back then, with the horrors that weren't near as long ago as they seem. She must be wondering how to close the door on them, and on him.

She's not too far off. Just that the question's different than what she's posing to herself. That kind of door doesn't ever close.

"So," she says from behind her glass, "what would you like to talk about?"

He can't see her mouth. Figures that's where she thinks her tell is. She's wrong.

"It's your eyes."

"What?" She frowns, covering a little.

"Your eyes. How I can tell what you're thinking? It's not your mouth, it's your eyes."

She sets the glass down naturally, like she was going to anyway. "That's how you found me then?" She tears at the corner of her napkin. "You haven't touched your beer."

"Good point." The Minister takes a long drink, not having to pretend to enjoy it. "Mmm. Tell you what, it has been a good long time."

"What, gonna tell me how you haven't had a beer since you got saved? Or, what, born again? Are those the same thing? I've never really been clear."

"No, I meant I haven't had one in a couple weeks." He sets the bottle down, slides it around in the growing rings of condensation on the table. "And I'm maybe not quite what you think I am."

"Minister Jim, right?"

"That's right.

"And you're, what, not a minister?"

"No, not exactly. Not the way you're thinking."

"But you are a minister. After a fashion."

"After a fashion." He lets it lay and she doesn't pick it up again. She does, however, pick up her glass, draining the rest of it. Lifts it toward the bar, at the waitress looking over.

"Figured you wouldn't mind," she says.

"No, go ahead. Maybe make it a double."

She looks at him with hardening eyes and raises two fingers. "That bad?"

He shrugs. "I imagine it's about things you'd rather not be talking about after work."

She opens her mouth, about to ask how he knows she just got off work, then stops herself. The waitress materializes, takes her glass and puts a full one in its place. Stacy drinks, slower.

"So," smacking her lips, "you were saying. Or you were about to."

"I was. I understand you were there when a person named Keane ran into something bad out Boston way."

She trembles but gets steady after a second. "How is he?"

The Minister narrows his eyes. "He's dead. Would come to, time to time, and he could talk, too, but he only spouted the kind of thing the nurses can barely remember."

"He didn't say anything?"

"He said plenty. But they weren't tracking most of it.

The way they told it to the police, he was saying all sorts of things. The only words they remembered were about sticky ashes and tentacles and a big yellow eye. Sound familiar?"

Stacy stops trying to control her face, tightens her hands around the glass. "Yeah. One or fucking two." She drains the rest of the whiskey, ice clicking against her teeth. "The yellow eye, though. Can't place that."

"You ever wonder where those tentacles were leading?"

She shakes her head.

"They're animals. Sort of."

"Like you're sort of a minister?"

"Just exactly like that."

CHAPTER NINETEEN

It doesn't take much for Stacy to convince the old man she's leaving for a job opportunity, that he won't see her again soon. He grunts and nods in an about-time way, and she bites her tongue about how she's been fending for herself for enough years that he can stow that shit.

He'd only remember the last couple months, though, her ass under his roof. His words.

She claps a hand to his shoulder in a way she doesn't feel and leaves, for the Minister's car and the freeway.

Enough miles pass that she doesn't recognize the names of towns. The Minister looks his part—calm face, ten-and-two hands. Hair combed back in a salesman sweep. He signals before changing lanes and checks his blind spots assiduously.

Stacy waits for him to slip but he never does. The sense of a hardness underlying his pleasant act she felt in the bar, it's not there now. She saw it, though. Enough to make her believe the kinds of things he said. She doesn't let down her guard.

The silence stretches. Stacy lets it. Waits for the Minister to break it first. He, too, lets it grow. The tension could just be Stacy's nerves ringing in her ears. She flexes her hands, keeps her eyes peeled.

The Minister gets them through a clump of traffic and into a little bubble of their own. He looks around, sighs. "I do prefer having the road to myself, a bit."

Stacy nods.

"Anyway. You probably have some questions."

"But you'll answer those when we get where we're going."

The Minister smiles. "That's the idea."

They burn a path south. Don't say a word until they've passed enough corn that Iowa City signs start showing up, turning off into a labyrinth of old farming roads, unlit. She doesn't know how the Minister knows where to turn. He taps out ten beats with his finger on the wheel before pulling off the dirt road into a patch of trees.

"Here were are."

"Where?"

The Minister gets out and opens her door. Leads her through the trees to a big wood shack—roof dipping in and one wall just the supports. Thick mat of leaves on the roof. If she hadn't been looking in exactly the direction they were walking, she'd've never seen it.

"Holy shit. You want to go in there?"

The Minister shoots her a crooked grin. She lets him walk ahead, a far-too-late burst of self-preservation. He opens the door for her, motions her inside. Stacy peers forward, but she can't see anything through the dark. Shakes her head: no, after you.

He leads the way. Stacy enters just before the blue flutter-and-catch of fluorescent bulbs turning on. When it takes, the inside of the shed gleams.

Blackout curtains over the windows. Corrugated steel walls laid overtop the originals, cut to reveal the windows, but with curtains screwed into the steel to cover them again. On the steel, charcoal smudges scraped real careful, so they go into the ridges without the lines breaking. Stacy gets caught up in them, one in particular, right by the door. It's the lines at first, the way they look scrawled but are actually carefully drawn. As she focuses on it, it tries to squirm out of her line of sight, just enough that it gets blurry.

It's the way they're drawn so close to one another that makes them hard to focus on. She squints at a few of them, gets a similar effect. Tries to bring a couple into focus, but they won't sharpen. She looks over at Minister Jim.

He's staring at her harder than she's ever seen anybody stare at anything.

"You recognize those pictures?"

She shakes her head. The word *picture* doesn't seem appropriate, rings in her ears.

"But you look like you see something."

She squints again. "Yeah. I mean, no. They kinda blur, you know?"

Minister Jim stares. Nods.

She saw the blurring of the sigils and she's staring at the Minister like she doesn't know what that means. She doesn't look like she's faking. He couldn't be sure, until now, how much she'd been holding back. Turns out, not much.

She was close to it in Boston but didn't get involved. She knows something happened that she can't explain, but as to what it was or even who was really involved, she wouldn't be able to say.

It's a relief. Better this way than the other, and less common.

He pulls a metal folding chair from the corner, skids another across the floor for her. "You say they're blurring."

"Yeah. It's a drawing technique, right? Like those optical illusions?"

"Like that."

A slow smile over her face. "But not quite, right?"

"Right."

He rehearsed this moment in the car, through the freeway and the old roads and the winding path his colleagues assured him no one else could find. That he couldn't find, probably, without the sense in the back of his mind that he's tried to hone, terrifying though it is. It's a tingling that he can't get rid of, the way a stranger's eyes feel on your back across a hotel bar.

Stacy's frowning now. He brings himself back around. He wanders lately. Not used to being around people anymore. Tracks back a little bit; they were talking about the symbols.

"They look like crude drawings, to most people. Which is exactly what they are. But to a certain person, if they've been exposed to the beasts, they look different." He pauses, scopes her careful non-reaction. "Which puts me in the position of trying to gauge that. How close a person's gotten."

"Sounds like a conundrum." Stacy's voice gone low and small.

"It can be, yeah." The Minister swallows, braces himself. "Thing is, once a person gets close enough, they start to get a taste for it. Start seeing the pictures shift. And then they start to follow the beasts, and it changes who they are. It's hard to tell, though, how dangerous a person has gotten. Without getting to know them, of course."

He sees it click for her—that he's trying to figure out if she's a threat.

He smiles as comforting as he can manage. "Look, hey. You saw some things, right? Things you're not sure that you know how to deal with and move on. I'm not saying I know what that's like for you. But I do know what that's like."

Stacy looks in his eyes, knows just the kind of bullshit he's spinning.

He dials it back. "I've seen them, too. You've figured that out by now."

She stares him down, waiting for him to flinch. He raises his eyebrows. She looks about to turn and run, but something clicks and her eyes soften.

"Okay then. Can you explain to me what it is you do?"

"I'm a minister."

"'After a fashion,' right. And I'm sure your real name's definitely Jim."

He smiles. "After a fashion. And, no."

She nods, ready to listen. He's getting somewhere.

He speaks slowly, seeming for the first time like a youth pastor and not a dangerously reserved traveling salesman. The more she listens to the Minister's story, the more Stacy's torn between two reactions: her gut tightens with recognition while her mind hardens against the impossibility of what she hears.

The Minister starts with a fable about the world. It sits torn between two realms, the one we see and touch and another—black slate and red skies and a seething, twisting presence at the edges of your vision. A world pushing back against this one, dragged behind unknown limbs through holes under major cities.

She waits for the key to the fable. The Minister pauses, watches as the blood drains from her face.

There's no key coming.

"Another realm? Like, what, another planet?"

"No. It's . . . not really clear. Like another world alongside this one. Under it. You can get to it if you know how to go there, and from where. Or if you're one of them."

"So, what, it's—"

The Minister shakes his head. "We don't know. That's as best we can guess, from what we've seen." He swallows. "And from a little bit of research."

Stacy wants to ask him what kind of research, but wants more to hear where he's going with this.

"Anyway," the Minister says, "it's hard to know what exactly they are." He tells her that not many people get the kind of exposure necessary to know what the beasts are, or their natural environment, and far fewer come out again in any shape to share their knowledge. Most are corrupted by them, or become obsessed with them.

He says that used to be the worst thing—to be corrupted by them, eaten away or worse. But lately some people seem to have formed an alliance—to worship the things.

The Minister and his friends have talked to enough of those people, after their encounters, to collate what they've got in common, eliminate the bullshit.

"And what else? You've talked to people, sure. But you're pretty certain."

The Minister nods. "Yeah. Pretty certain. Some people who run into them, they don't experience enough of their influence to be changed. Not completely."

He unbuttons his shirt, spreads the fabric before her instinct can turn her eyes away. The scars on his chest look like a burn at first, but then she's able to discern their edges, definite divisions and lines between.

And he's got a pendant around his neck, hung on a thin chain. It's a twisting circle of metal, strands swirling inward in impossibly intricate patterns. Against the back of the pendant, a large square of gauze shielding his chest from it.

Beneath the gauze, a flat, continuous scar.

Her eyes lose themselves trying to track the twists of the metal, taking in peripherally the damage to his torso, until he buttons up his shirt.

"So, yes. More than hearsay, I think."

"So that's what you want with me."

"What's that?"

"You want to interview me. About what I saw in Boston."

"Not quite." The Minister's hands go from his buttons to his already-fastened cuffs, then flutter and settle in his lap. "You've survived an encounter. Not many people have lately."

"Really."

"And fewer have escaped unscathed."

"I wouldn't say *unscathed*."

That smile again, understanding. "Yes, it's relative, I suppose."

She nods. It makes a certain amount of sense that the carnage in Boston wasn't standalone. Something like that wouldn't happen in a vacuum.

But the Minister didn't bring her here just to tell her a story. This is all leading somewhere.

"So. What is it that you all do? You Ministers?"

"It'll be easier if I show you."

* * *

Nathaniel runs his fingers along the inside of the window frame, over the tin foil. Presses it down again, making sure. He thought blankets might work at first, but you can't press them into the ridges of the window the same way. There's always a stream of light finding its way into the room. The foil takes care of that. It fills all the space.

He presses it down again to make sure. And to grind some comfort from the sharp ridges that don't ever quite smooth out against the pads of his middle fingers.

The time is coming, he's certain of it. The feeling's receded, true, but it's swelled and faded before, and always like an angry tide, sliding back before the biggest surges. The way his bones have rung hollow for months, the feeling of desperate bodily tension . . . this wave will be the biggest yet.

He braces himself, flops in the ragged armchair that makes up half of his living-room furniture. Takes out a dog-eared notebook and runs his finger along the thick pencil markings on the page. The hand that scraped them was light but careful—barely any ridges pressed into the paper, except in some of the darkest parts.

He spent weeks tracing those indentations with one hand, sketching what he felt on napkins using a ballpoint pen before satisfying himself that the ridges weren't the point—it was the spaces *between* the graphite. From there the process came naturally; the pen turned pretty easily into a needle.

Out in front of the house, a dull hum of tires rolling very slowly.

Nathaniel's ears have grown attuned to the silence. The glare from the headlights don't find any space to enter around the foil, but he hears what he hears. There's someone coming.

Nathaniel sets down the ballpoint-turned-tattoo-needle and reaches under the recliner for the revolver. Checks it's loaded. Cocks the hammer and watches his hand shake. He breathes until the barrel steadies. The tremors are growing, and he doesn't see what's around him as much anymore, but he levels the gun at the door.

This range, hopefully his shakes won't matter. Or that he hasn't fired a gun since he was a teenager at his uncle's farm.

The tires slow and stop. He hears a door open outside. His gut tightens. The tattoos itch furiously and pleasantly on his arms. The air tingles around him. He answers the knock at the door with the first round from the revolver.

The shot punches through at knee level. Particleboard drifting through the air in shreds. Lower than he meant but pretty well centered. No body hits the ground, though. No one comes through the door. Just gun smoke and the burnt smell of cordite and sunlight blazing through the hole into the dusty air.

Burst of glass and a window shatters. Rock clomps onto the carpet. Nathaniel pounces to his feet and glides to the door as softly as he can. Catches his mistake too late.

The front door slams open, smacks Nathaniel. His shot goes into the floor. A small man with a look like an insurance salesman drops the branch he must've used to knock.

Nathaniel reaches for his gun but the man's foot is a breath ahead of him, sends it clattering off into the kitchen.

"Clear," the man says to the door.

A woman steps in. Careful, distinct steps. Like she's walking over landmines.

She looks around. Nathaniel can tell she doesn't belong. In the searing sunlight, the man shimmers and vibrates. She holds steady in his sight at first, but the shimmer starts with her, too.

"You there," Nathaniel says. "You don't look like you're a part of this."

"You know, men keep saying that to me."

The little man looks surprised.

Nathaniel forces a smile. "I don't think your friend knows what you're talking about." He rubs his hand over his bruising face. "Go ahead and explain. It's none of my business, but I have nowhere to be."

The words coming from his mouth feel good. As he speaks, they cruise through his body and don't so much calm his shakes as soothe them into a more reasonable rhythm.

Even sprawled on the fraying carpet, blood trickling from the corner of his mouth, the posture creates what it imitates. The tattoos tingle something he takes to be agreement. The lesson's pretty obvious.

"I was saying," the man says, "it will be easier if you co-operate."

Nathaniel rides the feeling. "Fuck you, boy. You know who I am?"

The man offers a gentle smile and flicks the toe of his boot across Nathaniel's face. Nathaniel's head whips back, warm drip in the back of his throat.

He turns and spits blood on the carpet.

The man's foot is still hovering in the air. He pulls it back, sets it down.

Message received.

"What," Nathaniel's words, coming out muddy around split and swelling lips, "can I do for you, Minister?"

The girl's face flashes. She tries to hide it, isn't quite that in control.

"Oh, you didn't tell her? You don't think it's something she needs to know?"

The man looks genuinely impressed. Nathaniel hadn't been sure he was one until now. The bluff worked. Not long to wait then.

"No," the Minister says around a smile he can't or doesn't care to hold back, "not quite. I'm telling her now. You see?"

"Yes."

"Unless you'd like to help me explain?"

The pain comes in waves, rocking Nathaniel the way the Minister meant. "No. I think you've probably got it under control."

The Minister pulls the black chalk from his inside jacket pocket. He drags it along the wall and sets Nathaniel's mind to screaming.

Stacy braces herself against the doorframe. Lets the horror inside the dank little house play out. Watches it all, thinking she'll have to look away at some point, that she won't be able to take any more.

She can, though, and does. Even feels, against the twisting objection in her stomach, her eyes peeling themselves open. To take more of it in.

Old Minister Jim has a way about him. The second he touches that thin, midnight-black stick of chalk to the wall, the man on the floor starts writhing around like the Minister's twisting in thumbscrews. By the time he gets the shifting narrow symbol sketched out, the man's not drawing enough breath to scream.

His face, though. His face is screaming.

The minister goes methodically wall to wall and draws one on each of them. They're all different, and the man's face shifts with each. Like he feels them as distinct but perfectly complementary forms of torture.

By the time the Minster bends down to retrieve the stick from the floor, Stacy's already edging toward the notebook on the recliner. Looking at how it's full of sketches, at how they're the inverse of those on the wall—lines flipped with space and upside-down.

The man's muscles contract and his screams get lost further down his throat. Stacy puts her palm up against the door that she never thought to close. She keeps it there until the Minister steps toward Nathaniel and does what he was always going to do—with his hands, not a knife or a gun—and she stands there until he's wiped his hands off on the bathroom towel, which he carries with him back to the door. She follows him out across the front yard and into the car.

She sits in silence as long as she can take it. It's a long time.

Finally, turning onto some numbered stretch of highway she doesn't recognize, she finally lets some air over her vocal cords. "What the fuck."

Jim looks over, like he hasn't been waiting for her talk. "Hmm?"

"The fuck. Was that?"

"What do you think? Look familiar, any of it?"

"I've seen murder before."

Though not a pair of thumbs prying gore out of a set of eyeballs. No screaming. Just a wide mouth filling with blood runoff it couldn't spit out.

Minister Jim's face darkens. "Not quite murder, no."

Stacy leans into the opening. "You seem to think that we know each other well enough that I'm going to watch you turn some guy into a puddle of fucking—"

"Fair enough, but are you really gonna play the innocent card? You're gonna say you don't know why he had to die, why I wanted you to come along?"

The opening was more of a cul-de-sac. "I may have an idea."

Minister Jim slides over the white line into the right lane and clicks the signal to get onto some junction, some other highway. Stacy doesn't even know what direction they're heading anymore.

"Well then maybe you understand that I'm the only friend you've got right now," the Minister says.

"You make it sound like you're not dragging me into something. Like, say, the bloodiest room I've ever seen. And I've yet to hear what it is I have to gain from you."

"Or what I have to gain from you, hmm? You think Boston just fades into the past? That the things you saw don't have tails on them?"

Stacy doesn't have anything. She did think that. She thought that pretty hard.

"So, as we were saying." The Minister runs his hands over the steering wheel. "Did what I did in the house remind you of anything?"

"I think I've seen similar drawing somewhere, yeah."

"But you don't remember where."

"Not quite." Stacy frowns. "I mean, it happened fast, but no, I think I'd remember." She looks to the Minister. "Is that something you can fix?"

The Minister shakes his head. "That's an effect you'll have to live with." His face doesn't move, but something in the air shifts. "You probably won't get used to it."

The decision Stacy's suspected she has to make seems to have already been made, without her input. Nathaniel was involved, *some*how, and closer to her than she would have thought. There are more of them than she would have thought.

And the Minister doesn't seem to like people who've gotten close to the action. Stacy allows herself to reconsider the obvious possibility that he's here to kill her.

It seems elaborate, though. He wouldn't bring her to the site of a killing if he was planning on making hers next.

Still, there's no way to get a read on his thoughts. His face doesn't seem to correlate with what he's thinking, and he's got a mean streak she wouldn't have read from his dour look.

"So what do you want with me?"

The Minister smiles. "Isn't it obvious?"

It is, but she doesn't want to say it.

He arrives at her door, knows more than she does but doesn't want to show it, and then takes her to the scene of a killing.

He's showing her what he's about, what he does.

This is a recruitment.

But he doesn't seem to have any problem with cutting down people who got to close to what he refers to as "the beasts." That Nathaniel in the little house, he didn't get the same pitch she did, if that's what it's been.

And Minister Jim, he's watching this happen on her face without seeming to look away from the road. Which makes her think she's not the first he's approached.

"So then," she says, tiring of the back-and-forth, "you travel around and, what? Not-murder people?"

"Not murder, no." The Minister frowns. "Word we use is *purge*, usually. Or *cleanse*, or *banish*. Because it's not just about the person, their heart stopping."

"That action with the chalk."

"Yeah."

The way the shapes seemed to cut into the man, tear something loose in him.

The Minister said that those who could be affected by that are those who'd been exposed. And if he was, or still is, unsure what to do with her . . .

"That's why you kept yourself standing against that wall? And me in the doorway?"

The Minister's eyebrows climb. "Yes. They would have affected us, too. Not the same way. It matters who's writing them and why, and who they're writing them at, but the effect is there anyway."

Meaning the Minister's been exposed to the beasts. Stacy had somehow not guessed that.

She presses her lips together, tries not to let it get her down—the feeling of being a step or two behind, finding out what she needs to know far too late for it to influence what she's already done. It's coming back. And it feels a lot like Boston.

"So how did they get to you, Minister Jim?"

He cocks his head over to her, back to the road.

"How did you get exposed?"

He smiles, more at himself than at her, and shakes his head. "Long time ago. Time doesn't work the same way anymore for me, but I was exposed a long time ago."

Which isn't an answer to her question.

But it isn't nothing, either.

CHAPTER TWENTY

The Minister's house hums with sound. Stacy hovers in the doorway, reluctant to walk through to the little dining room. Radios trickle out sound in streams that come together to form a fluid wall, one with something on the other side of it.

Minister Jim looks like he knows what she's thinking, steps into the room backward. Letting her come in on her own. It takes her a second and more than a couple deep breaths, but she does. Closes the door behind her.

What's waiting for her, not on the other side of the sound wall like she'd thought but inside it, enveloped by it, is the put-together version of Nathaniel's place. The windows are covered, but by pinned-up blankets instead of tin foil. On the ledges this side of the makeshift blackout curtains, a couple radios in the corners of a five-sided star. The other points stand on an end table and an unvarnished nightstand, a long desk along the far wall covered in loose papers.

Sound bleeds out, none of the radios synched but all the same volume, syllables seeping into one another before Stacy can track any sentence longer than a couple words. She walks across the room and it's perfectly calibrated. No one radio ever predominates. There's always at least two in range.

Stacy frowns. Looks to Minister Jim. He smiles and nods, but Stacy's not sure about what. The sound comes through. The Minister says something, but it's just another layer of noise, shifting the pattern of sound. He's talking in his voice, but forcing it down into a lower register, from the chest. The radios are his voice, too. Five different recordings, saying different things at the same time. She can't make out his speech over the radios

"What in the world?" Stacy tries to get follow what they're saying with no success. "They're you."

"Yes." Voice clicking back up to normal range.

"What . . . what are you talking about?"

Minister Jim shrugs. "Some things. Some of them are important, some aren't. Initially I tried to keep the words themselves impersonal, but you know, you eventually run out of innocuous things to say if you want to keep talking and not repeat yourself."

"Not repeat yourself?"

"You could, but it's easier if you don't."

"So all the radios are, for sure, saying different things, yeah? So you don't have to check they won't synch up."

The Minister nods, smile shifting from encouraging to pleased. "Yes, exactly."

"What's it for?"

"It's to keep me from being heard."

It's funny, at first, because as long as he keeps speaking normally like this, she can hear him fine, but she realizes that's not what he's talking about.

"This has to do with the Boston monsters."

"Not just Boston. But yes, the way the sound works, it keeps the beasts from picking up on . . . well, that depends who you ask. The thoughts of people on their radar. Who they've touched."

The room is starting to look a little less like a commando base and a little more like a bunker.

"There was a man in Boston," the Minister goes on, looking at the floorboards, "who had a system like this. It worked, too."

"He's still alive?"

The Minister shakes his head. "But it wasn't because his system didn't work. Just, he used radio. Never music—music doesn't work, for some reason—but talk radio, sportscasts, that kind of thing. He had to keep adjusting the dials, rechecking the volume for changes, shifting his little radios around."

"This guy, he was someone you knew?"

"I never met him, no." Minister Jim says it kind of quiet, like there's more to it.

Stacy's starting to get used to that.

The Minister gets them a motel room for the night and sleeps on the couch. Stacy lies atop the bedding, convinced she won't be able to sleep. Brief flash of darkness and then the sun is up, the Minister shaking her awake.

"What time is it?"

"Almost noon. Time to go."

The Minister has already paid for the room. Into the car again, on the road. Stacy's back aches against the passenger seat. She hasn't had time to stretch out the stiffness from their driving yesterday.

The Minister tells her they're going to a site he's been meaning to visit, that might help explain things to her. He seems unhurried and not particularly intent on elaborating, so Stacy lets it ride, watches the landscape. The country fades, and the beginnings of habitation start to filter in.

"So, less the middle of nowhere this time?"

The Minister nods. "They set up under cities, mostly."

"That last guy was in the sticks, though. Nathaniel?"

"Not . . . yes, some of the touched drift as far as they can. Which isn't often far. But the beasts themselves, where they come through, it's under cities, usually."

"Huh. More people that way, I guess. Food or fuel or . . . whatever."

"As far as we can tell, it's probably 'whatever,' but yes. They need large numbers of people and some kind of decay."

"Gotcha." Stacy frowns at the dash, running through how many places that could describe, the scale of things. "That doesn't really narrow it down."

"No. No, it doesn't."

She should be wondering about Nathaniel, about how exactly the Minster knew he was there and what he had planned, but the radio spread at the Minister's base—*home* wouldn't be quite right—is playing on a loop in her mind.

There's something else to them. If he wants her to think that the reason he's using his own voice for the tapes is consistency, that's fine. But he could have used anything else— talk radio or books on tape or recordings of old baseball games. There'd be no chance of the kind of overlap he says he wants to avoid.

Minister Jim flicks the turn signal. It clicks for a second, two, three, the sound leading her back to this car in time for a wide left into a suburban outpost. Stacy looks around. She can't be seeing it right. Must have dozed off and missed the transition into town. But no, behind them is the same nothing road; ahead of them, the street curves around itself before straightening into a clearer view of houses looming large and dense. The kind of development you get on the outskirts of a small town—the illusion of old ranch homes, the developmental convenience of packing them all in on top of each other.

"This doesn't seem like your usual surrounds."

"'Surrounds.'" Minister Jim smiles, takes a minute to taste the word. "But no. I suppose not."

He drives them around the back of the subdivision, to a road curving along a green belt, houses on only one side. They get out.

"Wait." Stacy looks behind her, at houses for millionaires who never came; ahead at the hill they're heading toward. "What's out here?"

"I'd imagine you have a guess."

"Thought it'd be one of the spots we talked about."

Minister Jim nods.

"I thought they tended toward populated places. Busy places. This is an empty neighborhood."

Minister Jim points to the top of the hill. Stacy waits for him to start up and follows. The trees thin as they ascend, until they reach the bare top of a little hill with a view of a stream running down toward them.

Stacy looks from the stream to the Minister. There's nothing special about the water. The plants are just plants, but upstream there's a thin white line of smoke rising, drifting on the wind. Stacy makes out the low outline of an old industrial center in the distance.

The buildings under the steam trail fade fast. The factory is on the edge of the industrial sector, with the green belt dividing it from the houses. Probably a winding road running from there to here, sufficient trees to form a barrier for the illusion that the neighborhood is far from all that dirt and noise.

It irritates Stacy that the trick worked on her. "So we're close to a populated area, sure. But they're not *under* it. They're not living in it."

"Look a little closer." Minister Jim tramps down to the shore, levels his eyes upstream. "The plants up there, they're still running. Manufacturing something. Paper, steel." He shrugs, humble-pastor look on his face so sudden it cuts. "Or something."

"Not really your area, I guess. Somewhat less than ecclesiastical."

"Somewhat. But the plant produces runoff. The runoff goes, in theory, to a processing plant on the other side of town. There, any dangerous byproducts of the manufacturing process are removed, and clean water is introduced back into the city's water supply."

"And in reality?"

"In reality, the absolute first thing to go when the budget gets cut is the people who check . . . well, who check pretty much anything. So the water runs from the plant down this creek, carrying whatever it's got in it when there's factory runoff."

"Which is?"

"Unimportant. Officially, nothing harmful."

"I bet there's a piece of paper in city hall that swears it's all safe."

"Actually, yes. Exactly."

Stacy looks up the creek, back to him. He's wearing this expression like he's waiting for her to catch on to what he's suggesting. Like a high school teacher with a leading question.

"The runoff comes through *here*. It looks like there aren't any people here, but—" he scuffs some bushes and twigs to the side, shows the oily scum collecting in the water underneath "—really, this is the center of the town. Or a part of it."

"Okay." Stacy's voice drops in a way she doesn't like. "They could be nearby."

Minister Jim holds her eyes. "More than that, yeah."

Stacy's gut clenches. She follows him down along the riverside toward a cavern invisible from the ridge. The lip of the cavern is only a foot or two down from the ridge, but it's set in at a slant, grass and vines growing over it. Completely undetectable, if you don't know what you're looking for. Minister Jim walks right to it, though, and pulls the foliage back.

"So you've been here before?"

"No."

For a moment Stacy thinks he wants her to go in first, but then he dips his head and disappears. The vines fall into place behind him. Stacy grabs them and pulls until they tear. She can think of nothing worse right now than getting stranded in some subterranean pit with plants blocking the light, hiding the exit. She throws the fistful of greenery into the river and follows.

She has to crouch to fit in the space, but it's far larger than she expected from the gentle slope of the riverside. There's a smell, something reminiscent of a factory—of the paper mill she lived in with her father after the divorce. Stiff metallic tang underlying a wet, organic stench.

She stops breathing without noticing it, has to force her lungs to inflate, suck that air down into her chest.

Minister Jim crouches and pulls a penlight from his pocket. He clicks it on, holding it close enough to the dirt wall of the cavern that she can't see what it illuminates, just a tight circle of light. She strains but gets no detail.

His sigh is quick, excited. "Oh. Oh, we've got something here."

Stacy's curiosity burns off in an instant. She does not want to see.

Minister Jim pulls the flashlight back. The circle widens, glistening off of something that's not dirt. Stacy can't track what she's seeing at first. When she does, she sucks in air, making a noise she immediately regrets. The flashlight shows a wall coated in a thick layer of something wet, moving.

"Fuck."

She turns toward the exit. The wavering of the beam warns her that Minister Jim is coming to stop her. She doesn't fight him.

"What the fuck? Why did you—"

"Bring you here? Come, look."

She follows him back to the wall, noting for the first time the way her feet squish into the ground. She hadn't thought about it before, figured it was just dirt, but now her attention is focused on surfaces and she suspects that the substance is on the floor, too.

She can't bear to look at it, already wants to try and run again. It's only separated from her skin by a layer of sneaker rubber and an odor-eating insole.

Minister Jim guides her to the wall, raises the flashlight again. The coating moves, accelerates under the light. Stacy stares at it. It's thick and green, oozing something between its nodes that doesn't reflect enough of the light to describe a color. It shines, though.

"It's really something when you see it, isn't it?"

"What *is* it?"

"You've seen it before, I think."

Stacy steadies herself. She's pretty sure she hasn't.

"It follows a certain kind of creature around. Where they make themselves a more or less permanent home. When they settle in and their presence is felt for a long time, the mold starts to spread."

It does look like mold. Except no mold she's ever seen moves like that—like flayed skin under a gently oscillating fan.

"And, I think, where the mold goes, it makes it easier for the beasts to go. For the . . . for the *tentacles* to slither their way in and pollute our world. That's why it starts so often with violence; they have to establish a foothold, so to speak, in our sewers, in our gutters and our forgotten places. Once they have, though—and I think this first happened a long time ago—the mold keeps their place for them."

"Like a welcome mat." Stacy speaks without really processing the words.

Minister Jim smiles at the joke she didn't mean to make.

"So, if there's this mold here . . ." Stacy reaches out to touch it, catches herself. Minister Jim doesn't seem concerned. She braces herself and runs a finger along its surface. It feels dry, powdery, but as she rubs it between her fingers it grows sticky and flakes drift off.

The stuff is a contradiction. Another impossibility, presaging all the other impossibilities.

"Or whatever it is. If it's here, that means they're nearby."

Minister Jim nods. "And that they've been here for a while."

"And that means someone's come into contact with them. Like they need somebody, to pull them across?"

"No. It means it's more likely that someone's been touched by them. They start bleeding over on their own, though usually not this far west. But things have been changing. Either way, the longer they're in a place, the more likely some unfortunate soul might stumble onto them. So, we're here to find out."

We're. The word makes Stacy's skin crawl. "And how did *we* know they were here? Some of your friends? Like a network?"

"More of a loose association. And no, none of us have seen this before."

"Then . . .?"

"We do have some tools at our disposal."

Minister Jim clomps down the passage without another word. The procedures he talks about, the tools and the association and the rituals and the knowledge, would, from another source, seem like the self-serving ravings of some solipsistic madness looking for a second mind to draw into its influence. From Minister Jim, though, Stacy doesn't have that reaction. They seem more like religious mysteries, some secret and terrible knowledge that she can't have access to until she's committed to them.

It makes sense, if the Ministers are looking to keep themselves a secret force. But it makes her decision uninformed, too.

She wonders what Nathaniel would have decided, if he'd had the same pitch.

But he seemed to know about them, too, so maybe they *had* approached him and he said no. In that case, there's even less of a decision to make.

"You're somewhere else," Minister Jim says.

She doesn't know how long he's been watching her. "Trying to fit the pieces together."

"Anything I can help with?"

Stacy shrugs. "What else is here?"

Minister Jim swings the light forward. "You're not going to like it." Then, quieter: "I certainly don't."

The Minister has never seen anything quite like it. There has been any number of subterranean pits discovered, from sewer grates, to holes unearthed by construction sites, to one abandoned building in what used to be industrial suburbs. But the cavern they're standing in, where he would expect to see what they came here to see, empties into a narrower channel, a tunnel little more than a shoulder's-width for a large man. The Minister is not a large man, but the cramped passage makes him anxious.

He rarely gets anxious anymore, logs the feeling away to interpret later.

He's reacting partially to the size of the tunnel, but also to what's growing on it. The demon mold, thicker than anywhere else, crowds the passageway from all sides.

They'll have to squish and crawl their way through the foul stuff if they are to see what's on the other side.

And they have to see it. The Minister has responsibilities, and he's going to keep them.

Stacy's staring at him. He can feel it, but he's not going to look her way. He's having a difficult enough time getting himself ready for it without getting into a conversation.

He's not going to ask her to go first, but he does expect her to follow him. She's come with him this far. It hurts a little, to admit to himself that he's gotten his hopes up.

He crouches, thrusts his hands into the tunnel. Follows with his head, shoulders. The rank smell of spores bursting, leaking their unholy fluid all over him—wet, burning stench, rot and fire. The tunnel swallows him. Forcing his torso in, then his legs, he has the feeling that the fungus is pulling him in as much as he's pushing. It gives under his weight, the pressure of his wriggling, and slurps closed behind him. He's ensconced in the very guts of the enemy now, and for an endless moment he feels like he's being digested.

His feet come in and he's swimming. He pulls himself along in a savage breaststroke, hands never quite touching rock. The mold gives up to a point, then flattens hard and slick before his hands can puncture it.

The Minister's heart races like it hasn't in years. He opens his mouth to scream, chokes on a viscous flood of mold and slime.

His fingers break through first. He forces his hands through, briefly terrified that he won't be able to get leverage and will suffocate this close to the other side, but he finds the edges of the exit hole and pulls as hard as he ever has. He inches forward and bursts through with a vulgar slurp, crashing to bare rock.

He takes a halting breath. Shoves it out and sucks in another, feeling like the oxygen isn't getting through.

A few more breaths come and go before he realizes that he's hyperventilating, that this is how people start to lose their grip.

He inhales again and holds. Forces himself to count a slow ten before letting it out.

Blood surges through his temples and sound returns. Slime turns to ash between his teeth and he spits, rolls over on his stomach, spits again. His throat jumps into his mouth and he retches, sprays chunky gray bile onto the rock floor. He's still sputtering when Stacy breaks through the wall of mold and plops next to him.

She recovers faster. Much faster—they find their feet at the same time.

They stand next to each other, shaking off the gray second skin of dried ooze. It flakes off in huge chunks that waft into dust before they land. The two of them emerge like flesh statues from a block of clay.

The Minister stares at her. She breathes through clenched teeth, vibrating with tension, but doesn't seem overly fazed by the experience. He scouts the new room as best he can, blinking against the slime stringing from his eyelids.

It's a small pit, not unlike the cave they initially entered, but the rock ground is bare, the walls dirt. If the Minister stood on his toes and reached his hands up, he'd touch the ceiling with his elbows bent.

A body sits curled into itself along the far wall, directly opposite the hole they crawled through.

The Minister regards the body hesitantly. Turns and checks the passageway. The mold has expanded, blocking the exit entirely. No marks remains of their pressing through, and the green filth glints in the sparse light.

The light. By rights, the little cavern should be completely dark. Nothing in the room explains its visibility until Stacy touches his arm and points at the ceiling.

Light filters through little holes. They aren't far underground then, despite the incline they had to climb over—directly over this room, the Minister estimates—and how the crawl felt as if they were going deep down. Directions betray them, and the Minister briefly reels with disorientation.

"That's something, at least," Stacy says.

"We can see."

"Sure, that, but I don't want to go crawling through that shit again. We can break through the ground, crawl out that way."

That all depends, but the Minister doesn't say so. He creeps toward the body. It's perfectly still, hasn't shown any sign of awareness of their intrusion, or indeed of even containing a person, but that doesn't prove anything. His footsteps are light but nonetheless echo in the tiny space. The figure is dressed in loose denim—worn jeans and a newish jacket, black socks and work boots. Matted hair that could have been any color at all, once, but is now coated so thoroughly with dirt and the ashen leavings of the fungus that it's impossible to tell.

Stacy's right, though. Much as the Minister doesn't want to disturb the ground, open this place to the air, to anyone walking through the woods, this person had crawled in here the same as they had and gotten trapped. The light filtering though the ceiling would have provided a way out, had they seen it.

He presses the figure's forehead. It resists at first then rolls back all at once. Yellow eyes gape at the ceiling, blackened around the edges where they've rotted away. The throat looks strained, tendons locked in place with some misplaced perimortem effort. Dirt clumps to a light stubble on its cheeks, the only sign the body was a man.

This certainly looks like the beasts claimed him. Why, then, is there no sign of them inside this room? Why has this body not been claimed, made to jerk along on the impulses of the tendril that would have done it?

He rolls the head to the side and finds his answer: a long, jagged tear in the base of the skull. He calls Stacy's attention to it. It looks as if someone took a trowel or blunt shovel to it.

"Do you know what that is?"

"Somebody killed him. I don't know, with some kind of improvised weapon, looks like. Smashed his skull with whatever was handy."

The Minister shakes his head. "It's not something pushed *into* the skull. Look at the skin, how it's sticking up? This was something pulled *out*."

Stacy stares at the wound. "What is it, then?"

The Minister's surprised. If she got through the Boston disaster without seeing what happened to this man, then she's had an uncommon experience indeed. But then, he's heard rumors of hallucinations, of people claimed by the beasts marching along the streets, even attacking. It would seem a lot about Boston was uncommon.

He holds his hand out, wiggles his fingers to indicate the beast's hairy limbs. It's perhaps superstitious, but he's loath to mention them specifically. As far as they can tell, they feed on the ways in which people signify, make meaning. Their influence materializes prayer and makes weapons of symbols. Who's to say that spoken words couldn't work the same way?

Stacy nods at his fingers. He sets them on the dead man's skin, just below the edge of the wound. Checks if Stacy is following; the tentacle inserted itself into the man's head. She frowns, waiting to see where he goes with this.

"So then the man *pulls*—" yanking his hand away "—and frees himself. Kills himself, too."

Stacy's shocked. Clearly she didn't know how people were taken. "And if he hadn't?"

The Minister shakes his head. "Not here. This man, though, he died heroically." He looks around for a lighter, something they might try to burn his body with, comes up with nothing. "It's a shame to leave his body here with . . . with them."

"They why don't we—"

"Do you want to try to explain to some cop what happened to him? How we knew where to look for the body?"

"I don't *know* how we knew where to look. But no, I suppose I don't."

"Okay." The Minister crouches down, laces his fingers together. "Let me give you a boost, then you try and pull me up after you."

Stacy gets set fast, well past ready to get out of here. The Minister has to agree. She plants a foot on his hands and he pushes her up. Her hands hit the dirt, don't go through. She falls off his hands, reels back into the rock wall. Gasps when she sees how close she came to the moldy tunnel and runs back to him. He barely gets his hands set in time to lift her.

Her hands punch through the dirt this time, find enough traction to haul herself up, above the surface.

The Minister waits. No voices follow, no one surprised to see a woman hauling herself up from the earth. He was half convinced that someone would be waiting, would make the situation worse with questions.

Stacy's hands appear flecked with wholesome dirt, not the adulterated, bastardized stuff down here, and the Minister seizes them with an eagerness that embarrasses him.

She pulls him up. It's a struggle, but only a bit. Sprawled on the ground, looking at Stacy in the sunlight, he lets slip a boyish smile. Feels it on his face like a welcome if suspicious visitor.

They tramp their way back to the car. He opens the driver's side door and hesitates. Doesn't feel like driving. It's a mistake, this early, but he holds it open and steps aside to let her drive, if she wants.

She does.

They pull away. She gets them out of the subdivision and he tells her which way to turn.

"I can't believe what we just saw."

"Yes?"

"I mean, sure, it's a lot like . . . it's a lot like Gutter Street."

The Minister doesn't recognize the name, but he knows what she saw there.

"God, how many of those places are there?"

"It's hard to say. Until recently, there were only a few of these sites off the east coast. We don't know why. We've sent people to as many parts of the world as we can, but the sense of them that we have always fades. If they're out there, we can't find them. It's like there's a fissure, here, between the worlds."

"'Until recently?'"

The Minister feels his face go grim. "Yes. I just came from Los Angeles. There was a situation there."

"You resolved it."

The Minister detects a note of revulsion, ignores it. "Of course."

"And that situation. Same kind as with Nathaniel?"

"Very nearly. Much more developed." The Minister swallows. "And more than one. A group has formed. Groups form, sometimes. I think that maybe this is the reason for the new developments. Or the new situation encourages them. It's hard to say. But we're starting to get groups, where in the past we only had to contend with individuals."

A long silence.

Some twenty highway exits later, Stacy says: "This organization of yours. I think I'd like to know more about it."

"Yes. You will."

Mercifully, she lets it stand at that. The purpose of this little trip is to show her what they do. It's the first step to showing her who they are. The Ministry.

To making her one of them.

CHAPTER TWENTY-ONE

Elijah stirs the pot. He's been spending time in the kitchen lately. A surprising development for him, but the curry in front of him rewards specificity, attention to detail. Deliberate action, receptive to new developments, but not too hasty. The slow, methodical movements he's grown to savor express themselves best in the kitchen.

He lays a fish filet on the cutting board, smooths it down with his hand. Places the knife a couple times, finding the length he wants to cut, and then drives the knife down and forward, down and forward. Dissecting the fish into long, thin strips.

It's perfect control. None of the dangling problems that have become so commonplace for them—no mysterious presences or uncertain outcomes.

Still, he feels how hard he drives the knife through the flesh, into the board. It's a channel for the violence that still vibrates through his bones, calls for his attention.

There was a moment, the other day, when a well-dressed man came up to the door of the trailer. Elijah tensed. Armed himself with the baseball bat from their bedroom doorway and waited. Nervous and flashing-back, but a little relieved. A little grateful to slip back into the life-or-death frenzy of six months ago.

The man was distributing religious literature. He rang the bell, rang it again, and tucked the pamphlet into the door handle so that they'd see it when they came home.

When Elijah realized what was happening, he relaxed. But he was a little disappointed, too.

Lorelei's out. He's taken to having dinner ready when she comes home. There's comfort in cooking for your partner. It's tricky with the schedule she's keeping, adapting her life to the people she's tracking down and interviewing, trying to get a lead on Slim's network. She's convinced Slim had a network, or that there are more people like him, and she's determined to take the fight to them before they can find their trailer.

Elijah wonders why these people would necessarily come for them. He's asked her more than once.

Her answers vary, but usually she mentions the people she met in Boston, the way they'd been keeping themselves safe for fifteen years, but eventually the things came for them. Like they'd been trying to all that time, and finally found a way to break through.

She's been pouring over the notebook she got there, finding answers in between the lines. She says the things feed on how people make meaning by imbedding it in symbols. That their development was tied into humanity's, that most likely they can't live without us. That this means Alan had to record his notes in something approaching code, so the things—"beasts," he called them—wouldn't key into his records and adjust their plans accordingly.

And so they'll pursue them, forever, to make sure they maintain their influence, secure their source of materials. Alan knew that, but couldn't convince his friends.

Elijah has to admit the idea has a certain resonance. But there are a few leaps built in that he's not quite ready to make. Nothing's bothered them since they came to Nebraska, for instance.

And so he makes this fish curry. Most days it's hard to know when Lorelei will be home, so slow-cooking dishes are key. He's struck on a coconut milk recipe that he can simmer forever, more or less, and will still be palatable whenever she comes in.

He stirs the sauce fast and shallow for emulsion and drops the fish in.

The internet helps with this. The service is still registered with the trailer's original owner. The company doesn't seem inclined to ask as long as the money comes in on time. It keeps him from having to brave the public library for research purposes. Crowds were never his thing. His social anxiety didn't used to terrify him, didn't used to make him not want to leave the house. He knows what did that. It's started to feel like he and the things were made for each other. Like they just brought out the traits of his that were waiting in the wings all along, for just the right situation, just the right stimulus to let them blossom and take over.

He wishes Lorelei would get home soon.

The curry smells fantastic. He holds off, though. Turns on the television. Cycles through but doesn't want to watch anything.

The front door finally opens. Lorelei climbs the steps and slams it behind her. "Hey, big day."

Elijah looks at her over the edge of the recliner. "Yeah?" Not really wanting to know.

"Yeah." She stops next to the stove. "Shit, smells good. Anyway," she says, coming into the living room and sitting on the couch, "I met this guy who's a part of this group, right? A bunch of kids who knew each other from the hard-core scene in Wisconsin. They've started sort of a gang."

"You want to join a gang?"

"No. Oh, goddammit, no, but are you listening? There's this group of kids, and they're—I swear to god, they're do-ing what Slim did."

"Then why would we ever get involved with them?"

She gets up from the couch, springs squeaking. Walks to the kitchen, pours herself a stiff one from the bottle in the cabinet and a slug for Elijah. Comes back to the living room.

He thinks this is probably not a great thing, but he's will-ing to hear her out. "Why the hell are we still drinking this stuff?"

"It's perfectly serviceable," Lorelei says, something he's said so often over the years.

"How much money do we have in that bag?"

She shrugs. Doesn't have to say, but Elijah wouldn't like it if they switched to some top-shelf brand, anyway. "Look. Eli. We need to take a trip."

Elijah tries his best not to hear that. "I thought we were going to settle here for a bit."

"Eli."

"You know, lie low, let the shit outside burn itself off."

"Do you think that's really happening out there?"

"I don't know. You tell me."

She sighs. Drains her glass. Looks at it maybe a little dis-gustedly. "I need you with me. I need to you to come."

303

He's known it was coming. Here, on the brink, the moment after the moment where he decided it was time to follow her where she thinks they need to go, he thinks maybe all his resistance was just waiting for her to push the idea hard enough. "Where are we going?"

"Wisconsin."

He nods. It won't take him long to pack.

Lorelei drives, of course. She considers having gotten Elijah out of the trailer to be a minor if long-overdue miracle. He sits in the passenger seat, hair blowing around, and stares at the horizon like it's a drunk about to swing at him. He hasn't said a word since they left.

She's okay with that. She understands, up to a point.

This last month, though, his apparent agoraphobia has gotten almost aggressive, like he's proving something by rooting himself to that couch.

The sun arcs around the dark side of the earth and peeks up over the horizon again. Finally he turns to her. "What's in Wisconsin?"

"This group I mentioned. They're doing something like Slim did, but they've got their own fucked little approach. And there's more than one of them."

She fills him in on what she heard, about the group around this Carter guy, his tattoos. It's not a new thing for a crew of scene kids, especially scene kids with whatever drug connections they're surely disproportionately proud of, to have matching tattoos.

What's different is *how* matching the tattoos are, and when they show up.

"So, what, you think the tattoos are the same thing as Slim was doing?"

"I think that they're after the same shit, yeah. But how Slim lost it, started hunting *every*-fucking-body, these guys have gotten organized. They're putting it in the tattoos. What he carved into his arms. They're putting it in ink."

"How the fuck did you find this out?"

More than a small note of appreciation in there, she's glad to hear. "I've made a couple of connections, you know? Met a few people."

He lets it go.

"Anyway. I've got it from a couple people that this Carter and his people—Carter's Commandoes, if you can believe that—are planning something big."

"What's that?"

"Depends. Guy thinks it's a big score. Adderall, he said. There's a few colleges around there."

Elijah rolls his forehead along the window. "But you don't think so."

"I don't. I think if there's trafficking, that's their business, but that probably isn't what they're all about anymore. I think—based on the tattoos—that they've got some other shit going. That they're going to do what Slim thought he was going to do."

Elijah sits up straighter, sighs. Stares ahead, for once, at the road instead of the fields. He nods. "Well. Fuck it."

It's not much agreement, but it's what Lorelei needed. If he'd given her some head-in-the-sand answer, if he'd refused to deal with the information she's been gathering for months, something permanent might have snapped in her head.

She twists her hands on the wheel. Nothing feels right except moving forward. The plan after that is a bit nebulous. She's got the tools she's been working on in the trunk, though she hasn't been able to get that black paste the notes talk about.

She's pretty sure she knows what it is, though, and will have a chance soon to get some.

Viv strips her jacket off, flips the sweat from her hair in an arc. The band's not done brutalizing their instruments yet, but Maria doesn't mind following her to the bar in back. The boys on stage have feedback in lieu of a second guitarist and an apparent contract with the ibuprofen industry.

Viv raises two fingers to the bartender, jogs them between herself and Maria. "Weird night, huh?"

"Yeah." Maria looks back to the floor, to the slam dancing bleeding out of the pit and into the crowd. "Band fucking blows."

"Not what I meant."

"I know."

Maria does. A better band might help, but the evening had an edge from the jump. Someone's gonna bleed and maybe it won't be inside the venue; maybe it will.

Two vodka tonics appear in front of Viv. She slides one to Maria. Maria looks at it, at Viv.

Viv shrugs. "Hey, fucking free drink, right?"

Maria tries to make nice with the gift but quinine's always turned her stomach. She slides it over next to Viv's and waves for a beer.

Viv shrugs and gets rid of her drink faster, plops the second one in the dry cup, where it sits crookedly atop the ice.

Maria's beer comes and a pause between songs inspires false optimism. Feedback squeal and a guitar-pick slide and someone leaps off an amplifier stack, lands a beat before on-time. Stumbles back into the drum riser and the rest of the band launches into it.

Viv chuckles, leans back, elbows on the bar. "Tell you what, the kids are kinda growing on me."

"Graceful."

"A certain charm, right?"

They look around and Maria thinks she sees something pass behind Viv's eyes, a skepticism or a reaching. Like maybe they don't belong here anymore. Places like this. Then a screech from the guitar's cord coming unplugged cracks the moment. Viv covers her mouth and giggles, braces her head against Maria's shoulder.

"Fucksake, man," Viv says. "Let's get out of here already."

Maria nods and Viv starts darting her head around, looking for Mitch. Maria expects him to be caught up in the proceedings, but Viv's eyes click on something. Maria turns, sees Mitch coming up behind her.

Mitch leans on the bar with no shortage of theater. "You see that?"

Viv wraps her arm around his. "Shitty band?"

"No, the crowd. See who's here?"

Maria shakes her head. "Haven't seen anybody I know."

"That Buddy kid. Throwing himself around, making himself known. Posing around the fringes, you know. Got some of his friends with him."

Viv stiffens against Mitch. Maria lets them have their concerns. Buddy's not the threat they think he is. She knew him back home.

Viv goes to the bar for their tabs. The bartender shows up quick for her, looks a touch crestfallen when she cuts her hand across her throat—the universal signal. They sign and stow their cards, flatten themselves against the bar and push around the back, toward the door.

Night air carves the sweat off their skin. Viv skips ahead a step and turns to pull Mitch after her, jacket in her other hand, sweeping the parking lot. They lean like they're being pushed by a strong wind, glowing yellow as they slip in range of a streetlight.

The sweatshirt meets them at the edge of the light. Body materializing from the shadows around it. Hand flashing out, fast, for the jacket Viv's not wearing—finger through the scissor dip in her tee shirt.

Viv starts. The pull on her shirt jerks her down toward the asphalt. She gets her footing, but the collar's below her arm now, throws off her balance when she tries to stand back up.

Mitch darts past Maria, drops his shoulder to hit the guy in the stomach. Air whooshes out of him but he doesn't fall. Just doubles over in place and then comes down atop Mitch. Hand flies out to catch Viv's face. Her shoulder finds the ground and a brand new angle.

Maria gets her knife out of her pocket and steps forward, butterflies it open. Crackle of blue from the man's outstretched hand and Maria's muscles seize and her breath catches and her vision goes white.

Squeal of tires. White van in the side of Maria's vision.

Mitch's fists swing wildly until one finds a face. The man tries to step back, but slumped over Mitch's body as he is, he just tips over sideways. Scuttles back and finds his feet, moves right back in.

Viv meets him halfway but he's got something new in his hand and she trips back. Fingers pressed to her throat, blood spurting between them.

Maria can't quite move but blinks, and again. Sees Viv bleeding.

The van's door scrapes open.

Mitch pivots to look. Mistake.

"Fucking shit, man." Speaker unseen. "Christ, we said to—"

The sweatshirt man shouts vowels and drives a knee into Mitch's chest. "Shut up. Help."

Footsteps from the van and a second pair of hands helps the man drag Mitch inside. The door slides shut, and before Maria's caught up she hears the squeal of tires leave her and a very silent Viv in the parking lot.

She glances at the van as it peels out onto the street. Repeats the license number to herself. Knows it won't help.

#

Mitch blinks himself cogent, expecting a parking lot. Gets the inside of a van instead. Four men sitting in it, at a vertical enough angle that he knows he's on his side. The rub of plastic against his shoulder nearly as strong as the bite of the twist-tie handcuffs cutting into his wrists.

None of the men look at him. Least of all the sweat-soaked sweatshirt punk who jumped him in the parking lot.

He seems less imposing now, dripping and bleeding from the nose, blanched by the yellow dome light.

Mitch tries to wriggle his hands loose. Maybe bracing his back against the rear door of the van will lend sufficient leverage. They only draw tighter, though, and he realizes, with a distinctly sinking feeling, the toughs actually know how to use the things.

The van makes a few turns. Mitch doesn't know where he first came in, but it takes a few turns from there and shifts to a stop. Driver hits the brakes too early and the chassis rocks, shaking everyone around.

No one as much as Mitch, though.

The door grinds and slides open as he reels. He wrenches his eyes wide and hands are already reaching and clutching for him. He's pulled out, the floor of the van scraping his legs.

No one covers his eyes. He does his best not to register what this probably means.

They drag him for yards, into another, very similar-looking building. A warehouse, a storage unit. White paint flecking off industrial steel. The footsteps ahead of him grow an echo.

"What the fuck is this?" From somewhere far ahead. "Where's the girl?"

Hands on his back and Mitch tumbles to the floor. Steel girders above him, bare concrete walls. Lighter patches on the floor where big heavy things used to sit. Surely this used to be a factory.

All eyes present whip toward Sweatshirt.

He shrugs, scuffs his toe on the floor. "You know. There were three of them. Grabbed who I could get."

"The girl?"

"There were two. One left in the lot. One I was after's dead."

Mitch draws a trembling breath. The toe of a boot rams his sternum before he can scream. He only gets out a quavering whimper. He gets his feet up under him—gets kicked again. Lies still. Tears and blood.

"Jesus. How did you— We told you to grab the girl."

"Yeah. I fucking know."

Mitch gets yanked up and dragged by his shoulders and shirt.

"We talked about this. The woman would be easier to control. We can't afford distractions."

Sweatshirt makes a noise of consideration. Blast of pain at the base of Mitch's spine, and the heavy steel chair they're dragging him toward dims and shimmers.

"Doesn't seem like it'll be that hard to me."

The hands spin Mitch around and shove him into the chair. Leather straps emerge from pockets. They're fastened around his ankles and knees and elbows and wrists and forehead and he can't move. Fingers tingle.

They're fast, efficient despite their appearance. Mitch dimly imagines them practicing on a crash-test dummy, weakly sneers.

Voice of the new man, thoughtful, unquestionably the leader: "Well, so here we are. We've got a maiden who's a man, and a dead girl in a parking lot. And a witness. And—" lifting Mitch's head to peer into his eyes "—he's fading. Who knows how long we have."

"Better get to work, then," Sweatshirt says, a bit of confidence creeping back in.

Mitch spits what he can muster in the leader's face. It's not much. The man just smiles through it, leans in close.

"I suppose you're right."

Mitch's head hangs heavy. Click and whir of a machine. The sounds waver around, side to side. Handheld then—dry drag of a power cord against the floor.

Dull burst of recognition from the back of Mitch's brain. It doesn't connect with anything, just flares enough for him to feel it and fizzles, drowned out in the industrial clang.

He hasn't the strength to strain against the restraints. They itch where they're stuck to his skin with some drying fluid.

His eyelids weigh tons. They catch and drag and scrape his eyeballs on their long, slow rise. Blurry legs in dirty jeans and combat boots come through. Their leader crouches in front of him. Ecstatic grin like a prolonged muscular spasm. It's the face of a man who expects to see God soon, vibrating numinous anticipation.

A ramshackle tattoo gun materializes before the arm holding it. The rattling sharpens.

Mitch's skin tingles. The needle stabs through the air.

The assembled men stand behind their leader in a semicircle. Mitch can't make out their faces. Can't feel himself breathing, either.

He tries to read their faces as the needle finds skin and blood beads up from lines he can't distinguish anymore. The assembled hoodrats pant.

Mitch's head sags again. Nerve firings surge to his fingertips, carrying numbness instead of pain.

Something is coming and its greeting is taking shape on Mitch's flesh.

Someone lied to Colorado Jack and now he's dead and whatever he did out east is coming back around. Bodies in a bunch of different cities—never any witnesses. It had to be Slim, but now Slim's dead, too. Some blanks are going to be left blank, some are going to be filled with the effusions of Carter's Commandoes, the militant indie rockers of the Midwest.

Buddy doesn't mind that. They do business.

But Slim did, too, once upon a time. Until the people he did it with started getting dead.

So Buddy did his year for possession and then fled Florida, found a place here. Friends of friends, but immune to Slim's brand of insanity.

There was no way they'd all gone down that road, after all. Blood clots and wide eyes. But now Carter's out of prison and it's not really clear how his sentence got shortened. The judge assured the newspapers and the good people of Minnesota that Carter would under absolutely no circumstances be eligible for parole.

And he's got those tattoos. They seem to be spreading. He'll see them on the arms of people at shows, in alleys and living rooms, and he seems to remember Slim having one not dissimilar. Carving over it with a sharpened pocketknife.

So maybe it's all starting again and Buddy will have to skip town. Again. He thinks he's probably running out of fresh starts.

He looks to Maria in the passenger seat, cool as you please, gun barely showing under her jacket. The winter's taking its time coming, but Buddy has to focus to keep from shivering.

"Hey," he says, "you hear from that Eli cat? Or his lady?"

Maria up-and-downs him, looks to not believe what she's seeing. "Maybe. Maybe not. You looking for more people to set up?"

"I told you I didn't do anything to Viv. Mitch, either."

"Not directly, I know."

"Indirectly, either."

"You seem to have a pretty clear idea of where they are."

"Look, I said I had a guess. I hear things, yeah? Have a lot of friends. And you weren't about to take no for an answer."

Maria smiles. "What're you looking for Eli for, anyway? You don't still think he burned you to the cops?"

"I never really did. I said that to try to shake out the person who did." It's a lie and Maria knows it. Buddy waits.

She lets it ride. "Anyway, I hear from him, I'll be sure to let him know you'd like to talk."

"Not what I said."

"Well?"

"Sure. The chick, too."

Maria snorts, shakes her head. "You never do know what tree to bark up, huh?"

Buddy flips the turn signal and eases off the interstate. He's had his eye on her the whole time, waiting for her right hand to get far enough from the revolver for him to make a move, dive across the console and send the truck careening off the side of the road in some truly thrilling heroics, one of them to rise from the twisted metal gun clutched tight. The other not likely to rise at all.

No such window, though. He's starting to come to terms with how he's not going to get one. Will have to take Maria to where she thinks she wants to go.

He makes something of a show of keeping his eyes on the road.

She doesn't want to go there. She just doesn't know it yet.

Buddy's jumpy, and Maria doesn't think it's the gun she has to his ribs. He pulls the car over a few blocks from even the vague area he'd named and sits clutching the wheel. His look's not in keeping with how he likes it. Gone for a brief glimpse the freewheeling, easy-money gadfly; in its place, a white-knuckled kid, shaking, in far over his head.

But the old face slips over before Buddy turns to look at her.

"This where you were taking me?" she asks. "I didn't think this was where you were taking me."

"It wasn't."

"Well?"

"I wanted to check you still wanted to go there."

"You know what they did?" She waits for him to nod. "Then you know that, yeah, I wanna go there. So, is there anything I need to know about where you're taking me I don't already know?" She moves the gun side-to-side, just enough for him to register the movement. "That you, I don't know, maybe forgot to mention for some reason?"

She thinks Buddy's going to see how little she feels this avenger persona, but he's staring straight ahead like he might spot something through the brick wall at the end of the alley. He grinds his palms into the wheel slower and slower until he comes up with something to say.

"Might be a thing or two you don't know, yeah." Licks his lips like all's well.

"Yeah? Here I thought I was pretty clear before, with my asking."

"Yeah, yeah, no confusion."

"Well?"

"You gotta understand what Carter's been up to."

"Carter," she says. Maybe he's thinking something good, maybe something bad.

"Yeah. Carter. Guy named Carter. Everybody just calls him Carter."

"And?"

"And Carter's got him a group of guys, understand, a group of guys he's kicking around with."

"Everybody does, seems like."

"Yeah." A shadow passes over his eyes. "But maybe not like this."

Maria takes a deep breath. The way Buddy's talking, it's not his tone of voice so much as it's the way he seems to be having to force the words. He's breathing a little faster than usual and won't make eye contact. She's pretty sure it's one of his tools for success, always making strong eye contact.

If Buddy's looking less like a self-help practitioner and more like a scared young hustler, something serious is happening. And he looks young and scared.

"Different," she says. "Different how, you think?"

"Different weird, is how. Weird. Fucking disaster, except they get things done."

"Meaning they pay."

"Shit yeah, they pay. They can pay, because they make money. They're organized, you hear? Fucking organized, and I dunno how they got themselves that way, but they are. They hit and they fade away and then they get back together a little richer. Nobody talking, from their side or any other."

"'They hit,' you say. How do they hit? What's their deal?"

"Drugs, I think. Probably. I mean, what else? Where the fuck else is there any money?"

It's a pure-Buddy line, and Maria's thinking it's not too far off. The spaces between his words are gone, and with them much of the impression that he's lying with every breath.

Maria's known him long enough that even that puts her on guard. If Buddy seems like he's not lying, it's probably a sign he's lying. Plenty of people have made the mistake of underestimating him in the wrong situations.

He does seem to find ways of pulling people in.

"So," she says, "assuming that you're not bullshitting me, you're, what, afraid of leading me into a few drug dealers?"

"That's how they make their money. The Commandoes— that's what they call themselves, Carter's Commandoes— that's not what they're about. That's not what they do."

He sounds sincere, but he's still staring straight ahead through the windshield.

"All right, I'll bite: What is it they do?"

Buddy shrugs. "Hard to tell. Fucking weird, though."

Maria nods, in spite of herself. Her finger starts to itch on the trigger guard, so she makes sure it's pressed there, not where she might kill Buddy before she means to. She collects herself, gets ready for some kind of move from him, but he draws a long, loud breath and slumps into himself.

"Okay, look, I don't know all of it. Don't want to. But they've got these tattoos."

"Tattoos."

"Yep."

"Like gang tats."

"Like, I don't know." He turns his eyes toward her and they're some dark, hollow things. "But they keep adding them, and people keep going missing. Roughly the same rate, I had to say."

Maria clenches her hand around the gun. She twitches. Buddy reads the signal, puts the car in gear. Drives them to an industrial park.

Mitch doesn't feel a thing. Could be there's nothing more to feel. They took the restraints off a while ago, and he didn't think of running until he started thinking about how he wasn't thinking of running.

Warmth rises deep in his chest—a burrowing from else-where, a benediction.

He tries to chalk it up to blood loss, trauma, but doesn't think he's in shock anymore.

It's the slow-growing touch of a foul but ingratiating god.

The blood's seeping through cracks in the waves of clotting already drying on his arms, his torso, now his legs. It's a wonder his body keeps trying to heal itself, but that's the point, he supposes, of using the human body as a ritual canvas.

Everyone calls the leader Carter. Ragged jeans and a sweat-yellowed white tee-shirt tucked into them, blond crew cut. No one you'd remember looking at unless you'd seen the look on his face floating in front of Mitch's vision, all open nostrils and mouth and eyes, taking in the moment as much as he can, needle gun dangling from one hand and pocketknife from the other. Intricate tattoos on his arms—indecipherable shapes drawn one over the other like they're moving. Writhing. Mitch focuses on one forearm and thinks the shapes look familiar. Would feel familiar. He doesn't know.

Carter's smile stretches. "You remember that dude Slim?" he says over his shoulder to one of his boys. "How he said a knife would be better?"

Some sound from further off than the narrow bubble of Mitch's hearing.

"Well, if he was here he'd feel a bit the fool, I think. All his big words about taking things to the next level, but he never could do this.

"This is something," he says, turning to face the semicircle standing rapt behind him. "Beyond what we've ever done. Beyond ourselves." He sighs. "This is our sacrament."

Mitch senses the group nodding though he can't see them. He pulls himself off the floor as best he can, only gets halfway to sitting. His muscles won't take him any farther—the numbness pervades.

Carter puts his boot on Mitch's shoulder and slowly, gently pushes Mitch onto his back. The knife and the tattoo gun come up. He flips the power switch for the gun, turns the knife in front of Mitch.

"Let us begin."

CHAPTER TWENTY-TWO

Buddy drives them with lights off through empty lots, to the one in back for a building made of steel and cinder blocks. There's only one car in the lot. Buddy looks at Maria. She doesn't think anything of it. But Buddy knows the other cars should all be around back, invisible from the road. Two figures unfurl themselves from the vehicle. Buddy's breath catches.

"Slow down," Maria says, nudging his ribs not very lightly with the barrel of the pistol. "Don't tip them off."

Buddy nods. "They'll know me."

He flicks the lights on. Both figures from the other car shade their eyes, but Elijah and Lorelei Sirko are clearly visible.

Maria finally sees them. "Holy shit, what are—"

Buddy stomps the brakes. Maria's flung into the dash, shoulder crumpling.

She keeps her grip on the gun, though. Gets off one shot. Pulverizes the window on Buddy's side—and his eardrums.

He pins her wrist to the dash and gets the gun loose. She opens her door and gets one foot on the ground. Buddy lets off the brakes. The car lurches forward, pulling Maria's leg under it.

She screams.

Buddy picks up the gun and fires, but it's hard to aim with the car in motion and Maria thrashing to free herself. He stops the car, puts it in park, and puts the last round through her neck.

Her blood soaks the floor mat. The Sirkos fan out, moving to either side of the car. Buddy sighs. They've always been a pain. No idea how they showed up here, how they found the place, but it has to be related to Slim.

Unlike Elijah to have taken up with him, though. Which means they were probably involved with his downfall, picked up a few tricks along the way.

He gets out of the car.

"Drop the gun," Lorelei shouts.

Buddy does. "It's empty anyway."

"Who was that?" Elijah asks.

"Who cares?" Lorelei says, pointing her revolver at Buddy. "He was tight with Slim, wasn't he?"

Elijah reaches across and guides her arm down. "Wait, wait. Maybe he can tell us something."

Lorelei nods, but doesn't put the gun away. She walks to Maria's body.

Elijah waves Buddy closer. "What the hell are we walking in on?"

"You don't know? Good. Walk away. Don't go in that fucking warehouse."

Elijah's face gets hard. Like he can see straight through Buddy. "That's not what I mean."

"What then?"

"Who was that in the car with you?"

"Jesus," Lorelei says. "It's fucking . . . what was Maria doing in Wisconsin?"

Buddy winces. Elijah deflates, eyes pleading.

"Eli, it's—"

"I heard you." Elijah pulls a long knife from his back pocket.

Buddy swings the gun—too late. The knife bites into his arm, yanks back out again. Elijah stabs the blade through Buddy's face. He blinks, not registering the pain, but everything's getting blurry. Over the encroaching white static he hears Lorelei shouting for Elijah to stop, but Buddy's sure he's wanted his blood for a long time. Whatever's happened since they last saw each other has made him willing to take it.

The last thing Buddy sees is the warehouse door opening and another car creeping along the back of the building, unseen by the Sirkos.

#

Milwaukee is more what Stacy had been anticipating as a place to search out the beasts' followers. An old city, the feeling of history weighing on all the buildings. The Minister navigates seemingly by feel. He'll say a direction, sometimes when the turn is apparent, sometimes not, and Stacy will try to make it. He doesn't have street names to offer, and they once wind up having to double back when the route she takes leads in a circle onto the highway back the way they came. It costs them an hour, but she doesn't get the sense that time is of the essence.

When they've been in the city a couple hours, though, the Minister develops a twitching urgency that she wouldn't notice if not for the long week they've spent together so far.

So he navigates and she translates his directions as best she can.

Whether she wants them to get where they're going is another question. One she's increasingly unsure of the answer to.

From what she can piece together, the Ministry is a tight organization, loosely connected, of people exposed to the creatures but un-swayed by them, who try to recruit those like them to the cause, and eliminate those who've turned. But how they determine who's lost and who's not isn't clear. Far as she can tell, it's by instinct. Which leaves her wondering how many potential allies they've left in unholy graves.

She asked him after they left the suburb why they don't tell people up-front what they're doing, who they are.

"It's for safety," he said. "We have to know whether someone is reliable before they can know what we're asking of them."

"You sound like you don't see the contradiction."

"We don't have a choice. Ours is, of necessity, a guerilla resistance. An ecclesiastical underground."

She's unconvinced, but is certain she can't let him see that. So she keeps to her driving, tries to look like a committed new recruit.

But what he did to Nathaniel, what he was ready to do in the cave by the stream, puts Slim in her mind—what he did to Colorado Jack in that apartment. She imagines Slim and Minister Jim locked in a shadow war, one in which the people they're fighting over are never given the chance to take a side.

It feels a lot like her last weeks in Boston, all around. Only one of those sides, after all, would stand to benefit from a full knowledge of the beasts.

In some old neighborhood, Minister Jim sits up all of a sudden, touches his fingertips to his temples. "My God. They're so close."

"Who?"

Minister Jim shakes his head. "Something big is happening. Here, get onto the freeway here."

He leads her to an industrial park. The setting sun paints the ancient cinderblock structures, squat and flat and pasted over with a half-dozen layers of company logos, a luminous orange. Everything seems to float, warmed and elevated by the moments before dusk. He has her weave through the parking lots as the sun goes all the way down, finally insisting they're in the wrong place, that Stacy needs to turn around and cross the street.

It looks more like offices on this side. Stacy's doubtful until Minister Jim tells her to steer around toward the back of one building, rougher than the rest, all tall, corrugated steel. She sees a cluster of cars around back, parked to make them tough to spot, which makes them all the more obvious once you've seen them.

She lets her foot off the accelerator and idles toward the cars, making sure to keep an open lane to the exit. Minister Jim leans forward like he's able to peer into the building from out here. His forehead shines with sweat in the dim light. He tilts his head, and it takes Stacy a moment to realize he looks like he's listening.

There isn't anything to hear, but she holds her breath anyway, hoping. Gets nothing.

Minister Jim shakes his head. "Too many people in there. I don't— Pull around the other side."

"We'll be more visible. Are we leaving?"

"No. But it won't matter." He squints, focusing. "We might have already been spotted."

Stacy fights the urge to peel out of the lot as fast as she can. Idles around the side of the building instead, to a clear patch of pavement she missed on the way in.

She sees the glow of a car's dome light and a gunshot shatters the night like thunder and lightning. The Minister's out of the car before it stops. Stacy goes to follow. The car drifts forward as she exits. She curses and grinds the gearshift into park.

Three people: one by a truck with its headlights on, the other two staring each other down. The one by the truck straightens up, shouts something. The words are lost. Knife flash from a distant hand and one of the other two goes down. The other follows him. The victim's hands go up, but flesh can't stop steel.

They haven't even seen what Minister Jim felt coming from inside.

Stacy follows the Minister, walking slowly toward the two still standing. Slowly, deliberately. Like he's out for a little walk, just taking the night air.

The woman runs from the truck toward the man, shouting Her words start to come into focus, and it's all about how they might have needed him, how now they're going in blind. How he should have waited for one fucking second before pulling a knife, and where does he get off looking at her all the time like *she's* the one who's gone around the bend. She calls him Elijah.

Her voice is familiar. Stacy loses the feeling in her feet. Feels like she's floating across the lot to the end of a dream that was only ever going to go one way.

They hear Minister Jim's footsteps and turn.

The man, Stacy doesn't know. The woman, though, is the tall woman from Boston. The woman who put a knife into Stacy's leg, and somehow she struggles to come up with the name.

Lorelei. The tall woman is called Lorelei. Putting a name to her face sharpens it. Stacy feels like vomiting.

Lorelei stares at her, hands frozen where she'd been gesturing. Elijah raises the knife, settles back into a defensive stance. Minister Jim shows his palms, doesn't stop.

"What the fuck?" Lorelei says. "You're from Boston. You're that chick."

Stacy nods.

Minister Jim glances between them. "You've met."

"You all need to walk away," Elijah says. "You don't want any part of what's happening here."

The Minister chuckles importantly. "You don't know what's happening here."

"The fuck I don't."

"Not half as well as you think you do."

"Why don't we—" Lorelei starts.

Elijah's done. He springs, but Minister Jim moves impossibly fast, lays him on the ground. Elijah moans, knife forgotten. The Minister picks it up, turns it over in his hand like he's never seen one.

"The two of you," he says, "should not have come here. You've been touched. They know you're here."

Stacy suddenly knows that Lorelei and her husband are on the Minister's list—that he's having to improvise.

She swallows hard. Lorelei was good to her. And the Minister is ready to cut her down, because of her proximity to Gutter Street.

She starts to say something but never gets the first word out. The door to the warehouse bursts open. One man sprints out at first, then jerks back and twitches where he stands. Bent backward so far it's impossible he's still on his feet. Hands up about his head, scratching at something. Lorelei can make out what looks like an arm wrapped around his neck, shifting and twisting around itself.

The hair. It's a limb made from that hair. The things are inside.

A second man, in a tight white shirt, comes out of the building and places his hand gently on the strangling man's back. Like a father. The man relaxes and the hairy tentacle tightens. The second man turns the first around, guides him back inside. Stops in the doorway and stares at the four intruders. Stacy's guts twist icy and the man slams the door behind him.

Minister Jim runs for the door. Stacy hesitates, looks to Lorelei. Lorelei grabs a backpack from the car and runs after the Minister.

"Who in the hell are you?" Elijah asks.

Stacy follows Lorelei into the building.

It's like walking into a demented painting—red light and bending architecture and somehow immeasurably old. Ancient. Hot wet smell of sloughing skin and too many men to count, screaming.

One man glows. Strapped to a chair, geometry burning on his arms. Tentacles running from the far corner of the ceiling to pulse in his head.

Lorelei rubs her hands over her face and backs up, runs into Stacy. Can't make the sight of the room make sense. Can't process it.

"Where's Minister Jim?" Stacy screams into her ear.

"Minister . . .?"

He emerges from the crowd, crouches next to the body in the chair while clutching Elijah's goddamn knife. He runs a hand down the body's scalp, fingers working the hair away from the tentacle wound.

In the corner of the ceiling, a gaping hole leaks sickly red light. More tentacles crawl through, something massive lumbering behind.

The Minister whips the blade across the tentacles attached to the head. The body opens its eyes and stands, dragging the Minister with it. He hacks again, again, and the walls bend inward more. A sub-aural throb—a ripple through the world.

Lorelei opens the backpack but her hands freeze.

The body from the chair stands up straighter. The Minister's hacked halfway through the foreign hair. The body lifts up onto its toes then floats up into the air.

No. Not floats. It's being lifted. The illusion of life fades from the body and Lorelei sees it for what it is: a near-enough-dead puppet sloughing rot onto the chair. The restraints dig into its wrists as the body rises, holding it in place a second, but then the skin gives and scrapes off along the restraints. The body rockets toward the ceiling, the Minister still clutching to the hair, cutting.

Lorelei takes the black chalk from her pack and runs to help him. She doesn't know who he is, but he's after the beasts and seems to have some idea how to fight back.

She doesn't get even halfway to him before two other bodies hit her around the waist. She scratches at their eyes, jabs at their necks. They're not cold like corpses but rather far too hot. Inorganically hot. Their eyes strain and their lips flap.

Then she blinks, and for an instant they're gray bodies. Then people again, pin-cushioned with the tips of the tentacles, mold spreading out from their wounds in advance of purple infection.

She takes a breath and holds it. The world slows down. Her veins strain like tense steel cables and she settles into the new calm she's been riding for weeks, through bars and living rooms and the scene where these people's twice-removed friends circulate, and she remembers that the bodies she's struggling against aren't people anymore. She can't hurt them the same ways she could people.

The shock of the realization balances the shock of the figures themselves, and she settles into a comfortably vicious numbness.

One of her attackers claws his hand across her face. She can't raise her chalk hand, so instead she grabs the pendant from her backpack, letting the pack fall. Presses the metal to the forehead of one attacker.

His head whips back. The motion isn't distinct at first from the body's general movement, but then the flesh where the pendant touched flashes impossibly black and glows, burning dark. The body slumps to the floor like all its bones are gone, leaving a stomach-churning cloud of foul decay in its place. Lorelei expects the second assailant to see her weapon and back off, but it just wraps its other arm around her neck and pulls itself close. The pendant touches its shirt, pressing into the flesh. The body goes limp. Lorelei folds under it.

Atop her, the assailant twitches, deep in his muscles. Skin softens, bones bend. Lorelei gasps for breath, chokes on its gaseous putrescence. She drives the pendant harder into the chest and her hand breaks through the back. The body comes apart around her in gray-green strings and white mold, screaming all the louder as it ceases to resemble anything human.

She stands, dripping, and the room has fallen into calm. The Minister whips around from his ceiling-ward perch and cuts the last of the connections between the body and the beast. Falls the ten or so feet to the floor, staring at her all the way.

The Minister hits and rebounds, lies as still as everything suddenly is, save the remnants of a person at Lorelei's feet. The tissue ripples, contracting and relaxing in waves like a slow-motion muscle spasm. The rot soup sifts down over thin, tight tendrils of hair, coated over with white mold and moving green fungus. Black ooze drips from the bends in the strands.

The hairs lift up, allowing the rest of the body's remains to flump onto the rubberized floor. Lorelei can't look away; they're beautiful. But the moment of calm passes and a terrible shriek fills the room, one so low she can't hear it so much as she feels it, from somewhere deep and instinctive inside her.

The delicate weave of the hairs still mapping out the Commando's body ignites where its chest used to be. The flame flashes white for an instant. The strands whip apart, breaking rank and thrashing back fast enough to put out the fire.

The Minister's glares up from the floor. Lorelei holds the pendant out, brandishing it as much at him as the used-to-be-people turning slowly, facing her.

When they move, it's all at once.

They flood toward her and she grips the pendant tight, looking for the pair of arms that will reach her first. It's an impossible calculation, and a half-dozen hands land on her simultaneously. She staggers back.

The door opens. She feels Elijah there, gaping.

As the hands start to rend her clothes—practice for her skin—the walls of the wide room bend further, with everything following suit. The rot-soaked chair, the bodies, her own hand with the pendant still clutched tight all warp and distort on some savage geometry projected out from the portal in the corner of the ceiling. Only the hellish world lurking there beyond the concrete remains in proportion to itself. If she lives through this, she will never be sure whether it's her focus on the portal or its own agency that causes it to light up like frames in a film strip, one instant an intrusion into the warehouse, the next the opposite, the warehouse a dim, visual memory detectable in the shadows of this new place in which she finds herself.

The air is red and carries the copper smell of blood.

She breathes deep but the scream never comes.

\#

Elijah stands for a long moment in front of the warehouse door, finally gets himself solid enough to fling it open and step through. He whips his head around but can't take in what he sees—blood and decay and churning violence—before the whole setting blurs and shifts and he's somewhere else.

The air glows red, like some colored light bulb burns out of sight, bright enough to reflect off the stone walls and the dirt ceiling. The floor squishes underfoot, and looks in this light like expensive carpet. The sucking sound as his weight settles into this new place makes him sick. He remembers Lorelei reading from Alan's notebook on the long drive to Florida. The memory makes him feel cramped and stiff and road-blind.

And, though he wouldn't quite cop to it then—wouldn't call it by name—scared.

The people from the warehouse stood out previously in what he briefly saw of them, run through with strands of something and twitching like marionettes. Here, though, they almost seem to blend into the dirt—natural extensions of it, creatures returned to their proper environment.

But he saw their faces before, clearer than he can now. There's nothing natural about them. He has to assume the same about his new surroundings.

The people, if they're people, jolt erratically, breaking their momentary stillness. They surge toward him and he jumps back. His feet slide and the mushy ground catches the back of his skull when he lands. The men jerk against the ends of their hair. The cords of it are coming out of crevasses in the rock. The bodies look around at each other, or appear to, and settle down on their haunches.

Elijah takes in the surroundings as best he can in the sanguine light. The two walls he can see make him think it's a cramped space, as does the ceiling inches above his head, but the way the red light darkens in the distance somehow gives him the impression of a massive space indeed.

It doesn't matter, though. The corpse-people are ahead of him, and there's a steep drop coated in that not-carpet behind.

And he's lost sight of Lorelei.

She'd been standing, he thinks, in some puddle of desiccation back in the warehouse, but he's sure he must have seen it wrong.

He's sure of it.

Still, he can't shake the conviction that she had somehow *dissolved* one of the attackers and was standing in its remains when he came in.

The man she'd followed in there was crumpled on the ground. Elijah remembers the look on his face. It betrayed no fear but was nonetheless fixed on Lorelei, even amidst the charnel house the room had become.

Then something opened in the wall, in the world. Hair and blood and mold and screaming and now here.

Staring down these bulging faces, animate but putrid. He realizes these are the scene kids Lorelei had gotten a tip about, who were on the verge of some kind of breakthrough.

From the looks of things, they got their way. He wonders how many of them knew what that would look like.

CHAPTER TWENTY-THREE

Carter breathes deep. He feels every one of his Commandoes, tastes their fear and their doubt turning warm, growing contented. The bloodlust rising in their throats.

He flexes his fists and smiles.

The Minister finds his feet. The passageway is familiar in the secondhand way of the setting of a vivid story heard thousands of times over the years yet never seen firsthand. Its dirt and rock and cramped expansiveness fits the descriptions, but not the picture he'd drawn up for it in his head.

The reality is much worse.

Some of the faithful, the hip young people whose communion they'd interrupted, stalk him in odd reverse semicircles. He waits for his eyes to adjust. They're connected to the wall by long strands of the beasts' hair. It's like they've become part of the rock.

But the Minister knows the tentacles don't end in rock. He knows what it is that each man here is tethered to, more or less willingly.

He moves forward, tentatively, expecting the faithful to find some slack and pounce on him, but they remain where they are, straining. Flailing hands in front of them, desperate to spill his blood. They're being assimilated, but the Minister has never seen so many people taken at once. And they've done it on purpose.

The Minister doesn't know where their leader is. Carter. Stacy and the touched couple, either. They were within loud-talking distance of each other when the border burst, but if they're in this tunnel now, they're far outside his range of sight.

He looks around. He's only seen the beasts' realm once, and secondhand at that, through the doorway over the shoulder of a comrade who must have suspected his trip was one-way. But this isn't that. The Minister expected the red sky and the black rocks once they settled in wherever the beasts were taking them, but this is dirt and darkness, and a much dimmer red permeating the air.

They're underground, seems like. Under the ground of this world. But somewhere, light from the other is sinking through.

The nearest human marionette dives toward him, still can't get past its restraint; the hair's dug deep into his skin. It can't be torn out by the entirety of his heaving weight.

Minister Jim hugs the far wall past that one then ducks across to the other side for the other. Stays on that side and gets past most of them. No way to know that the direction he's heading is the right one, but everything in him screams that staying still is worse.

It's a bad mood to get in. He saw it in Lorelei when she showed up, working reactively, letting her rushing energy carry her from crisis point to crisis point. It's a good way to feel pretty indestructible. A good way to find out you're wrong, too.

Still, she'd pulled out that pendant.

The Minister didn't think any of those existed anymore. She'd been in Boston, though. And if she picked that up there, that means Stacy was in proximity to that scene, and Boston was a good deal more important than even he thought. He'll have to reevaluate his interview with Stacy.

But for now, there's the problem of the last couple Commandos. He's weaved his way past the rest, each pinioned at some distance to the stone wall, but these three are new. They're skinny kids, men in their very early twenties, in jeans and hooded sweatshirts in different states of disrepair. Where presumably they once had normal eyes stare blindly blooms of red—aneurysm-burst-bright blood inset with gaping pupils. The Minister would swear that he's seeing through those pupils, to the rot already working its way out from the puncture wounds on the backs of their necks.

He catches himself. These puppets aren't just stabbed through in the neck. The tentacles sprout from raised sores all over their bodies—thin, sticky strands that wind around their partners, braiding before condensing further into the thicker ropes that the Minister is more used to seeing. Plunging into the rock that way.

The beasts are developing. Or they're developing *something*. The Minister has never seen bodies this tightly tied in before.

The skin of the three in front of him is deathly blue. They're strung together, coarse hair splitting out the side of one and into the neck of another before bursting through the other side. A network like that—a web, of the thickest beast-hair the Minister has ever seen. For what might be the first time, he doesn't think of that hair as portions of tentacles, but rather as a fluid appendage of its own. Forming now tentacles, now smaller limbs. Sometimes thinning down almost into single strands, an almost-invisible piece ramming straight through one ear of the right-most man and through the other, into the wall.

They're dexterous in a way the Minister has never had the misfortune to know before. His usual approach won't work here. None of the fallbacks, either. There's too many of the beast's puppets, and too many uncontrolled variables beside.

He'll have to improvise. He does not like to improvise.

He crouches against the wall and gets out the black chalk. The three corpses ahead of him jerk back. He sketches quickly on his palms, trying for a sigil of protection. Tells himself that it will work, that his flesh can carry the violence through the bodies of the faithful.

He marks a circle around himself in the dirt, rises and strides toward the three linked bodies. They lunge for him when he gets within reach, their fear of the chalk lost in their bloodlust.

The Minister grabs the head of the nearest one with both hands. The hair slurps loose from the necks of the other two and slithers toward him, trailing long strips of skin and muscle. His palms tingle. Hair crawls along his arms, growing stiff and pointed at the tips. The strands soil his skin with slime and rotten blood and stab into his flesh.

He grips the head harder. The tingling in his hands grows to a burn and spreads up his arms. Like he's dipped them to the elbows in molten iron.

The man rocks against his grip, no longer trying to get closer to him. Bucks backward, trying to escape. Jagged patches of skin come loose. The gore underneath boils. The tentacles tear their way loose, leaving their host to flail and collapse under his own weight, helpless without the hair to support him. He settles in a heap against the wall.

To the Minister's horror, the desiccated man's chest rises and falls, still somehow drawing breath.

The other two men stagger. It takes the Minister a moment to realize that they've been thrown off by the broken contact with the third man. The tentacles scramble to re-establish control, piercing new holds into the bodies. The Minister slinks between them, farther down the tunnel.

Stacy rounds a corner gasping . The corpse-bodies around her had been looking the other way, but she got a good enough look to dread seeing their like again. The darkness of the passageways triggers something deep inside her and she sprints.

Around the corner, the Minister fends off a row of them. The things. She sees him break through and run—and the man lurking in the shadows, cheeks sinking around their own decay, revealing yellowed teeth. The Minister can't see the man.

In Boston, Lorelei dragged her from the street to safety, put a knife through her leg to keep her that way. And now she's some kind of wild card, killing her way into that warehouse, ready to leave the Minister in the dirt of that parking lot.

She knows the impression this is supposed to leave on her, the effect that the Minister hopes for, is horror. The need to push back the progress the beasts have made—to reset the world to its equilibrium: them on one side, us on the other.

And the idea has a certain appeal. To stop the predatory

incursions is paramount.

But how to do it? Retreating to a more comfortable reality, one in which the beasts don't exist, seems bafflingly impossible.

The question is whether this subterranean plantation—the apex of their gains, with people as raw material—can be put to use in opposition. Can be seized.

She thinks about Nathaniel, about how he might have answered that question. She thinks that probably the only way to fight back is to take the ritual tools of these monsters and use them against them. The Minister's sneaking around has done nothing to stop this incursion. If anything, Milwaukee has been worse than Boston.

Lorelei cuts and burns, slogging through hallways of the men from the warehouse. They've turned to something more and less than they were. The pendant warms in her hand, and she begins to wonder whether she's cutting down these men because she's faster than she thought she was, or if it's because the weapon itself knows what to do.

It doesn't matter.

She breaks free of a rotting crowd and sprints downhill, finds Carter with his head back and his arms out to his sides. Beatific. Bloodied.

He doesn't even resemble a person anymore. He looks more like a shadow, overlain with an outline of Slim's face. Lorelei knows it's not what's in front of her eyes she's seeing; it's what's really there. What *isn't* there.

The distinction is new, and she needs time to acclimate to it. Time she doesn't have.

This is something that Elijah talked about more times than she had patience for, that the quick response is often the wrong one. He wanted her to calm down, to approach things a little more methodically. He never understood how a person could be methodical by reflex, could let a knee-jerk feeling carry into a mental process. She did, but she didn't know how to explain it to him.

Maybe it will save her.

She could back out without Carter seeing her, but she knows he's at the center now. That something is happening around him—he's a fulcrum. She walks toward him.

His head whips down and his eyes open, and a sound like a train crash bellows from his mouth. She doesn't flinch. The pendant kisses the soft meat of Carter's neck. The flesh gives, flays out. Long strains of black hair are underneath, twisted and knotted into the shape of a human spine.

She hacks at the hair with her knife.

Carter's hands grab Lorelei's hand holding the pendant. Fingers push through skin, tear at muscle. She swings her knife wide, twisting. It doesn't work until suddenly it does, and Carter comes apart.

The beasts' limbs tear free from his body and Lorelei skips back not quite fast enough. One tendril burrows under the skin of her hand and she sees everything in an unbearable flash.

She sees the South Carolina plantation they've found themselves under, white-gone-yellow marble and thriving weeds.

The Minister, trying to crawl along the same rock floor, Commando teeth and fingers welcoming him violently to their fold.

Stacy, sprinting as hard as she can. Lorelei's heart leaps until she turns another corner, right into a wall of the enemy.

Elijah, backed into a corner, Commandos surging forward. The hair gets to him first, tunnels and rends as he swings a rock around, trying to dislodge it, but it's in too far.

Lorelei screams, but wherever Elijah is, it's too far to hear. She can't stop him, but she can feel the twisting animal revulsion he feels, fighting off the tentacle's visions to crack the rock against his own skull. It doesn't break the bone, though, doesn't plunge him into a darkness even these beasts can't penetrate. It only stuns him, knocks down his defenses.

The hair finds purchase in his neck.

Lorelei knows all their minds in their last moments: takes in everything the Minister told Stacy, everything she deduced; knows for the first time Elijah's mind, and nearly buckles with love; feels the Minister's plan, the insurmountable mountain of bodies he's left behind—people who'd been touched by the beasts.

She glances down at the hair piercing her skin and she feels the innumerable bodies held here in rotting stasis. More than just the Commandos, though they are the first of a new breed.

It makes sense. The men she met in Boston were stuck in place. Not a part of the beasts' machinations, but still kept in check by them—limited to one space.

Slim, they needed mobile. But he became so loose a cannon that he burned himself out, came crashing down when there was a skip in the process.

But the Commandos—and, she knows, Hector—they're to be more mobile. An army of rot.

Her shoulder cracks and dislocates. The tentacle has wound its way there from her hand, is dismantling her body. She digs the tip of the knife into her skin and cuts across the molded hair.

The impossible pain that blots out her senses is the beasts'. They can feel pain. They can be hurt.

It gives her new life.

She cuts through the rest of the tentacle, leaves its length inside her arm. She skips over its mates, all lunging for her. Presses the length of hair protruding from her wound to what's left of Carter. Pulls a lighter and sets the fire there. The hair melts instantly into a chalky black substance.

She was right, at least, about where Alan's writing material came from.

She keeps the flame going, scrapes a symbol she knows from long hours of practice tracing with a pencil on Carter's chest, the tendrils seething there.

Rush of hot sulfur and the tunnel begins to shake itself apart.

Lorelei pulls at the melted end of the hairy tentacle in her arm. It's fastened to something inside her. She pulls harder, eyes watering, knees buckling. Her vision starts to go hazy before the strand comes loose, slides out of her body with a sensation like marbles rubbing together, nails on a chalkboard. Visceral and invasive and abrasive.

But she gets the invader out.

Next to Carter sits a small glass case with an antique tattoo gun inside. Lorelei doesn't think. She dumps the gun, stuffs the tentacle inside. It pierces her skin in the process, but she finally gets the lid closed over it.

A chunk of the ceiling falls. Lorelei covers her head. Tucks the case under her arm and claws her way skyward.

It's a long time coming, but eventually her hands break through the ground and she crawls, gushing wounds and spasming lungs and burning muscles, up through the ground.

Lorelei chokes on the air—sulfur and blood. The smoke from subterranean fires wafts faster into the sky. The plantation is not an environment fit for human habitation, not anymore. It never was. What people did here wasn't habitation, it wasn't life. This was the ground for the conversion of human beings into raw material, into the fuel for some infernal industry.

She wipes at the blood on her face but only manages to spread it around. Her hands are covered, too. Her arms, her clothes. Everything doused in the blood of a long process she's found herself in the middle of.

The tentacle still squirms in the glass case. She considers it awhile, and thinks better of it, but still presses her hand to the glass. The squirming turns its energy toward her hand, the idea or feeling of her flesh, her usability. The hairs press themselves against the glass. She can see the way the mold congeals on impact, forming a little fungal sucker where each strand touches the glass an instant before they flatten into a twitching pad.

But that's all it does. She wasn't sure before, but the things need actual skin contact. She waits for the tentacle to realize it's not getting what it wants and stop, but it doesn't. Its pursuit of her body is implacable, ceaseless. Without that glass to stop it, it never would.

And they never will. She's felt that in her bones since the trailer—probably since well before then—but somehow avoided putting it into words. But there it is. The beasts, Slim's masters, the Minister's demons, they won't stop coming for her ever. They had a taste of her, and now they'll pursue her as their property.

It took Hector and the priest, and it took Alan.

Stacy.

Who knows how many others.

Elijah.

She stands, shaking the tentacle under her arm, hoping the motion hurts it somehow. They won't stop coming for her, so she has no choice. She sees that now, the way the others had no choice, though they thought they could hide. In the end, the forces they thought they'd escaped came for them and took them. It won't take her.

She's armed now.

Lorelei walks for hours until she finds a highway, then longer to a rest stop, expecting her mind to change, but it doesn't. The only way out is through, as Elijah was fond of saying when drunk, when he was sprawled exhausted in their living room. When everything looked like it was dying.

It's not too hard to steal a car.

On the passenger seat next to her, as she puts the car in gear and heads toward Boston, where everything started and where she suspects it may well start again, sit the two weapons she needs:

The severed and captured tentacle, providing her the raw material to craft weapons for the fight.

And Alan's notebook, pointing the way to use them.

Armed with the past, Lorelei rides blood-streaked into the future. The beasts surely follow.

ABOUT THE AUTHOR:

Mark Jaskowski. Grew up in Florida. Lives in Kansas; less flat than advertised. First novel.

ACKNOWLEDGEMENTS

Inestimable and un-pay-backable thanks are due to people including but not limited to:

Roy Starling, because one year a seventeen-year-old kid walked into his classroom in August, and walked out in May damn well going to be a writer;

Craig Clevenger, for the Hotseat Reloaded;

Padgett Powell, for ruthlessly pointing out when I was trying to be clever, as distinct from being clever;

Richard Burt, for the critical theory and the even-more-critical pulp;

Pela Via, for the many rounds of edits on that story that time, pushing me to be less boring;

Stephen Graham Jones, Elisabeth Sheffield, and Paul Youngquist, for their eyes and invaluable criticism on the earliest version of this;

Logan Priess, for those early eyes as well, and for showing me how to fix so many of my stories besides;

The fine employees and regulars of the Outback Saloon in Boulder, CO, where a goodly portion of this book was written;

My family, for their admittedly perplexing yet unflagging support and enthusiasm;

J David Osborne, for saying "send me the first thirty pages;"

Andrew Wilmot, for repeatedly thwacking the manuscript with his mighty editorial hammer;

Matthew Revert, for putting the wrapping on it;

And to Caroline, for absolutely everything else.

www.ingramcontent.com/pod-product-compliance
Lightning Source LLC
Chambersburg PA
CBHW020931260626
47169CB00006B/1671